Read Good

Bernice Goedeke

NOT LONG
FOR THIS
WORLD

Also by Gar Anthony Haywood

Fear of the Dark

NOT LONG

....

FOR THIS

....

WORLD

An Aaron Gunner Mystery

Gar Anthony Haywood

ST. MARTIN'S PRESS
New York

Library of Congress Cataloging-in-Publication Data

Haywood, Gar Anthony.
      Not long for this world / Gar Anthony Haywood.
           p.   cm.
      "A Thomas Dunne book."
      ISBN 0-312-04398-8
      I. Title.
PS3558.A885N68 1990
813'.54—dc20   89-77953
                                                 CIP

First Edition

10 9 8 7 6 5 4 3 2 1

For
My Mother,
Barbara Jean.
Few men will ever know such love and faith.

acknowledgments

The author would like to thank the following people for their invaluable contributions to this book—and for their far more invaluable friendship:

Lin Bolen-Wendkos, the North Star
Bill and Joey Sommers, the innkeepers

NOT LONG
FOR THIS
WORLD

prologue

Ironically, Darrel Lovejoy wasn't looking for trouble the night he found it for the last time. Had the world in which he lived been just, he would have died a far more noble death, been cut up or shot down in the midst of performing some laudable act of gallantry and self-sacrifice, but the world was not just and life was unkind, and so he died instead somewhat routinely, as many far more ordinary men and women living in the ghettos of America die every day. The thirty-three-year-old black man was just minding his own business when his time came, returning from an innocent walk to the corner market for a paltry eight dollars in groceries, his antennae retracted, his defenses down. He didn't see the blue Ford Maverick or the shotgun barrel nosing out of its passenger-side window until his fate had long since been decided.

A South-Central Los Angeles youth gang known as the Imperial Blues was unofficially given credit for the hit in its aftermath, and this was a development no one familiar with Lovejoy's personal history, or the Blues's long-standing record of disservice within the community, rushed to question. It made sense—as it would have had any of a dozen other L.A.-based juvenile fraternities of terror been implicated in the Blues's place, because Lovejoy had been equally despised by them all. From the nineteen different chapters of Cuzzes on the Westside (among which were the Blues) to the sixteen tribes of their eternal enemies, the Hoods in the east, he had been a thorn in their collective side for years, a constant distraction and source of aggravation, and as such, it was generally assumed that the man was living only on whatever time they chose to loan him.

He had earned such unenviable disfavor as the founder and chief executive officer of the L.A. Peace Patrol, a nationally publicized, community-sponsored band of volunteers who made it their business to monitor and control gang-related violence in the low-income Los Angeles neighborhoods where gang warfare ran most rampant. Lovejoy's was the story of a local boy gone good, a college-educated escapee of the ghetto who in the fall of 1985 had abruptly scrapped a successful advertising sales career, double-backed on himself, and returned to his roots, all for reasons too altruistic for most people to take seriously. He seemed too good to be true.

In time, however, he proved to be exactly what he claimed to be: a man out to change the world. He was being driven by no great personal loss, past or present, and had little to gain as near as anyone could tell, yet Lovejoy was determined to see the streets of his childhood purged of gang violence, the ages-old tribal insanity that fed daily, and indifferently, on children and adults alike. He had no plan at the beginning; he wandered from one community-service group to another, learning firsthand what methods of communication and reform bore the most fruit or suffered the greatest amount of resistance. He worked side by side with police task-force officers and child psychologists, social workers and ex-gang members—but he never really found himself until he and the Reverend Willie Raines joined forces.

Raines was the dynamic figurehead of the Children of God Ministries, a black Christian juggernaut that had evolved over fourteen years from a small Baptist church in Inglewood to a powerful religious/political movement of nationwide scope and influence. The Reverend was a perpetual-motion machine, a charismatic leader with a gift for gab who was as adept at charming small donations out of his most impoverished flock as he was at shaming the minority corporate community out of much larger ones. His teachings, and most of CGM's programs, focused almost exclusively upon the underclass youth of America, its defense against modern-day social ills and its proper cultivation within a "morally sound" environment. He was a tireless opponent of drug use and pornography, and an inspirational salesman for education and the family unit. In the eyes of many black Americans, he was a role model forged in gold.

Lovejoy himself had not held that opinion immediately, but the more Raines sang his song, gaining more and more media exposure and financial momentum, the more it became obvious to Lovejoy that the two men seemed to want the same things for the future generations of their people. Deciding to seek Raines out, patiently waiting in a long line to see an increasingly unapproachable man, he eventually found that Raines concurred: Their ideals were, indeed, compatible.

The Peace Patrol was born soon after the pair's first meeting, backed by CGM's money and steered by Lovejoy's grit. The success the joint venture inevitably achieved did not come nearly as easily, however. Lovejoy's approach to defusing gang violence—direct and unarmed intervention—was wrought with peril, and much blood was spilled before the patrol earned the respect necessary to deal with gang leaders and their minions on any kind of productive level. Early on, the casualties among the ranks were high, including a pair of near-fatal episodes involving Lovejoy himself, and the community's faith in the program, not to mention its active participation in it, was on the wane.

Again, however, Lovejoy's persistence came into play. He was, after all, a man whose penchant for speaking the cold, hard truth could be ignored, or ridiculed, only for so long. The tide began to turn. His lectures started hitting home and the infallible logic upon which his rhetoric was based began to reach even the most jaded members of his daily audiences. In accordance with his agreement with Raines, the kids he was able to win over he referred to the Reverend and the Children of God Ministries for further instruction in the Word; those he could not, he merely endeavored to keep from killing one another, for however long that was possible.

A week was usually tops.

He was the best there was in the human salvage business, but the work was hardly lucrative. After three years of endless effort, he had little to show in the way of thanks for his good works, save for a dozen or so plaques mounted on the walls of his office, trinkets tossed his way by assorted citizens' action committees, and a *Time* magazine cover story that made him nearly as famous as Raines for all of three weeks.

His final reward, however, was murder. Only weeks before he was scheduled to moderate a ground-breaking peace conference between the two most dominant factions of the Los Angeles gangbanging tribal structure, an event that Raines had masterminded and arranged with great care and promotional fanfare, Lovejoy met with a fast death on a dark corner. It was a pitiful, ignoble end with no bravery or heroism attached.

Tamika Downs, the thirty-two-year-old mother of four who had witnessed his assassination from a nearby bus bench (and who, incredibly, had actually stepped forward to admit as much to the authorities), swore to reporters afterward that Lovejoy had deserved a far better conclusion to his life story.

But then, as so many of the man's friends mused in mourning, so did the average dog.

chapter **one**

....

On the fourth day of proceedings in the civil suit of *Compton* vs. *Hernandez* being heard in Room 221 of the downtown Los Angeles Municipal Courthouse, a full hour after the lunch break of which he had neglected to take advantage, private investigator Aaron Gunner finally took the stand on behalf of the defendant, Celia Hernandez. He had been on his way to the snack shop down the hall, in search of his second cup of coffee since noon and his fifth overall, when the bailiff called him inside.

Gunner's relief at the summons was only partially due to boredom. While Hernandez had paid him a fair and equitable sum to deal with the circumstances of her case in earnest, he found them laughable nevertheless, and was anxious to have his participation in the litigation come to an end.

Eighteen months earlier, Celia Hernandez had made the acquaintance of Lionel Compton in the dark and empty parking lot of the El Segundo aeronautics tooling firm where they both worked the late shift—she as a keypunch operator, Compton as a machine-shop trainee—and their introduction had not gone well. Gunner's client's description of the incident was attempted rape, plain and simple; Compton saw it as a harmless passing of two young and attractive coworkers in the night. The pair could agree on nothing that occurred during their brief exchange save for the way it came to an end—with two well-placed and highly motivated knees to Compton's groin, courtesy of Hernandez.

It was Compton's contention that the blows had cost him whatever sexual capacity he could have claimed beforehand, and if his police record was any indication, everyone involved in the case admitted, that was a sizable loss indeed, because the twenty-four-year-old black man had a history of sex-related arrests and convictions almost too long for a single machine to print out. It was a background that should have, and likely *would* have, invalidated his case long before it ever came to trial had Hernandez only been wise enough to press charges against him following their altercation. Sadly, however, Hernandez had not. She had tried to ignore the incident instead, mistaking her assailant's foiled attempt at assault for but an isolated if stupid blunder he would never make again, and Compton was using the abstention to lend credence to his argument that the woman's attack upon him had been as unprovoked as it was damaging.

He was suing for a cool million.

Hernandez's lawyer, a low-rent file-server twice removed from Kenya whose firm operated out of a department-store chain, chose to build his client's defense upon the assumption that Compton's claims of sexual incapacitation were vile exaggerations, if not outright lies, and hired Gunner to prove it. Gunner did. It took five weeks of surveillance and all the film a good Olympus camera could shoot, but the results were unmistakable. The prints were clear and self-explanatory; Gunner's photography was improving.

Compton and a hooker at the Red Robin motel, a Baldwin Hills flophouse on La Brea just north of Exposition.

Compton and two hookers at Compton's bachelor apartment in Hawthorne.

Compton, two hookers, and a male friend at the Red Robin.

Compton, two hookers, and a female friend at the Red Robin.

The eight-by-tens left little to the imagination—Gunner had shot them all outside one poorly draped window or another, his camera armed with a telephoto lens that could have brought the hairs on a fly's hind leg into razor-sharp focus—but his testimony was required to explain them, nevertheless. William Botu, Hernandez's department-store lawyer, asked simple questions, to which Gunner provided simple answers. The three *w*'s—who, what, and where—were covered in great detail; it was a tedious, if painless, affair.

Then Daniel London, the walking oil slick representing Compton, decided to go for broke and cross-examine. It had already been established that his client's only witness—Compton himself—was a highly unreliable source for the truth, and London was hoping the same conclusion could be reached about Gunner, with a little creative questioning.

Compton was dead meat otherwise.

Therefore, the square-jawed counselor in the finely tailored blue suit wandered about before the witness stand, hands behind his back, delaying his first question as long as possible so as to leave the jury with the false impression that he had given it a good deal of thought. Only when the Honorable Theodore J. Spillman, who was hearing the case, voiced his impatience with a dry and hollow stage cough did London abandon the tactic, in order to hand Gunner one of the twenty-seven photographs held in evidence, this one labeled Exhibit A-14.

"Mr. Gunner," London said, smiling effusively, "do you recognize that photograph?"

Gunner did the polite thing and glanced at the print before answering. "Yes. Of course."

"Did you take it?"

"Yes, sir, I did."

"At the Red Robin motel?"

"That's right. Outside of Room 11, in the north wing, as I said before. The stenographer can read back the date and time for you, if you missed that, too."

London stopped smiling. Somewhere in the back of the courtroom, a giggle was dying. "That won't be necessary," he said. He started to pace again. "I would, however, like you to take another look at that photograph and tell me, in your own words, what you see. Of my client, Mr. Compton's, anatomy, specifically."

"Your Honor . . ." Botu said, rising.

Spillman ordered him back to his seat with a firm wave of his right hand. "Let's see where Mr. London's headed before voicing any objections, shall we, Mr. Botu?"

"Thank you, Your Honor," London said.

Gunner gave Exhibit A-14 a thorough evaluation, said, "His head, in profile; his right leg and both feet; both arms, but only one hand, his right. Oh, and his joint."

"I beg your pardon?" London said.

Gunner pointed. "His joint. His penis. Right here."

London snatched the photo from his hands and pressed his nose to it. "Are you trying to tell the court that Mr. Compton's joint—I mean, his penis—is actually *visible* in this picture?"

"Well," Gunner said, shrugging, "I admit it's not that easy to see—I recall hearing the girl on the left there saying something to that effect, in fact—but it's there, all right. That sure as hell isn't a marital aid."

"He's lyin'!" Compton roared, leaping to his feet indignantly. "Shawanna never said nothin' like that! Shit, she couldn't get enough!"

"That will be all, Mr. Compton!" Judge Spillman shouted, trying to be heard over the din of the suddenly excited courtroom audience and the pounding of his own gavel.

"Your Honor," a red-faced London said, before the

laughter in the room had fully subsided, "I submit that these photographs prove only that Mr. Compton shared a room with some friends on four separate occasions, and that they do not in any way indicate an ability on his part to experience or maintain an erection!"

"I didn't say anything about 'maintaining,'" Gunner said. "You asked me to tell you what I saw in the photograph, not how many micro-seconds I had to photograph it."

Laughter again exploded throughout the room.

"He's a goddamn lie!" Compton cried at the top of his lungs, once more on his feet. Glaring at Gunner, he snapped, "I can outlast you any day of the week, motherfucker!"

Gunner just smiled.

London lowered his head like a beaten dog and returned to his seat beside Compton as Spillman's arm swung his gavel again and again, hammering out an order of silence that, London knew, was not soon to be obeyed.

"That was quite a performance in there," someone said with obvious amusement.

Gunner turned to find an attractive brunette in a pinstriped suit standing beside him, joining the crowd waiting for an elevator out in the second-floor courthouse hallway. The suit was a beige linen-blend number of little distinction, common and ordinary, but the same could not be said for the woman inside it. She was in her mid-twenties, Gunner guessed, and tall—an easy five ten—with a light mane of golden brown hair and a dark European face that was wonderfully ambiguous: large brown eyes and a full mouth, complemented by an understated, angular nose.

"My name is Kelly DeCharme, Mr. Gunner," she said, offering the black man her hand. "I'm with the Public Defender's office. The gentleman who answered your office phone—Mickey, I believe his name was—told me I could find you here."

Gunner accepted her hand without comment, silently cursing Mickey Moore—whose barbershop in Watts he had recently started using as an "office"—for making his itinerary a matter of public record. Then he waited for the catch. There was always a catch when someone from the Public Defender's office went out of their way to introduce themselves, especially when they looked like DeCharme.

"You put on quite a show in there, as I said. Compton's goose is as good as cooked."

"You really think so?"

"Please. The man absolutely crucified himself. You pushed all the right buttons, and he did the rest."

"You flatter me, Ms. DeCharme."

"Granted, Judge Spillman struck Compton's outbursts from the record, and warned the fine men and women of the jury to disregard his comments, but I think we both know how much good that's likely to do. Don't we?"

An elevator arrived. Gunner and DeCharme allowed it to fill and depart without them. The public defender had the kind of naughty-girl smile on her face that was, in the detective's experience, often best erased with a kiss.

"I'm afraid I no more know what that jury will do than I know the reasons for our discussing it," Gunner said.

"Which is your way of asking me to get to the point, I believe."

"Yes. As a matter of fact, it is."

"Would you mind very much if I did so over a drink?"

"A drink?"

"That's right. A drink. In lieu of a bribe. Or can't you be taken advantage of when properly intoxicated?"

She tried the smile on him again, and Gunner returned it with one of his own, openly intrigued. "Now *you're* pushing all the right buttons, Ms. DeCharme," he said.

• • •

They jaywalked across Grand Avenue to the Los Angeles
County Music Center's three-theater complex and found a
table at the bistro that lay directly opposite the courthouse,
snuggled into the eastward base of the Dorothy Chandler Pa-
vilion. The place was dark and languid, as full of life as a
Christmas tree on the third of January. DeCharme ordered a
Corona in the bottle, while Gunner stuck with his old
standby, Wild Turkey on ice, confident that DeCharme
would not tolerate any attempt on his part to pick up the
check.

They drank in a delicate silence until DeCharme grew
tired of it and asked, "Does the name Toby Mills mean anything to you, Mr. Gunner?"

Gunner decided it didn't, after some deliberation, and
said so.

"How about Darrel Lovejoy? You ever hear of him?"

This time Gunner nodded. "He was the anti-gangbanger
who was murdered a few weeks back. The one the press
made such a fuss over about a year ago. A couple of kids shot
him in a drive-by, supposedly."

DeCharme nodded her own head, spilling a wisp of brilliant chestnut hair before her face. "That's him. Founder and
CEO of the L.A. Peace Patrol, one of the most successful
anti-gang community-service organizations in the inner city.
He and the Reverend Willie Raines ran the program together. He did some good work and turned a lot of bad kids
around before he was murdered, but he pissed off just as
many in the process, so you can imagine how thin the ice
was he'd been skating on. Any one of the hundred or so
youth gangs presently operating in the South-Central area
could have 'done' him, as they say, and been thrilled to admit it.

"Ordinarily, sorting through them all to find the gang
actually responsible for his murder might represent a monu-

mental task for the police to undertake, but this time around they've had some rather unusual help. It seems they've found a witness who's positively identified the killers as members of the Imperial Blues, a local Cuz set active in the neighborhood in which Lovejoy was killed. Not far from your own neighborhood, if I'm not mistaken."

The observation didn't seem to mean much to Gunner. "I believe so. Yeah."

"Then you are familiar with the Blues."

Gunner shrugged. "I know only what I can't help but know. I bump into a few kids flashing their colors every now and then, and come across their spray-paint artwork from time to time." He stopped short, making the connection belatedly. "This Mills kid was supposed to be a Blue, wasn't he?"

"Yes."

"He's the one they have in custody? The trigger man?"

"The alleged trigger man. Yes. His prints were among several found on a weapon the police turned up a few days after the murder, but that doesn't make him the one who used it on Lovejoy. There's only the testimony of Tamika Downs to imply that, and for my money, that kind of evidence leaves plenty of room for doubt."

"Downs is the witness?"

DeCharme finished off her beer and nodded again. "She's an unemployed barroom dancer with four kids to support and no past history of humanitarianism to speak of, yet she's appeared out of nowhere to voluntarily identify Mills and a second Blue by the name of Rookie Davidson as the pair in the car. Which either makes her a very special lady or a very dishonest one, because I just can't see it. I mean, since when do unwed welfare mothers of four like Downs put their asses on the line for a dead man?"

"As a rule?" Gunner asked. "Never. But maybe she's a special case."

DeCharme waited for him to explain.

"You live in that part of the world—and I assume Downs does—you learn pretty fast that cooperating with the police in a murder case—especially one dealing with a gang-banger—is no way to enhance one's life expectancy. But"— he shrugged and took a sip of his drink—"every now and then you come across somebody with no interest in the odds. Somebody who's been hit too close to home and has decided they've had enough. Lovejoy *was* an unusual man. If Downs was among his many fans, her sudden show of good citizenship could figure."

DeCharme gave that some thought, momentarily forgetting to hold up her end of the conversation.

"Maybe," she said eventually, not sounding at all sold on the idea.

Gunner tossed another generous shot of Wild Turkey down his throat and said, "I take it you're either Mills's or Davidson's court-appointed attorney."

DeCharme rewarded his insight with a woefully hollow smile. "Give the man a cigar," she said.

"Mills is your client?"

She nodded.

"And Davidson?"

She shook her head. "Davidson doesn't need a lawyer— yet. As of this morning, he's still at large. Which, you'll no doubt be happy to know, finally brings me around to that point I promised almost an hour ago I'd get to."

She pushed her empty beer bottle aside to clear the space between them and leaned forward on her elbows to take advantage of it. "Toby Mills wasn't in that car the night Darrel Lovejoy was murdered, Mr. Gunner. If Rookie Davidson was driving, he was playing chauffeur for someone else."

"Uh-huh. And who says that? Mills?"

"That's right. Says Mills. And I believe him. Don't ask me why."

"No. I don't think I will."

"He was out in his mother's driveway changing the oil in his sister's car when they arrested him, for Christ's sake. That doesn't sound like a guilty man to me."

"So if the gunman in the car wasn't Mills, who was it?"

"That's where you come in. Because Mills doesn't know. He can drop some names and make a few guesses, but that's not going to buy him much, is it?"

"You need Davidson."

"At this point, yes. He's supposed to be something of a weak sister, just a junior flip; Mills says the police'll have no trouble getting the truth out of him once he turns up."

She passed a photograph across the table toward him. It was a blown-up mug shot of Rookie Davidson, as the name across his chest advertised. He was a dark-skinned kid with a jheri-curl haircut and a frail goatee who looked about fifteen years old. If he had posed for such photos before, he had yet to harden from the experience; the expression on his face was the kind a man generally wore just prior to wetting his pants.

"And if he doesn't turn up?" Gunner asked.

"We just need a name, Mr. Gunner. Proof of the real gunman's identity. If you could manage to get that without Davidson's help, that would be fine, of course."

Gunner smiled dourly. "Of course."

DeCharme saw the smile and said, "I say something wrong?"

The black man rolled the ice cubes around in his glass absently, watching them play leapfrog in a shallow sea of thinning bourbon. "Generally speaking, Miss DeCharme," he said, facing her again, "gangbangers aren't my favorite people. I don't much like their manners, or the heavy iron they're so fond of demonstrating in public places. They kill children in sandboxes and grandmothers on porch swings in the never-ending process of killing themselves, and that kind of fatal inefficiency pisses me off no end. So I do what I can to see that our paths cross as rarely as possible. You know what I mean?"

DeCharme said nothing, unwilling, at least for the moment, to argue with him.

"While I've never met your client, I'd imagine he's a hard-nosed little man-child I'd dislike immediately. Big and bad, cold to the bone, a master of the scathing, monosyllabic cry of social protest. Abusive and cynical; a postadolescent wound looking for a place to bleed.

"The reason I don't have to meet Mills to safely assume all this is because I deal with hoods like him every day, down in our little war-torn corner of the world. I see the bloody messes they make up close and personal, hours and sometimes days before they make the evening news. All it takes is a walk around the block, any time of day or night, whether I'm in the mood for the carnage or not."

"So what's your point?"

"My point is, I can't see why I should have the slightest interest in what happens to your client, counselor. Can you? You want me to help such a fucked-up antisocialist get his act back out on the street—my street, remember—you're going to have to explain my motivation for me."

"You have a job to do as a licensed operator for the state of California," DeCharme said pointedly. "How's that for motivation?"

Gunner laughed, an abrupt, guttural edge to his voice turning heads around them. "I'm going to need a little more incentive than that, lady," he said.

"I'll pay you what you're worth, for as long as it takes. That's incentive enough for most people."

Gunner's laughter ground abruptly to a halt. "Maybe. But you're not trying to hire most people. You're trying to hire me. And the thing about me is, I have to give a damn about the people I represent. Otherwise, I do piss-poor work, believe me."

The public defender stood up quickly, fished through her purse, and tossed a twenty-dollar bill on the table. "In that case, Mr. Gunner, I'm afraid I've wasted your time. Because Toby Mills obviously fails to meet your high standards in people. And quite frankly, you fail to meet mine."

She said the last in passing, already executing a fast retreat. Gunner had to do some serious hustling to catch up with her out on the sidewalk, where she stood at the curb waiting for traffic to clear on Grand, trying to get back to the courthouse. It was after 6 P.M. and the sky was growing dark, giving up the ghost of day ever so grudgingly. DeCharme seemed not to notice Gunner at her side.

"Guess I blew the interview back there," Gunner said dryly.

"Don't worry yourself about it," DeCharme said, eyeing the street. "I should never have come to you in the first place. We have our own detectives. One of them will help me."

Gunner shook his head. "You don't want to deal with those clowns."

"No," DeCharme agreed. "I don't. They're overworked and not very good. But they're at least willing to deal with *me*, and that's something, isn't it?" She turned to him at last, glowering. "Toby Mills is *twenty-two years old*, Mr. Gunner. He's just a child, to most people's way of thinking. He has time to wise up, to turn his life around. Yet you want to write him off, sight unseen, because you think you know him and every kid like him like the back of your proverbial hand. Well, join the club." She clapped her hands sarcastically. "The world's full of experts like you. And they're all just as amenable to seeing the poor bastard hang for one thing or another . . . even if it has to be something he didn't do."

"That's a big 'if,'" Gunner said defensively.

"Not for me it isn't. I've spoken to Mills. Have you?"

Her eyes wouldn't leave his, throwing down the gauntlet, and he could actually feel himself diminishing under the weight of her gaze.

"No," he told her reluctantly. "Not yet."

He took the public defender's arm and led her across the street.

chapter **two**

....

The prisoner-visitation room at the Los Angeles County Jail facility on Bauchete Street in the heart of downtown was a three-ring circus, sans clowns, at noon the next day, a Friday.

The room was bad enough any other day of the week, the heavyset, baby-faced guard at the door said, but Fridays were always the worst. For the endless procession of prisoners and visitors that packed the little room to its maximum capacity from dawn to dusk, it was harder to be on the inside looking out on Fridays, and almost as hard to be on the outside looking in. The weekend was waiting, two days of endless promise under the bright light of Southern California sunshine, and the incarcerated were all too aware of the pleasures, both sacred and profane, of which they were about to be deprived. Tempers were short on Fridays, and physical violence was not uncommon. Sexual frustrations, erupting on either side of the conference tables, often led to some steamy and embarrassing scenes.

The garrulous young guard grinned at Gunner wolfishly. "*Real* embarrassing," he said.

Gunner and DeCharme were assigned to the only vacant hardwood table at the south end of the room's

long, evenly spaced row of six, near a pair of barred
windows and the warm wash of sunlight they provided.
They sat down on the cold aluminum of some cheap folding
chairs at the table and took in the crowded room while waiting for Toby Mills to be escorted in. As a motley crew of
gray- and blue-garbed prisoners conferred with friends and
family, lawyers and accomplices, a pool of mixed voices
speaking several different languages splashed off the flat-
latexed walls and rolled through the stale, smoke-filled air,
rising and falling in volume like an eccentric ocean tide.
Through the din, Gunner found himself eavesdropping on
the Hispanic couple at the next table, who were engaged in a
heated, bilingual debate on the merits of grand theft auto; the
uniformed inmate was defending the practice in English,
while his portly, swarthy wife was soundly denouncing it *en
español*.

Before a winner of the pair's exchange could be established, a lean black guard with a clean-shaven head dropped
Toby Mills into the chair opposite Gunner and DeCharme,
acting not unlike a man taking out the garbage. He frowned
at DeCharme, frowned harder at Gunner, then moved off
again, having made not even the most casual of introductions. Gunner watched him come to rest not far away, at a
spot along one wall where their table could be easily observed; he made himself comfortable there and grew still, his
eyes never leaving Mills for a minute.

"He don't like me," Mills said gleefully.

Gunner turned his attention from the guard to appraise
DeCharme's client, without concern for discretion. Mills let
him look, enjoying the spotlight. He was just short of average
height, somewhere around five seven or five eight, with jet-
black skin, lady-killer eyes, and an iron-man build too well-
defined for his undersized blue prison blouse to conceal. He
had high cheekbones and small ears, and his hair was cut to
an all-but-invisible length all the way around, with the ex-

ception of a tiny rat's tail hanging at the back of his head. His teeth were good, but his gums were discolored, and a meandering scar drew an ugly tan line from the corner of his mouth to the edge of his earlobe on the left side of his face. The scar did a dance whenever he smiled, and he looked like the kind of man who did a lot of smiling, for nothing but the worst possible reasons.

Gunner was immediately able to see the guard's problem with him.

"Who's this nosy motherfucker?" Mills asked De-Charme curiously, eyeing Gunner with the kind of amusement most people reserved for circus clowns.

"This is Aaron Gunner, Toby. The private investigator we talked about earlier." DeCharme was blushing slightly, and she glanced briefly in Gunner's direction, apologizing.

"No shit," Mills said.

"Toby, I've hired Mr. Gunner to find Rookie. He's on our side, all right?"

"Oh, yeah. I hear you. He's a cop, but he's on our side. He's here to help."

"Yes." DeCharme glared at him, the cords in her neck pulled taut and hard.

Feigning boredom, Mills yawned and said, "So how's he gonna do that? Man ain't asked me shit yet. How the fuck he gonna help me, he don't never ask me nothin'?"

His eyes were on Gunner, and the scar on his cheek was dancing again. DeCharme turned and joined him in waiting for Gunner's response, encouraging the detective to take the floor with a light shrug of her shoulders.

Gunner absorbed Mills's indignant grin with great restraint, his own expression a masterpiece of neutrality. When he finally spoke, his voice was barely audible above the room's throbbing wall of sound.

"How fast do you heal, sweet pea?" he asked Mills.

"Say what?"

DeCharme bit down hard on her lower lip.

"I take this chair I'm sitting in and crack your skull with it," Gunner said, "how long you think you'll be laid up? A few weeks? Five or six months, maybe?"

Mills's scar stopped dancing. Gunner pulled his chair up closer to the table and said, "I think you'd better give it some thought. Because your 'homeboy without a cause' routine is weak, and if I hear another ten seconds of it, I'm going to jack your smart ass up and explain it any way I want, with your partner over there as my star witness." He nodded his head at the guard who had dropped Mills off at the table; the bald man in the crisp Sheriff's Department uniform was still watching their conference with open interest. "Or do you think he'd side with you?"

Mills didn't answer. He sat in silence and allowed the last glint of charm to dissolve from his face like a serpent shedding its skin. He stiffened in his chair and glared at Gunner with eyes narrowed down to mere slivers of white, fingering the edge of the table with both hands, battling indecision.

Gunner and DeCharme let him have all the time he needed to make up his mind.

"What you wanna know?" he asked Gunner finally.

"For starters, where were you the night Lovejoy was killed?"

Mills looked at DeCharme. "She ain't told you that?"

"I'm not asking her. I'm asking you. I'd like to see if you still remember how the story goes."

Mills shrugged. "I was with a friend."

"Be more specific."

"You mean, what was her name?"

Gunner nodded.

"Sharice Phillips. My girlfriend. Me an' Sharice was together that night. You can ask her."

"Together where? Doing what?"

"We was at the movies. At the Baldwin theater, up in Baldwin Hills. They got three screens at the Baldwin."

"Tell me what you saw," Gunner said.

Mills made the scar quaver anew, seemingly remembering. "We seen a little of everythin'. We seen some of that new Sylvester Stallone movie, *Heavy Artillery*; we seen some of this love-story flick, I forget what they call it; and we seen almost all of that stupid-ass *Friday the Thirteenth, Part Eight*, or Nine, or whatever number they up to now. I think it's Eight. Yeah, Eight."

"So you were bouncing from screen to screen."

"Yeah. Right. From screen to screen."

"Anybody see you who might remember it? The cashier in the booth out front, or an usher, maybe?"

Mills shook his head. "Didn't nobody workin' there see us that night. We didn't see no cashier, 'cause we snuck in the side door, like we always do. And we didn't see no ushers, 'cause we didn't wanna see none. I didn't wanna have to bust nobody up if one of 'em tried to say somethin' 'bout us not havin' no tickets, or 'bout us sneakin' in all the theaters, some shit like that."

"You have any idea how long you were there? From what time to what time?"

Again, Mills shrugged indifferently. "We was there all night, is all I know. From 'bout eight o'clock 'til they closed, I guess."

Gunner looked at DeCharme.

"LAPD says Lovejoy was killed somewhere in the neighborhood of ten-thirty, give or take fifteen minutes," she said.

Which meant that Mills had a fine alibi, providing his presence in Baldwin Hills—no stone's throw from the site of Lovejoy's murder—could be verified.

"How did you get to the theater? You drive, or did she?"

"I did."

"What were you driving?"

"My mom's car. Seventy-nine Olds Cutlass, gold with a white top. What difference do it make what we was drivin'?"

"If no one saw you or Sharice in Baldwin Hills that night," DeCharme said, before Gunner could reward Mills's curiosity with an insult, "maybe they saw your mother's car, and will remember it. Although Oldsmobiles—"

"Don't usually leave lasting impressions on people," Gunner said, completing DeCharme's thought. "If you parked it in a crowded lot, it was probably only one Olds out of a hundred there."

Mills nodded his head silently, understanding.

"You see Rookie Davidson at all that evening?" Gunner asked him, shifting gears abruptly.

The teenager shook his head. "Uh-uh. Didn't see the Rook all that day."

"He wasn't at the movies with you and Sharice?"

"Hell, no," Mills said, disdaining the chance to hitch Davidson up to his comfortable alibi. "He was back in the 'hood drivin' for the man what popped Dr. Love, how he gonna be with us?"

Gunner paused, genuinely surprised by the admission. "You know that for a fact?"

"What?"

"That Rookie was the driver in the Lovejoy killing."

"Oh yeah," Mills said. "Had to be him."

"What makes you so sure?"

"The car, man. S'posed to've been a blue Mav'rick, right? That's Rookie's ride, a blue Mav'rick. 'Sides, that's what homeboy does, ain't it?"

"What's that?"

Mills looked at Gunner as if he were some low-intelligence life form too dense to be believed. "*Drive*, man," he said simply. "Rookie don't do nothin' for the set but drive."

He said it as if Davidson were capable of nothing else; as

if he had found his niche in life and could not possibly deviate from it. In the organizational matrix of the contemporary street gang, Gunner thought, one's very role in life was probably just as easily defined as that.

"Why would Rookie have been driving that night? He have something against Lovejoy personally that you're aware of?"

"Shit yeah, he did. We all had somethin' 'gainst Dr. Love personally," Mills said matter-of-factly. "The Blues, the Troopers, the motherfuckin' Tees—everybody. Didn't no set want Dr. Love in they 'hood, 'cause all he ever caused 'bangers was trouble. Always buggin' homeboys to give up they set, to stop gangbangin' and shit. Look at this bogus peace conference thing he was tryin' to get everybody to come to. You know about that?"

Gunner nodded.

"Shit. Peace conference my ass. That ain't gonna 'complish nothin', 'cept get a few more homeboys' heads fucked up."

"I take it you weren't invited to attend."

"Invited? Yeah, we was invited. Matter of fact, now you mention it, it was Dr. Love what invited us. In person. Came around the 'hood one day, tryin' to make his goddamn conference sound like somethin' fresh, like some special event was gonna change our whole lives, or somethin'. I told 'im, 'Sorry, Doc, but my homies an' me, we got other plans that day. Count us the fuck out.'"

He laughed.

"It doesn't sound like you two hit it off too well," Gunner said.

"No. We didn't," Mills admitted.

"But you didn't kill him."

"No. Not me."

"But the police have your shotgun, with your prints all over it."

"So? They didn't find it on *me*. Last time I seen that piece was four days 'fore I got hemmed up, 'fore some motherfucker busted into our crib in the 'hood and took everything. All the homeboys' gats got picked, there wasn't nothin' left behind. I keep tellin' the cops, whoever it was done it, musta been them what killed Dr. Love, not me."

"What about the witness who says *you* did?"

"You talkin' 'bout the bitch on TV? Shamika Jones, or whatever her fuckin' name is?"

Gunner nodded. "You know her?"

Mills shook his head. "Uh-uh. Ain't never seen her nowhere before."

"Then how do you explain her picking your mug shot out of the book? Why you and not somebody else?"

"Shit, I don't know why she done it. Maybe she made a mistake. Maybe she just seen somebody in the car looked like me."

"Yeah? Like who?"

"Hey, I told you, I don't *know* who. If it'd been one of my homeboys, I would've heard somethin' 'bout it."

"Then Rookie was driving for someone other than a Blue."

"I guess so. Yeah."

"Would he do that?"

Mills laughed at the question. "Shit. Why not? The Rook, man, he's a little pussy. A *mark*. Ain't never down for nothin'. He'd drive for anybody, anytime, they scare him bad enough."

Gunner paused, said, "That why you're so eager to sell him out?"

"This ain't sellin' out nobody, man. This is just tellin' you, *straight*, 'cause you asked me: It was Rookie what was prob'ly drivin' the car what rolled on Dr. Love, and it wasn't no Blue he was ridin' with. All right?"

"Then who *was* it? Give me a for instance, name names."

"Shit, I told you, I don't know who it was. His old man, maybe. The King. The King's crazy. One mean, drunk motherfucker. The King tells Rookie to jump, Rookie always say, 'How high?' He'd've told Rookie to drive that night, Rookie would've drove, no questions asked."

"If this King had a reason to want to kill Lovejoy."

"Yeah. That's right. If."

Gunner glanced at DeCharme wearily, then back at Mills. "Anybody else?"

Mills shook his head. "I can't think of nobody else. Rookie usually stays with his older brother Teddy, but Teddy ain't no gangbanger. Hell, no. Teddy, he's straight. Runs a tire store in the 'hood; man wouldn't't've had no part of no drive-by. I'd bet money on that."

"He and Rookie get along all right? Are they close?"

"Teddy be ridin' the Rook to stop gangbangin' all the time, but they get along all right, mostly."

"You think he might know where Rookie's been hiding out since the shooting?"

"Might."

"How about the King?"

"The King? Man, I don't know 'bout the King. If he was the one what made Rookie drive, he might know somethin'. But if he wasn't, he prob'ly don't know shit. 'Cause he don't wanna know shit usually, right? I mean, the King, he don't usually give a damn 'bout Rookie."

"And you? You have any ideas?"

"'Bout what?"

"About where Rookie might be holed up."

Mills parted with another dispassionate shrug. "He could be at our old crib, maybe. Place I told you 'bout, where we used to keep all our shit? Go see my homeboys; ask for Smalltime. Tell 'im I said to show you where it's at. He got any questions, they give you any trouble, you tell 'em to see Jody, my sister. She'll talk to 'em, tell 'em I say you're okay."

Gunner asked if Smalltime would be able to tell him where to find Rookie's father, and Mills nodded.

"Anything you want, you just ask 'im," the Blue said. "But don't bother askin' nobody but Smalltime nothin', 'cause he the only one gonna wanna talk to you, prob'ly." He looked at DeCharme, and the scar on his face began another dance as he grinned broadly. "Tell 'im 'bout Cube, Miss D. So he'll know what I'm talkin' 'bout."

Gunner turned toward DeCharme.

"One of his more misanthropic 'homeboys,'" the lawyer explained, with apparent distaste for the subject. "'Cube' is short for 'Ice Cube,' presumably because he has that kind of cheery disposition. I made the mistake of trying to interview him some weeks back, and very nearly got myself killed. You'd be well advised to give him as wide a berth as possible whenever dealing with the Blues."

Gunner nodded, filing away for future reference how gravely DeCharme had offered the advice. "I'll remember that," he said.

"All right, people. Time's up."

It was Mills's guardian angel, the walking frown in the freshly laundered sheriff's deputy's uniform. He was suddenly behind the inmate's chair, arms locked tightly across his chest, genielike, trying to make the point clear that he was not about to be kept waiting. Mills peered up at him and smiled.

DeCharme checked her watch and looked at Gunner helplessly. "Were you through?"

Gunner nodded. "Pretty much."

"Good," the guard said, lifting Mills to his feet.

"Though there is one more thing I'd like to ask him," Gunner said, before DeCharme's client could be led away.

He was staring directly at the man in uniform, issuing a wordless order to back off.

The guard hesitated, torn between duty and charity.

"Just one," he said to Gunner gruffly, careful to make it sound more like a directive than a question.

Gunner nodded.

The guard backed away, just far enough to be harmless, beyond the range of their voices. Mills watched him leave, sneering, delighting in his small retreat.

"This Cube," Gunner said to Mills, trying not to let the slithering scar on the young man's cheek enrage him, "he have any kind of hard-on for Lovejoy you're aware of? Did they know each other?"

"Cube? Naw." Mills shook his head emphatically. "He and Dr. Love, they knew each other, yeah, but they didn't never mix it up. Love knew better than to fuck with the Cube. Cube 'banged with some Patrollers once, Doc seen what he can do."

"Peace Patrollers?"

"Yeah."

Gunner asked what had happened.

"'Bout a year ago, Cube say he caught a couple Tees in the 'hood and was fixin' to pop 'em when some Patrollers got in the way. So he had to kill one." He sounded like somebody describing a memorable play in a football game. "Why you ask?"

Gunner shook his head. "Just wondered," he said.

He looked up to find the bald-headed guard starting back toward them, and made no move to stop him.

He was finally tired of asking questions he couldn't stomach the answers to.

"Well?" DeCharme asked.

They were standing in the County Jail parking lot, turning like weather vanes against an assertive but dry Santa Ana wind passing through April on its way into May. DeCharme's late-model Volkswagen Jetta and Gunner's borrowed Hyundai Excel both sat nearby, but they declined to take refuge in either car, preferring instead the freedom of movement they had outside on their feet.

"He's insane," Gunner said. "You know that."

DeCharme nodded, acquiescing. "Yes. I do." She produced a pack of cigarettes from her purse and lit one up, fighting the wind all the way. "But that doesn't mean he killed Darrel Lovejoy."

"No. It doesn't."

"You think it's a setup, like he says?"

"Maybe. Some things seem to fit too well, some things not at all."

"Yes. His being the trigger man, for example."

"Yeah. Like that. At twenty-two, he's too old for that kind of duty. A gang decides to take somebody out, they don't generally assign the actual killing to anybody over seventeen. They let a minor do it, somebody the state can't try as an adult."

"Exactly."

"Still, his Baldwin Hills alibi could have easily been trumped up. The girl will say it happened just the way he describes it, of course, but without an objective third party who can place them in the area of the theater at the time of the murder, his movie reviews aren't worth a damn."

"Tell me about it," DeCharme said.

"And it's hard to buy Davidson driving for just anybody," Gunner went on, speculatively. "If he's half the wimp Mills says he is, he should have been too scared to go on a drive-by with anyone *but* a Blue."

DeCharme nodded and blew a lungful of smoke over her right shoulder.

"Which only serves to prove your point: You need to find him."

"Yes. We do."

She left it at that, and waited. The gaze she turned upon him was steady yet undemanding.

Gunner shook his head and sighed. "I can't think of anything I'd rather do less than this," he said. "Because to do the job right, I'm going to have to get knee-deep in this gangbanging bullshit . . . and I can't stand the view of it I already have. But I made that abundantly clear yesterday, didn't I?"

"Abundantly clear. Yes."

"And yet I'm here, anyway."

DeCharme nodded wordlessly. She tossed her cigarette down and crushed it underfoot, then studied its flattened carcass absently.

"You're going to start with them, I assume," she said after a while, looking up. There had been a slight but detectable trace of dread in her voice.

Gunner shrugged noncommittally. "Maybe not right away. But soon, yes."

"In that case," DeCharme said, "I think I should show you something."

Even in the muted light of the parking lot, Gunner could see that some of the color had left her face. She moved up close and pulled the hair away from the right side of her throat with one hand, tilting her head back to give Gunner a good look at the underside of her jawline. There was a fresh scar there about an inch and a half long, running parallel to the jawline, healing well enough to fade but not well enough to disappear. Ever.

"Mills meant what he said about Cube," she said, quickly covering the scar up again. "And so did I."

Gunner didn't say anything.

Self-consciously, DeCharme shrugged and smiled, hoping she had done the right thing in warning the black man so graphically. "Just for the record," she said.

"Sure," Gunner agreed, nodding his head mechanically. "Just for the record."

It was highly pessimistic of him, but he was already detesting the week to come.

chapter **three**

....

I'm looking for something in a nine-millimeter auto," Gunner said. "Something lightweight but with plenty of stopping power."

"Uh-huh."

"Accurate and easy to conceal."

"Right."

"Moderately priced but built to last."

"Naturally."

"Know what I mean?"

Dee Holiday nodded her head. "You want something *cheap*," she said.

"Yeah. Exactly."

Holiday smiled in appreciation of her own clairvoyance, happy to see that Gunner's priorities were as easy to call as ever.

"Got just the thing for you," she said, winking, before ducking down to open the long, waist-high display case she was standing behind.

Dee Holiday was a handsome, ebony-skinned black woman in her mid-forties who could do more with a smile than most women could manage with their entire bodies, and she used the power sparingly, selectively. It was the smile

that generally brought Gunner into her place of business—
Holiday's Gun Shop on Rosecrans, just west of Long Beach
Boulevard in Compton—rather than any genuine need on
his part to actually shop there.

Today, however, the smile was a secondary attraction.
On this Saturday-morning visit, like everyone else in the
shop fingering Holiday's merchandise, he was here to equip
himself with some new and improved tool of death, to re-
generate his capacity to do one living creature or another serious bodily harm.

"This is the Ruger P-Eighty-five," Holiday said, resur-
facing from the depths of the display case to hand Gunner a
compact, smooth-skinned automatic pistol in a menacing
matte-black finish. "Nine-millimeter double-action, fifteen
rounds. Built like a tank and hits just as hard, with hardly no
recoil to speak of."

"Loads?"

"Practically anything. Hollow point, round nose . . .
you name it."

Gunner tossed the Ruger about in his right hand, testing
it for weight and feel, liking what he found. "What about
accuracy?"

"Inside of twenty-five yards, very good," Holiday said.
"Inside of ten, better than that. Excellent, even." She
laughed. "Even you could probably hit the broad side of a
barn with it, providing the barn didn't move."

Gunner ignored the joke, said, "Sold," and passed the
Ruger back over the counter to her.

They haggled over price for a while, Gunner trying to
make a steal, Holiday trying to make a profit, until a friendly
impasse brought them to a fair figure Gunner could almost
live with.

At that point, convinced Holiday had reached her dis-
counting limit, the detective laid a small bundle on the
counter before her, a handgun swathed in a ragged-edged,

makeshift blue pistol rug, and carefully peeled it open. His black, antediluvian Police Special was inside, a Smith & Wesson .357 with a stumpy barrel and a wicked, battle-scarred finish.

"What'll you give me for it, Dee?" Gunner asked.

Holiday looked at the gun and shook her head. "I don't want this," she said apologetically. "This is your Special. The one they gave you at the academy."

"So?"

"So it must have some kind of sentimental value to you, Aaron. You should hold on to it."

Gunner shook his own head. "I'm not that sentimental," he said. He wasn't going to tell her that the weapon had forever lost its special place in his heart because someone had only months ago used it to kill two people, one directly, one indirectly, and neither with his consent. It was a story of stupidity and professional ineptitude that hurt just to think about, let alone relate to friends.

Holiday studied his face earnestly, trying to see past the flesh clear through to the secrets of the soul. "You going to war with somebody?" she asked him eventually.

"Not if I can help it," Gunner lied, cursing his unfailing transparency. "But one never knows, does one?"

She tried to wait him out, but he wouldn't let her steady gaze pry anything in the way of further explanation out of him. "I'll give you fifty in trade for this," Holiday said, referring to the Smith & Wesson, "but on one condition: You hold on to it for me."

"Say what?"

"You heard me. Keep it for me. Put it in a safe place. I ever have a buyer for it, I'll let you know."

The terms sounded suspect to Gunner, but he shrugged, accepting the harmless compromise. "I can do that," he said.

Holiday nodded and took his money, then went off to get the requisite paperwork—state and federal forms in duplicate and triplicate—needed to complete their transaction. In many states of the Union, the paperwork would not have been necessary at this, the point of sale, but here in California, the law prevented Gunner from taking possession of the Ruger, or any handgun, until the proper agencies could be officially notified of its purchase, a process that in most cases took somewhere in the neighborhood of two weeks.

It was an attempt to make the acquisition of lethal weapons a more complex and troublesome proposition for the criminal element, one that would have been worth a mild round of the taxpayers' applause, if not a raucous standing ovation, were it not for the fact that rifles were wholly excluded from the ordinance's demands.

Perhaps it was this judicial oversight that accounted, at least partially, for Holiday's perpetually booming business. As he rewrapped his revolver, Gunner took a look around to survey the customary crush of customers milling about the store. Kids too young to shave were grinning at their reflections in the blades of huge hunting knives and men with tired faces were holding shotguns in their arms like new fathers cradling infants in a nursery. An old man standing at the end of the store's main display case was handling an American-made copy of the AK-47 assault rifle under the watchful eye of one of Holiday's expert salespersons. He looked to be in his early fifties, slow and easygoing; somebody's innocuous grandfather out treating himself to a new rod and reel. Only the thing in his hand was not for fishing. It was for killing, and on a grandiose scale.

Holiday reappeared and caught Gunner inspecting her clientele, his face clouded by a mild revulsion for the scene.

"It's crazy, isn't it?" she asked him, watching with Gunner as the old man at the counter, satisfied, began to lay his money down for the pseudo-AK-47.

Gunner turned around and said, "They're just looking for an edge, Dee. Same as you and me."

Holiday nodded, her mood having taken an obvious turn for the worse.

"When you're up against the devil, I guess you've gotta have *something*," she said.

Gunner caught the vacant look in her eyes and left her without saying much more than goodbye, certain that the smile that could lighten any man's load, no matter how despondent, was out of service for the day.

The Hyundai was a dog.

Gunner's cousin Del had picked up the payments on the car as a favor to an old flame's irresponsible son, a party-hopping college dropout who had neither the means nor the will to ever make them himself. Del was a man of simple tastes, an electrician by trade, who thought the silver and black Korean-made four-door would make an ideal company vehicle, but he soon developed a reluctance to drive it that made loaning it out to Gunner for a month or so no great personal sacrifice.

It had only taken a few days of unrelenting commuter boredom for Gunner to dislike the car as much as Del did, but the Hyundai's lack of power and panache was wholly outweighed by its suitability to his purpose. Gunner had finally conceded the fact that his own car—a classic, eye-catching red 1965 Ford Shelby Cobra convertible—was a surveillance vehicle of dubious merit, which, when combined with a black driver behind the wheel, often amounted to nothing less conspicuous than a large neon sign advertising his presence on the street. The Hyundai, on the other hand, was almost chameleonlike in its ability to blend seamlessly into any background. Advertising hype claimed there were more than a half-million of the boxy little cars on the American road, so its appearance in the rearview mirror of someone Gunner was trying to tail was almost guaranteed to go unnoticed—as Del's had during its first tour of duty under Gunner: the Lionel Compton surveillance.

All of which served to explain why it was the Hyundai and not the Cobra that Gunner edged up to the curb in front of Ted's Tires, the discount tire store Teddy Davidson owned and operated on Main and 137th, less than thirty minutes after his visit to Dee Holiday's gun shop Saturday morning. Kelly DeCharme had supplied the detective with a wealth of information with which to do his job, including the names and present addresses of all the principal players involved in Toby Mills's case, so hunting Davidson down had not been the difficult process of phone-book scanning it ordinarily might have been.

Rookie's older brother had converted an old gas station into an off-brand tire supermarket, plastered the architecture with bright paint and exuberant sale signs, and in so doing had apparently found the formula for success, because the place was teeming with people and cars as Gunner approached the service desk. A short Jamaican with lidded eyes and too many teeth stood behind the counter there, taking orders and fielding complaints with equal panache, and Gunner had to brave the sneers and brush-back blocks of the horde before him to ask whether Teddy Davidson was in. The Jamaican nodded his head and made a faint gesture with his right hand to indicate the service bay, never looking up for a moment from the catalogue he was studying.

There were three men laboring heavily out in the crowded service bay when Gunner entered, each wearing identical blue overalls that lacked the customary breast-pocket name tags Gunner was hoping to see, but one of the three was giving all the orders and the other two were taking them, so Davidson was nevertheless easy to identify. He was circling a late-model Pontiac up on one of the bay's four racks, pounding the hubcaps back onto its freshly refitted rims, when Gunner came up behind him. He turned once at the intrusion, then returned his full attention to his work.

"You're not allowed back here, sir," he said simply.

He was a clean-shaven man in his early thirties, expertly

groomed and mannered; the grease on his hands and face clashed with his gentlemanly presence, like white socks paired with a brown suit.

"I'm looking for Teddy," Gunner said, staying put.

"I'm Teddy, but any questions you have, you'll have to ask me in the office. Not out here."

"I'll ask them wherever you want," Gunner conceded, stepping around the elevated Pontiac to show Davidson his investigator's license.

Davidson didn't give the license much of his time; he saw the wallet come up in Gunner's hand and got the gist of things right away, letting the mallet he was using on the Pontiac's hubcaps drop to his side as if he had suddenly lost the strength to wield it.

"Jesus Christ. Not another one." He looked thoroughly disgusted. "You guys never quit, do you?"

"Read the fine print. I'm private," Gunner said.

Davidson glanced at the license again and shrugged. "Okay, so you're private. What difference does that make? You're still going to ask the same ten thousand questions about Rookie the cops did, right?"

"I don't have the stamina to ask ten thousand questions. Even on my best days, five hundred's my limit."

Davidson didn't much care for the joke. He had a booming business to run and Gunner was keeping him from it. Still, experience had taught him about the persistence of these people; if he didn't comply with the detective's demands now, he'd only have to do it later, perhaps at an even less convenient moment than this.

"I'll give you ten minutes," he said.

He barked some hurried orders to one of the two men working in the bay and led Gunner off to a tiny office in the rear of the building. It was sparsely furnished but classically decorated, with a small metal desk and a calendar featuring naked women hanging on the wall behind it. Gunner took a seat in a wobbly wooden chair opposite the calendar and, flipping through its pages, tried to find a nude-of-the-month to his liking. He couldn't. It looked as if most of the girls would have been better suited to working for Joe Lanier's Transmissions than posing for its calendar.

"You say you're a private cop?" Davidson asked Gunner, taking his seat behind the desk like the CEO of Texaco sitting down for a board meeting.

Gunner nodded. "I'm working for an attorney named Kelly DeCharme. Toby Mills's court-appointed lawyer. I've been hired to find out who was riding in the car with Rookie the night he rolled on Darrel Lovejoy, if it wasn't Mills."

"And if it was Rookie who did the driving."

"Yes. If."

"But Mills says it *was* Rookie, I imagine."

Gunner nodded again. "He can't seem to see anyone else doing it."

"But he can't prove that Rookie did, can he?"

"No. He can't prove anything."

"Uh-huh. That's what I thought. He knows it was Rookie who was driving the car, but he can't say who Rookie was with. I love it." He forced himself to grin. "They call themselves honorable, these kids. One for all and all for one, and all that brotherhood crap. A Blue would never rat on another Blue, they tell you. But let one of 'em mess up, find himself squarely behind the eight ball, and you see what happens. They get religion. They finally feel the need to confess . . . to someone else's sins, of course."

"You obviously don't think your brother had anything to do with Lovejoy's murder," Gunner said.

"What should be obvious is that I don't have much faith in what Rookie's friends have to say about anything," Davidson said. "They're nothing but infantile thieves and liars, and murderers of women and children, when the mood moves them. As for what I think about Rookie rolling on Lovejoy, the truth is, I don't know whether he did or not, and I consider myself lucky that way. The less I know about his business, the better."

"He lives with you periodically, doesn't he?"

"Whenever he and the King decide they need a vacation from one another, yeah. He's my little brother, I love him, and it'd be un-Christian of me to turn him away. But the King is his legal guardian; he's the man you people should be harassing, not me."

"I just came from his place. Nobody's home. I expect I'll catch up with him sooner or later, but I've been told not to expect much help from him. I thought in the meantime I'd talk to you. But if asking a few questions is your idea of harassment . . ."

"I didn't say that. I just said that Rookie lives with the King, not me. The only reason Rookie stays with me at all is because life with that man is no picnic; the kid's got to get away from the drunken idiot sometime. And where else is he going to go?"

"Was he staying with you at the time of Lovejoy's murder?"

"No. Last time I put him up was back in February."

"But you have seen him since then?"

"A couple times, yeah. But not since the murder." He saw how his anticipation of Gunner's next question had surprised the detective, and said, "I've been through this line of questioning before, remember? I've got the routine down."

"So where do we go from here?" Gunner asked him.

"If we stick to the script, you ask me where else I think Rookie could be hiding. And I tell you I don't have any idea. I'm his brother, not his bodyguard. Then you ask if I'm aware of any grudge Rookie or the Mills kid may have held against Lovejoy, and again, I say no, I'm afraid not."

"It sounds like if we stick to the script, you're not going to be of much help to me yourself."

Davidson shrugged. "I don't think I did the police much good, either."

He didn't laugh when he said it, but the thought seemed to please him all the same. He had a serene look on his face that begged to be slapped off.

Gunner ignored that temptation and said, "They catch you harboring a fugitive, you're gonna have to run this place from a jail cell. I assume you know that."

"The police have promised me that would be the case, yes. But I'm sure, with God's help, I'd manage somehow."

"No. You wouldn't. You'd lose your shirt, and the pants that go with it. And for a man who looks like he's worked hard for what he's got, that's a hell of a lot to risk for an 'infantile thief and liar,' and sometime 'murderer of women and children.' Or does that description only apply to Rookie's friends?"

"It applies to any gangbanger. Anybody stupid enough to fall into that lifestyle and ignorant enough to stay in it. Rookie's no exception.

"These kids have choices, Mr. Gunner, despite what they and others would have you believe. I stand as evidence of that. I've lived in this part of the city all of my thirty-one years; I had the same obstacles of peer pressure and environmental deficiencies to overcome as Rookie, and you see how I've turned out, what I've managed to accomplish. Rookie should be encouraged by my success; he should see it as proof of his own potential, but instead he merely finds it laughable. He's a quitter and a fool, and I pity him for that.

"However, while the boy may be guilty by association of murder, he himself has never actually killed anyone before. And this is not just me talking; this is a matter of record. He's never even been accused of murder before. So I wonder, why is everyone so eager to believe he's committed one now? Because another Blue says he did?"

"There's the matter of his car. The blue Maverick,"

Gunner said. "And the witness who's placed both Mills and Rookie inside it."

"Yeah, the witness. I'd forgotten about her. She's something else to think about, isn't she?"

"How do you mean?"

"I mean that she's a real bolt out of the blue. A rare find. Most people I know see a man killed in a drive-by, they don't rush out to make it a matter of public record. They go home and try to forget about it, pretend it never happened."

"You trying to say she's lying?"

"I'm trying to say that maybe she's confused," Davidson said. "With a man like Lovejoy getting killed and all, maybe she saw an opportunity to be a star and jumped on it. All the police would've had to do was coax her a little bit. Convince her it was a Maverick she saw, and not a Pinto or a Comet. You know how things like that can happen."

Gunner did but chose not to say so.

"Or maybe she's just saying what she was told to say," Davidson continued. "Maybe the Blues are being fingered for Lovejoy's murder because it's so easy to see them doing it."

"You're talking about a frame."

"That's right. And why not? Where is it written that all of Lovejoy's enemies had to be gangbangers, that no one else could have wanted to see the man dead?"

Davidson was asking better questions than Gunner was, and the role reversal made the detective uncomfortable.

"I were you, I'd look at all the possibilities," Davidson suggested.

"Thanks. I intend to."

Gunner took a business card from his wallet and passed it across the desk.

"I'm getting paid to clear Mills of Lovejoy's murder, if I can manage it," he said. "But that doesn't mean I won't do the same for Rookie if the opportunity presents itself. All I'm after is the truth; I don't care who it condemns or vindicates.

If you hear from Rookie, tell him that for me. Give him my number; tell him I just want to talk."

"Sure," Davidson said, pocketing the card without even looking at it, like a street flyer he intended to trash at his earliest convenience.

"You love the kid like you say, you'll let me help him," Gunner said, standing up. "Because I don't think there's anyone else out there who even cares enough to try."

He waited for Davidson to nod before showing himself to the door.

chapter **four**

....

Harold ain't home," the little boy at
the door said.

"How about your mother? Can I talk to her?"

The boy shook his dusty head from side to side.
"Momma's at work."

There were five kids in all that Gunner could see from
where he was standing outside the decrepit two-bedroom
apartment in Willowbrook in which Harold "Smalltime"
Seivers lived: the boy at the door, who looked about five; two
younger boys and a slightly older girl watching television on
the floor; and a toddler of indeterminate sex dressed in blue,
pulling on the curtains of a window on the far side of the
room. The girl and one of the boys on the floor were playing
tug-of-war with a pair of pliers, fighting for the right to
change the channel on their knobless and archaic rotary-
tuned television set.

"Isn't someone watching you?" Gunner asked the boy at
the door.

"Gwen's watchin' us," the boy said.

"Gwen?"

Her tiny charge was nodding his head when Gwen finally appeared, rushing into the living room from somewhere

off in the back. She was a nine- or maybe ten-year-old, with a round face and uncombed hair, dressed in the same Pick 'n Save coordinates as the other children, only in sizes best suited for the not-so-pleasingly plump.

"Who you talkin' to, Byron?" she demanded, reaching the apartment door to yank the boy standing there behind her, shielding him from Gunner with her body like a huffy mother hen.

"I was looking for Harold," Gunner said, as if that explained everything.

"Harold ain't home," Gwen said.

"Are you his sister?"

She nodded.

"You know when Harold might be back?"

She shook her head. She wasn't going to elaborate, either. "What you want him for?"

"I want to talk to him. Regarding some friends of his. Toby Mills and Rookie Davidson. You know Toby and Rookie?"

She shook her head again. "I don't know none of Harold's friends. Momma says to stay away from 'em. You a policeman?"

"I'm a private investigator. That's like a policeman, only different."

The girl just stared at him, as confounded by his answer as she had every right to be. Feeling foolish, he changed the subject.

"Gwen, you know where I might find Harold now?"

"No. He could be anywheres."

She was distracted by a loud cry behind her. The toddler in blue had found a can of Michelob somewhere and had poured most of its contents all over himself/herself trying to down it.

"I gotta go, mister," the girl told Gunner, starting to close the door in his face.

Gunner stuck a hand out, said, "Waitaminute, wait-aminute. What time will your mother be home? Maybe I could talk to her."

"I don't know. I ain't supposed to tell nobody what time Momma comes home. I gotta go."

Against Gunner's meager objections, she pushed the door closed with authority.

Gunner stepped off the porch and raised his eyes for-lornly skyward, assessing the light of day as he let the sting of rejection slowly subside. He decided Saturday afternoon was probably good for another two hours in the sun, and was sure something worthwhile could be accomplished in those two hours, if he was to put his mind to it. However, he was not surprised to realize he didn't *want* to put his mind to it. What he wanted to do was fold up his tent and go home. So he did.

Something about having doors closed in his face always had that effect on him.

Working on the Sabbath day was one of the few sins Gunner had never enjoyed committing, especially during the football season. He had found early on in his investigative career that lethargic Sunday mornings spent staring at a color television invariably led to stuporous Sunday afternoons, days that sim-ply did not lend themselves well to the pursuit of professional accomplishment.

On this particular Sunday, however, less than twenty-four hours after the detective's interrogations of Teddy David-son and a pair of Harold Seivers's younger siblings, the usual excuses for deferring work until Monday did not apply. The football season was three months away and the Lakers/Super-sonics game at the Forum was an evening affair. If he wanted to live with himself, he had no choice but to start what most people would come to appreciate as a day of rest with a late-

morning visit to the home of Claudia Lovejoy, Darrel Lovejoy's widow.

He preferred to think of the move as his idea, but he was
man enough to know better. Teddy Davidson had turned his
attention to Claudia Lovejoy the day before when Davidson
had suggested the possibility that Darrel Lovejoy might have
had enemies outside the youth-gang hemisphere. It was a
thought Gunner would have come upon of his own accord,
eventually, but for now he had only Davidson to thank for it,
and the debt rubbed his pride the wrong way.

Perhaps it was this sense of ambivalence that led Gunner
to drop in on the Lovejoy home unannounced, a tactical
blunder that left him knocking on the door of an empty
house in Lynwood when he arrived shortly before twelve
noon. It was a mistake he had made before and had vowed
never to make again, but for once, all it cost him was time.
He had a hunch where he might find the widowed Mrs.
Lovejoy, and unlike most of the hunches he tended to play
whenever a racing form wormed its way into his hands, this
one actually paid off.

The Reverend Willie Raines's First Children of God
Church was a newly constructed oblique monument located
on the northeast corner of Van Ness and 104th Street in Inglewood, an angular architectural expression in red brick
and stained glass, and when noon services broke there at
one-thirty in the afternoon, Claudia Lovejoy was among the
mass of people who poured from its doors out into the
street.

Gunner had never met the lady, but since her husband's
death, she had had enough television-news minicams stuck
in her face to make her instantly recognizable, even from a
fair distance. Without the notoriety, however, she would
have stood out from the crowd all the same. Claudia Lovejoy
was blessed with the kind of beauty that held a man's eyes
longer than he wanted to look.

The secret to her allure was an unusual contradiction, a clash of physical characteristics as rare as it was mesmerizing. Her skin was the color of white chocolate, smooth and unblemished, yet the ethnicity of her facial features seemed to have been lifted from a woman much closer to her African ancestry: Her lips were generous and her cheekbones high and proud. Dark, slashing eyebrows were raised in perpetual skepticism over green eyes of limitless clarity, eyes that drew a man into their emerald depths and would not let go. She appeared to be in her early thirties, short and lean but not petite; nothing petite had that many curves in so many appropriate places.

She was wearing a white cotton dress with a cowl neckline when Gunner picked her out of the crowd, her black hair pulled tight and glistening across her scalp, away from her face, as if to give it room to glow. He let her get all the way to her car in the parking lot before approaching her; she had exited the church in the company of a pair of much older women in garage-sale hats, and he preferred to wait until they had said their goodbyes to introduce himself and state the nature of his business.

It took a while, but the two older ladies finally waddled off. Claudia Lovejoy slipped a key into the door of her wine-colored late-model Toyota sedan and started to turn it, then sensed Gunner standing nearby and looked up.

"May I help you?"

There had been no trace of fear in her voice, only an innocent, almost playful curiosity. Resisting the urge to put off his bad news as long as possible, Gunner explained himself quickly and flashed his credentials, then watched as the joy of God drained from her face like sand from an hourglass.

"You have a great deal of nerve coming here, Mr. Gunner. I suppose you realize that."

"I'm a little pressed for time, Mrs. Lovejoy. I'm sorry."

"The little hood you represent killed my husband."

"The kid's a hood, granted," Gunner said, "but he may not be the one who killed your husband."

"The police appear to be satisfied that he is."

"If you'll excuse me for saying so, the police find satisfaction in a great many things. The truth, unfortunately, is not always one of them."

"So what do you want with me?"

There were a number of possible answers to that question, but only one of them had no implication of carnal knowledge. Gunner kept things clean and said, "A few moments of your time. There are some questions I need to ask that only you can answer reliably."

"And I assume you want to ask them now?"

"If at all possible, yes. I'm a little pressed for time, as I said. Have you had breakfast yet?"

The woman in white shook her head, waiting in icy silence for the invitation she knew was coming.

"Would you like to?" Gunner asked, humbling himself for the cause.

She considered the question and stared at him while she was at it, finding no small pleasure in the spectacle of a man teetering on the brink of an embarrassing rejection. Then she nodded her head and waited demurely for Gunner to show the way.

Ordinarily, Ray's was no place for a man to go for breakfast if he didn't have all day to wait for it, but the rules that applied to the restaurant's general clientele rarely applied to Gunner, and so he took Claudia Lovejoy there anyway. A small, nondescript kitchen on the corner of Western and Forty-eighth Street, Ray's was a breakfast-only establishment as famous for its excellent food as its all-too-limited space in which to enjoy it; only its generous portions made it worth overlooking the annoyance of the intimidating line of people forever ringing its exterior.

No one had ever actually told Gunner he could circumvent the line whenever he cared to drop in, but it had worked out exactly that way ever since Gunner had saved a head-waiter's life at Ray's one afternoon two years before. Halfway through Gunner's breakfast, a drunken patron built like a small Caterpillar tractor became enraged by a whopping twelve-cent overcharge on his bill, and was about to find the waiter's jugular vein with a dull carving knife when Gunner broke a chair over his head. Gunner figured to get a free meal out of the deal, and he did. Every meal after that, however, he had paid for, though his name always managed to get him through the front door without the usual thirty-minute delay.

As it had today.

An overstuffed couple in line at the door made a brief show of complaint, but otherwise Gunner and Claudia Lovejoy were shown to a table quickly and without incident. Once they had settled into their seats, Gunner ordered ham and eggs, and Claudia did the same, but it seemed she had done so just to have an excuse to play with her fork at the table. Gunner watched her ruminate in silence for a few minutes, then decided enough was enough. He was going to feel like an ass for putting Lovejoy through another unpleasant interrogation whether he chose to procrastinate for five minutes or five days beforehand.

"Tell me about your husband, Mrs. Lovejoy," the detective finally said.

Lovejoy looked up from her food sculpting, her gaze cool and impassive, and said, "What would you like to know?"

"I'd like to know if his friends can be believed when they say what a fine man he was, for one thing. Call me a skeptic, but I can't help but wonder if anybody could have been as squeaky clean and wholesome as your husband was reputed to be."

"If you're asking me whether or not Darrel was perfect, Mr. Gunner, the answer is no. Of course he wasn't. He was, however, scrupled. Which is more than I can say for you."

"Me?"

"That's right. You. I know who you work for, Mr. Gunner. Remember? If you were a man of high principles, you wouldn't be here."

"My principles have nothing to do with this, Mrs. Lovejoy."

"No. Of course not."

Gunner eyed her coldly. "It should be obvious to you by now that I'm a man with some modicum of principles," he said. "Because you've been treating me like shit since our first hello, and I've yet to voice any serious objections. How much more 'scrupled' can one get than that?"

Lovejoy blushed, and for a moment Gunner wondered if he had pushed her too far. "If I've been rude to you, Mr. Gunner, I apologize," she said. "But surely my poor behavior needs no great explanation. I've only been a widow for three weeks now. It takes time to adjust."

Gunner nodded his head, conceding the point. She was a woman someone had only recently crushed underfoot, and as such her cheerless disposition should not have been unexpected.

"Look. This is just awkward for me, that's all," she went on. "You're working to get Toby Mills off the hook for Darrel's murder, and by my very presence here, I'm helping you, even though I share none of your reservations regarding Mills's guilt."

"So I've noticed. What makes you so certain Mills is guilty?"

"I read the newspapers, like everyone else. I know what kind of evidence the police have turned up against him. The gun alone should be proof enough of his involvement for anyone."

"Then your judgment isn't based on any personal insight or knowledge of Toby Mills."

"No."

"Ever see or hear of Mills before your husband's death? Did Darrel ever mention him by name, that you can recall?"

"No."

"How about Rookie Davidson?"

"No. Darrel rarely discussed gangbangers with me. He didn't like to bring his work home, and that, as you might imagine, was fine with me."

"Then you can't say for sure that Darrel even knew Mills or Davidson."

Claudia Lovejoy dropped the fork in her hand as if it had offended her in some way; the racket it made on her plate was enough to stop conversation three tables away. "Look," she said, "why is it so hard for some people to accept the obvious? Darrel made enemies of little hoods like Mills and Davidson every day of his life. He was playing with fire, trying to turn these kids around, and it finally caught up with him. It's as simple as that. It's how I knew things would end for him—for us—all along."

To Gunner's complete surprise, she was suddenly fighting back tears, anger and pain welling up in her eyes all at once, and the momentary lapse in her iron-woman performance only enraged her all the more. Refusing to draw any further attention to her plight by dabbing at her eyes, she said, "It may sound trite to you, Mr. Gunner, but I loved my husband very much. And while I wish I could speculate on the hows and whys of his death in a less emotional manner, I'm afraid I lack that kind of self-control just yet."

Gunner nodded his head and said nothing, watching her struggle to repair her misplaced cool. Her beauty, already overwhelming, had taken on a new brilliance now that her facade of hostile indifference was lifted, and its effect on him was as profound as it was unexpected.

All the questions he wanted to ask her now had nothing to do with her husband or the Imperial Blues.

"Maybe we should talk about something else for a while," he said.

"Such as?"

"Such as yourself. Tell me who you are. What you are."

"That sounds like small talk to me."

Gunner grinned. "I suppose it is. Anything wrong with that?"

She thought about it for a moment. When she decided there wasn't, she said, "Who I am is no great mystery. The news media have seen to that. I'm the bereaved widow of the late Darrel Lovejoy. The woman in black. As for *what* I am, I can't say. I used to be a wife and aspiring mother, but I'm neither of those things now."

"You could always be again."

"Yes. I could." She smiled thinly. "But in the meantime, I'm lost. I could go back to Minnesota to be with my family for a while, but I know that wouldn't last. I've been away too long to ever return there for good. When you've gone two years without shoveling snow, you're cured of the jones forever."

"Darrel left no family here?"

"No. No one. And that fact always surprised people, because they liked to think his motivation for the things he did came from somewhere outside of himself, when that wasn't the case at all. What Darrel did, he did on his own, by his own volition. He *was* the 'wonderful human being' everybody thought he was. No matter how bogus he must have seemed to some, he was a man who cared about people the way most of us only care about ourselves, and he loved me like no man I have ever known. So, if you came here hoping I'd tell you he was a wife-beater and an adulterer, a drunkard and a drug-abuser, I'm afraid I'll have to disappoint you."

"Then there's no reason to believe someone other than a gangbanger may have killed him."

"None. None whatsoever."

Gunner downed the last of a by-now-cold cup of coffee and said, "All right. Assuming that's true, we're only rounding the possible suspects down to every kid in every gang he ever dealt with."

"I'm afraid that's about the size of it, yes. Darrel had been shot three times previously, Mr. Gunner. He was a constant target of theirs. If it wasn't the Blues who killed him, it was the S.S. or the Little Tees. Cuzzes or Hoods from one set or another, I'm absolutely convinced of that."

"How is it they knew where to find him?"

"You mean at the minimarket?"

"Yes."

"Darrel was a creature of habit. He made that walk regularly, and I expect they knew that. I had wondered why they chose that location, too. I had always thought—I had always *feared*—that if something like that ever happened to Darrel, it would happen in front of our own home. But the police explained that it probably happened where it did because they wanted it to get a lot of attention. They wanted it *seen*."

"Then the attempt on Darrel's life did come as a complete surprise to him, you think."

"Of course."

"He wasn't particularly moody or on edge at the time of his death?"

"No. No, he wasn't." She thought about it. "He was a little more quiet than usual, but nothing more than that. Why?"

"Because warnings don't usually precede your run-of-the-mill gangbanger drive-by. They're too spur of the moment to allow time for all that. If Mills and Davidson rolled on your husband like everybody says they did, he shouldn't have been acting as if he knew what was coming."

Lovejoy nodded her head slowly, following his logic. Then her eyes lost focus, the way eyes always did when the person behind them had checked out of the present to revisit the past.

"You just remember something?" Gunner asked her.

She blinked twice, coming out of it, and shook her head. "No. It's nothing. He was just quiet that week, that's all. I thought . . ." She paused, then shook her head again. "Never mind. Really."

Gunner looked at her. He didn't like leaving such loose ends dangling, but she seemed determined to deny him the chance to pursue it. It was an odd way to act about "nothing," but the issue was only worth pressing if what she was trying to hide was something relevant to Gunner's case, and not something that was merely none of his business.

"What about parents?" Gunner asked eventually. "If Darrel was making enemies of gangbangers, he had to be bending a few of their parents out of shape in the process. Moms or Dads who didn't appreciate what they saw as his Patrol's constant harassment of their children."

"There were a few of those, of course. How could there not be? The parents of most gangbangers are masters of denial; they don't like it when strangers confront them with the truth about their babies. But these people aren't killers, Mr. Gunner. They're just weak. Ignorant."

"Many murderers are," Gunner said.

"Well, maybe so. In any case, as I've already told you, Darrel kept me pretty much in the dark where the Patrol was concerned, so I really can't say for sure whether or not he ever had a serious run-in with somebody's parent. If you want my opinion, though, I'd rule the 'angry parent' theory out."

Gunner did a little heavy thinking, then asked whether Darrel Lovejoy had ever locked horns with anyone, past or present, in the Peace Patrol family.

Lovejoy shook her head. "Darrel did too good a job of recruiting for that. The people he brought aboard were always people he could get along with and trust implicitly. He realized from day one that many of the people who would be attracted to the Patrol were going to be fanatics on the fringe, men or women with chips on their shoulders looking for an excuse to bust some heads, so he was always careful to weed those types out."

Absently, she started to nibble on a piece of ham, finally making some legitimate use of her utensils. "I suppose someone like that may have wanted Darrel dead, now that I think about it. You know what I mean? Someone with a grudge to bear because Darrel rejected them for the Patrol."

Gunner nodded. "Anybody specific come to mind?"

Lovejoy began eating in earnest now, fueling her sudden inspiration with food. She raised her empty coffee cup at a passing waiter, successfully getting his attention, and said, "As a matter of fact, yes. Somebody does. Only I never knew this person's name. Darrel never told me his name."

"It was a man?"

"Yes."

"How do you know?"

"I know because he called the house. Three times over a two-week period, if I remember correctly, and I answered the phone each time. All he'd ever do is quote Scripture and hang up."

"Quote Scripture?"

Lovejoy nodded. "Fire and brimstone, vengeance is mine, that sort of thing. A different passage every time, but always something dark and threatening. He once used a reading from the book of Deuteronomy, Chapter Nineteen, verses eighteen and nineteen, I believe."

"Which says?"

"You want me to recite it? Well, let's see. 'And if the witness hath testified falsely against his brother, then shall ye do unto him as he had thought to do unto his brother,' or words to that effect. I wasn't familiar with the passage at the time, but I came across it afterward in my daily readings, and I wrote it down. Apparently, this man who was calling felt Darrel had falsely accused him of something."

"And Darrel knew who he was?"

"He seemed to. He told me it was just some crazy who had a problem with the Patrol, a neighborhood nut he'd had some words with. I just assumed it was over a job or something. Darrel said he'd take care of it, that he'd put a stop to the calls, and I guess he did, because there were no more after that."

"How long ago was this?"

Lovejoy thought about it. "A year, maybe. Possibly longer. I'm not sure."

Their waiter appeared with coffeepot in hand and slowly proceeded to refill their cups, drawing the exercise out in order to prolong the look of definite disapproval he was casting Gunner's way. Lovejoy's earlier moment of distress had apparently not escaped his keen young eyes, and thinking Gunner was the cad responsible, he was boldly letting the detective know that he didn't care to see the lady in tears again, no matter what kind of weight Gunner pulled in the place.

Gunner removed a small notebook and a mechanical pencil from a coat pocket and allowed the reckless romantic his minute of chivalry without comment. Eventually, having poured all the coffee he could pour, the waiter wandered off toward the kitchen, freeing Gunner to ask Lovejoy to repeat the source of the Scripture passage she had accused the stranger on the phone of reciting.

"Deuteronomy, Chapter Nineteen, verses eighteen and

nineteen," Lovejoy said, watching as Gunner wrote this down. "But I'm afraid that's the only passage I've ever been able to place. I'm sorry."

Gunner shrugged as if he wasn't disappointed. "Providing the others seemed to follow a similar theme, this might be enough."

"Enough for what?"

"Enough for somebody with a better handle on the Old and New Testaments than I have to explain it. Perhaps find any hidden meanings a heathen like myself might overlook."

"And what will that get you?"

Gunner shrugged again. "Beats me. But this is what being a detective is all about. Sweating the details. Leaving no stone unturned. Taking wild shots in the dark."

He smiled at her, and Lovejoy surprised him by smiling back.

"However, there are less iffy ways of playing detective than counting on long shots like this to pay off," Gunner said, putting the notebook away. "If you could give me something more substantial to go on, I'd be a lot better off, believe me."

"Something more substantial? Like what?"

"Like a lead on some of the other people who may have gotten along less than famously with your husband. For all his aforementioned fine qualities, one disgruntled job applicant could not have been his only enemy in the world."

"There were people he had trouble getting along with at times, certainly," Lovejoy said, getting testy again, "but I would hesitate to call any one of them an enemy of Darrel's. Reverend Raines, for example."

Gunner raised an eyebrow.

"He and Darrel disagreed about a great many things, on a great many occasions, but they were not what I would consider enemies."

"By disagreements, I take it you mean spats. Minor squabbles."

The assumption brought another smile to Lovejoy's face, and it looked very comfortable there. "No. That's not what I mean. Darrel and I had spats. He and the Reverend had fights. Arguments akin to war, without the bloodshed. They were two very headstrong men, with opposite opinions on almost every subject, and working together on a daily basis toward a common goal . . . an exchange of words was a weekly inevitability. But that isn't to say there was any bad blood between them. They never let it go that far."

"What kinds of things would they argue about?"

"The same things all business partners do. Finances. Personnel. Delegation of duties. Never anything sinister."

"They ever talk about dissolving the partnership? Was control of the Patrol ever an issue?"

"No. Never. They'd make noises about splitting up now and then, but nothing would ever come of it. They needed each other too much. Darrel was the man with the know-how and the Reverend was the man with the money. They could never have duplicated the Patrol's success alone, individually, and they knew it. And despite all their differences, I think they truly loved each other."

"As a man of the cloth, Raines wouldn't seem to have any other choice," Gunner said.

Lovejoy smiled again, recognizing his cynicism. "You're one of those people who have an easier time believing in Santa Claus than in Jesus Christ as their Lord and Savior, aren't you?"

"My faith in Christ is merely on shaky ground, Mrs. Lovejoy. What's gone completely is my faith in some of his messengers. There's a certain slickness to Willie Raines I find inappropriate in a man with his supposed priorities."

"You think he's a fake."

"Not a fake exactly, no. I just think he's far more than advertised. He sells himself as a man of the spirit but exhibits more than a passing interest in things of the flesh. He might be committed to heaven, all right, but I think he intends to party awhile before he gets there."

Claudia Lovejoy shook her head. "You've got him all wrong," she said.

Gunner shrugged again. "Maybe. All I know is, Raines never met a camera lens he didn't like, and you generally find that kind of fastidious self-promotion in men looking to get ahead in this world, not the next one."

Lovejoy didn't offer a rebuttal; she could see that Gunner's mind was made up where Raines was concerned.

"The Reverend's a good man," she said simply. "He's been very kind to me since Darrel's death. Very kind."

"I'm sure he has."

"You'd feel differently if you met him, I think."

"Perhaps I would. Is that something you could arrange?"

"I don't see why not. Although he'd probably be no more willing to help your client's cause than I, at least initially. Would you like me to talk to him?"

Gunner shook his head. "Not just yet. But I'd like to be able to call you in the next few days should I decide it's necessary. How can I reach you?"

Lovejoy drew a business card from her purse and used Gunner's pencil to write her home phone number on the reverse. Gunner exchanged it for one of his own and turned hers over to glance at its printed side before sliding it into his wallet.

"You're a chiropractor?"

Lovejoy nodded her head modestly. "I don't look like one?"

Gunner shook his own head and grinned, his mind wandering. He had always been partial to massage as a form of sexual foreplay. Wouldn't chiropractic work just as well?

"Drive me back to my car, Mr. Gunner," Claudia Lovejoy said, eyeing him. "Please."

Without a word, Gunner did as he was told, thinking that she must have seen the dreamy look on his face somewhere before.

chapter **five**

....

Monday morning had rain on its mind. The sun was just an amorphous, impotent ball of light hiding behind a darkening screen of cloud cover when Gunner showed up at Tamika Downs's door, punching the clock at the outrageous hour—for him—of a few minutes past nine.

The steadfast memory of Claudia Lovejoy had followed him here, having unexpectedly made a sleepless shambles of his Sunday night, but Gunner was bound and determined to work his way around it. This was clearly the wrong time to become infatuated with a beautiful widow, and Lovejoy was clearly the wrong widow with whom to become infatuated. She was the kind of woman, he knew, with whom the point of no return was only one senseless, if blissful, step away.

Reminding himself of this, he knocked on Downs's door and willed the thought of Lovejoy into submission, focusing instead on his surroundings. The door before him was in fairly decent shape itself, but the two-bedroom home it was attached to was the kind of eyesore wrecking balls were invented to obliterate. It sat in the middle of a particularly desolate stretch of Croesus Avenue in Watts, a graffiti-marred, wood-frame lean-to with a water-based paint job and a busted-up chimney. The front yard was landscaped with dirt. It was as unsuitable a source of shelter for a woman with four children, Gunner mused as he waited for someone inside to respond to his incessant knocking, as it would have been for three little pigs trying to hide from the big bad wolf.

His arm had grown tired of pounding on the door when he finally heard feet padding around on what sounded like a bare wooden floor, and a voice said, "Who is it?"

Gunner shouted out his name and identified himself as a private investigator.

"A what?"

Gunner raised his voice another notch, moving closer to the door, and repeated himself. "I'm a private investigator! A detective! I'm looking for Ms. Tamika Downs!"

A long silence ensued. Then: "You sure you ain't no reporter? Let me see some kinda I.D."

The door cracked open and a bloodshot eye peeked out of the darkness. Gunner took his wallet out of his coat and displayed the license inside prominently, patiently. "I have some questions regarding the murder of Darrel Lovejoy I'd like to ask Ms. Downs, if she could spare me just five minutes of her time," he said. "You wouldn't be she, would you?"

"Who you workin' for?" the owner of the eye demanded.

"Toby Mills," Gunner replied.

Another long silence. "What if I don't wanna talk to you?"

Gunner shrugged. "I get in my car and go home. But if your testimony regarding my client is accurate, you'd have no reason not to want to talk to me. You've told your story to everybody else."

"Yeah. So what? You workin' for Toby Mills, you prob'ly just wanna try and catch me in a lie, to see if I still got my story straight, or somethin'."

Gunner shook his head softly from side to side. "I just want to ask you a few questions. That's all. To tell you the truth, you'd be doing me a favor if you could convince me that Mills is guilty."

"Yeah?"

"Yeah. I don't much like him. The only reason I'm here is because his lawyer's money is the right color." He held a twenty-dollar bill up to the crack in the door enticingly. "All-American green."

Downs let Gunner squirm around in a state of uncertainty for a full minute, then reached out to snatch the bill from his hand and pulled the door completely open, gesturing for him to come inside.

"I only got five minutes, like you said," she told him firmly.

She was a plain-looking woman in her early thirties, painfully thin and emaciated. Her dark skin was dry and ashen, and her hair was a short brush of brown that stood up on her head like an unwieldy bouquet of ragweed. There was no discernible shape to her body; the bland housedress she wore just seemed to lie there, as empty as it would have been on a hanger in her closet. She had shiny cheeks and a mouth full of large, disgruntled teeth.

She was right at home in her living room. It was a poorly lit rest stop for mutilated furniture and broken toys, tasteless wall paintings and empty beer bottles. A pie tin atop a wobbly end table served as proof that she had had a badly burnt omelet for breakfast.

"You can sit down, if you want," Downs told Gunner, directing him toward the crushed and spotted cushions of an old sofa at the center of the room.

"No, thanks. I'll stand."

Downs made a face and dropped into a high-backed wicker chair with more holes in it than a cheese grater.

"Where are the kids?" Gunner asked, trying to make preliminary small talk.

"At school. 'Cept the youngest, Dana. She's stayin' with my mother for a while." She frowned. "You wanna talk about my kids, or how I seen Mr. Lovejoy get shot?"

"You weren't kidding about the five minutes."

"No. I got things to do today, Mr. . . . What'd you say your name was?"

"Gunner. Aaron Gunner."

"Yeah. I got things to do today, Mr. Gunner. My time's valuable, just like yours."

"All right. Let's talk about the shooting. How much of it did you see, exactly?"

"I seen everything. From beginnin' to end."

"Tell me about it."

Downs took a deep breath, as if she was going to try to recite the story on a single lungful of air. "I was at the bus stop on the corner of Wilmington and a Hundred Twenty-fourth Street, about ten-fifteen at night, a Friday night, when I see this car come flyin' 'round the corner toward me—"

"You were waiting for a bus?" Gunner asked, cutting her off.

"That's right," Downs said. "The forty-one bus, the Wilmington bus. I was gonna take the forty-one up to a Hundred Seventh Street and walk home."

Gunner took out his notebook and pencil and started to take notes. "Home from where, exactly?"

"My sister's. Rhonda's. Rhonda, she lives on Blakely, near a Hundred Twenty-fourth Street. I got a ride over to her house that afternoon, but she couldn't give me no ride back, 'cause her old man took her car while I was there and didn't come back 'til late. So I had to try and take the bus home."

"You were alone?"

"Uh-huh. My mother had the kids that whole weekend; she takes 'em for me one weekend a month. Anyway, I'm standin' there waitin' for the bus, when this car comes flyin' 'round the corner, like I said. The Maverick."

"You know for sure it was a Maverick?" Gunner asked,

exposing his chauvinistic doubt that a woman could have knowledge of such things. "It couldn't have been some other make? Something similar in appearance, like a Pinto or a Comet?"

"It was a Maverick," Downs said. "I use' to work in a Pep Boys; I know the difference 'tween a Maverick and a Pinto."

Gunner nodded his head, allowing her to think he was conceding the point rather than merely choosing to move on. "Describe the car," he said.

"I told you. It was a Maverick. A Ford Maverick, I don't know what year. Dark blue, with them shiny wheels and big tires gangbangers be so crazy about. It had a dent in the front, a big one on the right side, like somebody done backed into it in a parkin' lot or somethin', and there was bumper stickers all over the back. KDAY and the RAIDERS, stuff like that.

"Naturally, I heard the car 'fore I seen it, but I seen it in time to get a good look at it and the boys what was in it. There's a streetlight right on that corner; I couldn't've missed their faces if I'd've tried."

"Describe them for me. The way you described them for the police."

Downs appeared to want to object, but said, "The kid in the front drivin', he was dark-skinned and scared-lookin', with a face like a girl's. Had a sharp, pretty nose and a thin mouth, and long curly hair fallin' all around his eyes, like Michael Jackson. You know, that jheri-curl shit."

"You're talking about Rookie Davidson."

Downs nodded. "Rookie Davidson, right."

"And Toby Mills?"

"Mills was darker, harder lookin'. Had bright eyes and a scar on his face, runnin' down his cheek like this," Downs said, tracing the exact path of Toby Mills's disfiguring trademark from the corner of her mouth to the bottom of her ear on the left side of her face. "And he didn't have hardly no hair on his head, 'cept for a rat's tail in back. He was sittin' in the back of the car, doin' all the shootin'."

"No one else was in the car?"

"No. Just them. Davidson drivin', and Mills shootin'. Mills leaned out the window and just started shootin', didn't shout 'Blue,' or nothin'. I thought he might be shootin' at me, 'til I turned around and saw Mr. Lovejoy lyin' there, bleedin' all over the parking lot, his groceries all out on the ground, and shit."

"Did you know who Lovejoy was at the time?"

"Not at first. But later, when the police came, I found out it was him. I couldn't believe it."

"And you were the only witness to the shooting? Nobody else at the bus stop, or in the store or parking lot, saw any part of it?"

"There was a man in the parkin' lot who saw it, I think, but he got in his car and took off 'fore the cops showed up. And I was the only one waitin' at the bus stop."

Nodding again, Gunner said, "You ever see Mills or Davidson before that night?"

"No. Never," Downs answered quickly.

"And yet you made a positive I.D. of both, based on what you were able to see one night inside a compact car traveling at what, forty, forty-five miles an hour?"

"I told you," Downs said, "there's a streetlight on that corner. A *bright* streetlight."

"I see. You must have gotten a pretty good look at what they were wearing, then, huh?"

"What they were wearin'? You mean their clothes? Uh-uh." She shook her head. "I didn't see nobody's clothes. The Davidson boy, he had a hat on his head, I can tell you that, but don't ask me what kind. It was a baseball cap, is all I know."

There was a pack of Marlboros on the table beside her,

and she picked it up to take one. She made the task of lighting up look arduous, but Gunner was unable to decide
whether that meant she was starting to come down with a bad
case of nerves or was merely a stumblebum with matches.

"You don't mind my askin', is this gonna take much
longer? I mean, like I said, I got a few things to do today."

The detective shook his head. "Not much longer, no."
He was watching her closely now, his curiosity piqued.

"Well?" Downs prodded.

"I'd like to know what made you stick around," Gunner
said. "For the police, I mean. Most people in your shoes
would have taken off, disappeared, the way you say some guy
in the parking lot did."

Downs shrugged and injected a cloud of secondhand
smoke into the room. "I thought about it," she said.

Gunner just looked at her.

"But, you know, I just seen a man get killed in cold
blood. A man wasn't doin' nothin' to nobody, just goin' to
the store for his family like I do every day. And I thought to
myself, that could've been me them boys done like that, shot
up and left in the street to die like a dog. Me, or my sister, or
my mother, or one of my children. Gangbangers 'round here
be doin' people like that all the time.

"So I guess I got mad. Mad for myself, mad for Mr.
Lovejoy, mad for everybody else gotta deal with these crazy
children, day in and day out. So I stayed. I stayed and told
the police what I seen."

"Even though you knew it could be dangerous."

"Yeah. I knew." She shrugged again. "I just didn't care
no more." A cloud of personal gloom lingered in her eyes for
a brief moment. "Life for some people," she said, "it's hard
enough without havin' to worry 'bout teenagers gunnin' you
down every time you stick your head out your front door.
What happened, I guess, I just got tired of livin' afraid all the
time."

It all sounded very noble, but she was making it work, lending it just enough credibility to hold Gunner's unqualified skepticism at bay.

"You ever have any trouble with the Blues before this?" Gunner asked her.

"No. Not the Blues, not the Seven-and-Sevens, not no set 'round here. I ain't stupid."

"You received any threats of any kind since the murder? From anybody claiming to be a Blue, specifically?"

"I got some calls at first, yeah, 'til I got an unlisted number. Ain't got none since, though."

"Then you're not concerned that somebody will try to harm you eventually."

"I just told you. I'm all through bein' afraid. Ain't gonna do me no good to be afraid, right?" She stood up. "I ain't no hero, Mr. Gunner. I'm just tryin' to do the right thing. For everybody. Them two boys killed a good man, maybe even a great man, and I just happened to be standin' there when they did it. Lucky me.

"Now, if you'll excuse me, I really gotta go."

She came toward him, moving on feet that seemed less steady than they had only moments before. Or was that only Gunner's imagination?

He put his pencil and notebook away and said, "I assume you've asked for police protection."

Downs shook her head and went right past him to the front door. "No," she said, her hand on the knob. "I don't want no police protection."

"I thought you said you weren't a hero," Gunner said. "That's playing it awfully heroic, isn't it?"

"It ain't playin' anything. I just don't wanna be bothered with police all over my house, followin' me wherever I go. That'd only create more 'tention than I got already."

"They have ways to be discreet, you know."

"It don't matter. I don't want 'em hangin' around. I can take care of myself."

Gunner nodded his head toward the living room window and said, "Then I think you'd better go out there and tell the boys in the Buick to go home. They probably won't, of course, but you never know."

"Say what?" Downs went to the window and pulled back the curtains, agitated. "What Buick? Where?"

"The green one across the street, near the end of the block. With the plain-Jane hubcaps and telephone antennae."

"There's two green cars down there," Downs said.

Gunner went to the window to join her and said, "The Buick's the one in front. I spotted it when I first pulled up. Unless there's a rock house next door, I think they're here for you."

"Shit," Downs said softly.

"You're really better off with them there," Gunner said, heading for the door without having to be given any more hints. "But if you insist that they back off, I expect in time that they will."

Downs turned away from the window, clearly perturbed. "It don't matter," she said, drawing the last breath from the Marlboro in her hand. "They wanna watch me, let 'em watch me. I don't give a damn."

It was the least convincing thing she had said all day.

chapter six

. . . .

Now came the hard part.

Working a case he had wanted no part of but had failed miserably to turn down, Gunner had made it past the sneering hubris of his client Toby Mills to this point by dealing with the case's peripheral characters first, leaving out of sight and out of mind the central ones he so dreaded meeting. As he knew it would eventually, however, this tack had finally run its course, and now there was nothing left to do but fish or cut bait, introduce himself to the rest of Mills's lodge brothers or admit to Kelly DeCharme that he wasn't up to it, after all.

Gangbangers.

He almost cared as little for the word as he did for those it referred to. It made Mills and his like sound almost innocuous, like a band of rambunctious boys who were sometimes prone to kicking up a little racket. The reality was, that was more than "banging" the Cuzzes and Hoods were out there doing every waking moment, from one end of Los Angeles's South-Central ruins to the next—it was killing and maiming, making widows of wives and orphans of babies, cripples of high school basketball stars and martyrs of straight-A students. Theirs was a dance of death, pointless and seemingly without end, and only a fool or a hero would expose himself to the insanity of it any more than his everyday circumstances already demanded.

Gunner sat in the idle Hyundai, at the far corner of a shopping center parking lot on Wilmington and El Segundo, and took an hour to decide how big a fool—or hero—he wanted to be.

Lunch break was less than an hour away when Gunner finally arrived at Centennial High School in Compton.

Kelly DeCharme's data file included a surprisingly extensive dossier on the Imperial Blues hierarchy, a nine-member-strong inner circle, and most of the teenagers it named were enrolled at Centennial. Gunner came expecting to find less than half of them here, knowing how rarely gangbangers abandoned the streets to attend classes, but this was as close to neutral ground as any upon which he was ever likely to meet them, and he preferred to conduct his interviews, at least for the moment, outside of what they liked to think of as their home turf.

He entered Centennial's main hall and asked a pair of chubby girls loitering near the door for directions to the Administration office. One of the two looked like someone he might like to see fifteen pounds lighter and a dozen years older, but the other one needed a lot more help than that. They giggled coquettishly upon pointing in opposite directions, then got their act together and charted an accurate course for him to follow, down the corridor to his right, second door on the left.

The Boys' Dean was a man named Benjamin Rafeed, a middle-aged, stocky black man with a pointed head and tiny eyes, eyes that worked hard to see past the smoked lenses of thick horn-rimmed glasses. He was a standard-issue hard-nosed educator in a white short-sleeved dress shirt, and he greeted Gunner's visit to Centennial as enthusiastically as a mob boss would that of an IRS auditor.

"You can't ask nothin' gonna stir these boys up, now," he told Gunner gravely, leaning as far back in the swivel chair behind his desk as he dared. His collar on one side was turned up slightly, exposing the solid blue clip-on tie hanging from his neck for the fashion fraud it was. "Their fuses are pretty damn short as it is, and I don't want one of 'em goin' crazy on the grounds. We've had two killings already this year, and I intend to see to it that there isn't a third. I've got other students to consider, you understand."

Gunner nodded his head agreeably, willing to promise Rafeed anything just to get him moving. The wall clock at the dean's back read 11:22; the lunch break from which many a mischievous student would not return was little more than thirty minutes away.

"You working for Toby Mills, huh?" Rafeed asked.

"That's right."

"You ever dealt with kids like these before? Kids who would just as soon shoot you in the face as shake your hand?"

"I've known my share of gangbangers. I live on Stanford and a Hundred Seventh, I don't have a whole lot of choice."

"Then you know what you're getting into, the risks you'll be taking."

"I'm a big boy, Mr. Rafeed. Don't worry yourself about me, please."

Rafeed just stared at him, worrying anyway. "We'll set you up in Room Two fifteen upstairs," he said after a moment. "I'm afraid Rucker and Mullens will have to do, though." He looked over a note on his desk. "Seivers, Henderson, and Clarke are all absent today. Same as every day."

Gunner couldn't help but grimace. The ever-elusive Harold (Smalltime) Seivers, the Blue Toby Mills had specifically recommended he seek out, had again managed to be absent when Gunner came calling. And the others were not supposed to be the talkative type.

"Still . . .

"Rucker and Mullens will be fine," Gunner told Rafeed, taking a chance on his powers of persuasion.

Room 215 turned out to be a combination English Lit./World History classroom furnished with thirty-four student desks, a teacher's mahogany desk and chair, and an out-of-round globe of the world with the word *fuck* emblazoned in red ink across the flatlands of Australia. The olive green chalkboard spanning one wall was similarly decorated, but the walls themselves were spotless and smooth and smelled of fresh paint. Rafeed let Gunner in and left him immediately after, promising to send LeRon Rucker and Phillip Mullens up just as soon as they responded to his summons. Gunner sat down at the teacher's desk and looked out over the room while he waited, trying to imagine it filled with thirty-four teenagers packed together like clowns in a Volkswagen bug at the circus, children caught in a game of fiscal numbers that made individual attention and tutoring, not to mention breathing space, an impossible favor to ask of any one teacher, underpaid or no.

It wasn't a pretty thought.

"You look like a cop," somebody at the door said.

Gunner turned around. Two teenage boys stood at the edge of the room near the door, appraising him from a safe distance, one seeking shelter behind the other, both seemingly in no hurry to get a closer look at the man they were here to see.

"I'm a private investigator," Gunner said, standing up, "not a cop."

It was a distinction he was forced to point out to people with amazing regularity, and for some reason, it always made him feel small.

The shorter of the two boys near the door, the brave one taking the point, came forward and collapsed into one of the student desks in the middle of the first row, just off to Gunner's left.

"Mr. Rafeed says you wanna see us."

"You LeRon Rucker and Phillip Mullens?"

"Yeah. 'Cept don't nobody call me that, LeRon. They call me Cat."

"Like in Fast Cat," Rucker's friend Mullens explained, abruptly cheering up and taking a seat next to him. "'Cause he got spots all over his ass, like a fuckin' leopard."

"Fuck you," Rucker said, trying to reach Mullens's face with an open hand, laughing at their inside joke.

Rucker was only sixteen, according to Kelly De-Charme's dossier, but he looked much older than that, even to Gunner's imperfect eye. He was heavy-boned and light-skinned, with a freckled (or "spotted") face that seemed capable of growing much more than the reddish stubble presently shading his cheeks. There were lines under his pale gray eyes and at the corners of his mouth, etchings of time that seemed borrowed from a man who had had more than sixteen years to grow so discernibly tired of living.

Mullens, by comparison, looked like a six-foot-two baby waiting for a diaper change. He was reportedly a full year older than Rucker, but nowhere was that apparent. He had full-moon eyes and a flawless, dark complexion, and the kind of slight build most men could break with a good insult. Twin lightning bolts had been formed upon both sides of his almost hairless head by an artistic barber. Like Rucker, he wore tattered denim pants, a silk-screened T-shirt, and a sixty-five-dollar pair of unlaced hi-top Reebok basketball shoes, but in his case, the shoes suggested something more than a trendy fashion statement. He had the moves, the mannerisms, of a bona fide player.

Which could explain why the Blues called him Phi, short for the name the freewheeling Houston University basketball team of the early eighties went by: Phi Slamma Jamma.

"I take it Mr. Rafeed has explained to you that I'm here

on Toby Mills's behalf," Gunner said, trying awkwardly to get his show on the road.

"He said you workin' for his lawyer," Mullens recalled, "an' you wanna ask us some questions."

"That's right."

"What kind of questions?" Rucker asked.

Gunner took the direct route. "I'm trying to find Rookie Davidson, and I don't have the slightest idea where to start looking. I thought you two might be able to help."

"Look, man, we done already told the cops we don't know where homeboy is," Rucker said, agitated. "How many times we gotta say it?"

"Maybe you didn't hear me the first time, LeRon. I'm not a cop. I'm a private investigator. You know what a private investigator is?"

"Yeah, I know. I heard you. So what? Don't matter what you call yourself, ain't no Blue gonna start talkin' to nobody 'bout one of the homeboys just 'cause he say he workin' for Toby. We ain't that stupid."

"I'm hip," Mullens agreed enthusiastically.

"This could all be bullshit," Rucker said. "How we s'posed to know it ain't all bullshit?"

Again, Gunner was reminded of Mills's warning that Harold "Smalltime" Seivers was the only member of the Blues set Gunner was likely to find cooperative, and now the investigator was beginning to regret not having taken his word for it.

"Toby says if you have any doubts about me, you can talk to his sister Jody," Gunner said, unable to keep a slight edge from his voice. "She'll vouch for me."

Rucker, doing all the talking now, put both hands up in a mocking gesture of disappointment and grinned. "Ain't no Jody here," he said. Mullens cracked up and the two exchanged a hearty series of low- and high-fives.

Gunner walked around the teacher's desk to stand before

them, close enough so that they both had to look up to meet his gaze. "You little jokers are wasting my time," he said.

"Say what?" Rucker asked, still grinning.

"Either answer my questions or tell me where I can find Smalltime. One or the other."

"You think he gonna talk to you, man?"

"I think somebody had better. Because I can't do jack shit for your boy Toby until somebody does, and I don't care enough about his sorry ass to even try. If he really is innocent of Darrel Lovejoy's murder, I'm going to have to find Rookie to prove it, and I need the Blues's help just to get started. It's as simple as that."

"Toby didn't kill Dr. Love, man," Rucker said.

"I'll believe that when I hear it from Rookie. *If* I ever find him."

He was looking for an excuse to quit, and they knew it. He was placing Mills's fate squarely in their hands, granting them the power to choose his own course in the process: perseverance or surrender, hanging in or walking away. Everything was suddenly riding on how easy they were willing to make the next ten minutes for him.

Still, even cognizant of what hung in the balance, their choice did not come quickly. The silence was threatening to curl the corners of the homework assignments hanging from the classroom walls when Rucker finally broke it.

"All right. You wanna talk to 'Time, we'll take you to 'im. After we outta school. An' if he say he wants to talk to you, we'll talk to you. That's the deal."

"Right. Cool," Mullens agreed.

They waited for Gunner to show some sign of appeasement.

Gunner just nodded his head, feeling like the winner of a million dollars' worth of nothing and a year's supply of grief.

• • •

At a quarter past three Monday afternoon, they found Smalltime Seivers the first place they looked, and in Gunner's
mind a mystery immediately presented itself: To what did the
Blue owe his nickname?

Because there was nothing small about him.

Harold Seivers was a six-foot-six stack of fat and muscle
who must have tipped the scales in the general neighborhood
of 250 pounds. He had arms like the pillars supporting a
freeway overpass and a beer-barrel torso that deserved its own
ZIP code. He looked out at the world through a pair of glossy
eyes set deep in the shade of a hard, protruding brow, and his
slick, knobby head rose from massive shoulders with nothing
resembling a neck to support it. He was wearing a black fish-
net tank top and navy blue sweat pants, and a pair of off-
brand tennis shoes set off with blue laces, all in the largest
sizes Gunner had ever seen.

He was standing among a group of men gathered out in
front of a liquor store at the corner of Central and 121st as
Gunner and his two tour guides parked their separate cars
nearby. Smalltime was lifting his tank top up and out of the
way, using both hands, in order to give the diverse crowd of
old winos and gangly youngsters surrounding him an unob-
structed view of his stomach and the hideous serpentine scar
dissecting it. Running diagonally across his swollen ab-
domen, moving northeast by southwest past his sunken
navel, it was clearly the work of a knife, perhaps even several—but not of the variety one could find in the average
kitchen drawer.

A hurried surgeon wielding an arsenal of scalpels had
left this mark upon him, Gunner knew; it was the signature
physicians often left behind when repairing the damage rendered by gunshot wounds to the lower torso.

If Smalltime saw his friends approaching, he didn't ac-
knowledge it; he was too busy reveling in the amazement of

his drunken elders and the adulation of his starry-eyed juniors. The scar was just another way of holding their interest, maintaining their awe-inspired worship, which was his most consistent daily purpose, so monotonous had the twenty-year-old's already-stagnant life become. Rucker and Mullens described this form of occupation for Gunner as simply "chillin' out"; Gunner's name for it was something altogether different, and one he decided would be better left unsaid.

The members of Smalltime's audience finally caught sight of Rucker and Mullens advancing upon them and the party was abruptly over. The old men took their liquid lunches and wild exclamations a few yards farther down the block, while the younger men crossed in scattered formation over to the other side of 121st, in a hurry, against traffic. They had all been perfectly willing to risk spending an hour or so in the company of one unagitated Imperial Blue, but life in the shooting gallery that was South-Central Los Angeles had taught them that standing out on an open street corner with two or more gang members of any persuasion was tantamount to a death wish very likely to be fulfilled.

Mullens and Rucker reached Smalltime first, but it was Gunner the big man had his eyes on, even throughout the trio of Blues's ritualistic greetings. His expression was not easily interpreted, but his interest in the investigator seemed to carry no malice or overt mistrust; he appeared merely to be studying an anomaly, trying to identify an unfamiliar object in his path before it could identify itself.

Rucker spoke to him briefly, whispering, and then attempted to announce Gunner formally, but Smalltime waved the effort off.

"I know who he is," he said, moving forward until Gunner was close enough to breathe upon. He appraised the investigator for a long, silent minute, then said, "You the private eye, right? The one come by my house lookin' for me Saturday?"

Gunner nodded his head uneasily. He didn't care much for his low-angle view of the big kid but could think of no way to improve it, short of standing on a milk crate.

"Jody told me to be lookin' out for you," Smalltime said. "She say Toby's lawyer done hired a private eye name a Aaron Gunner to try an' get Toby off, some brother gonna be lookin' for whoever it was what really killed Dr. Love. She say the man gonna need our help, so we should do everything we can to cooperate."

He let the comment lie there, without embellishment. Gunner tried to wait him out, hoping Smalltime would go on in his own time, but that approach didn't work, and he came to doubt that it ever would.

"So what'd you tell her?" he asked finally.

Smalltime shrugged, flexing his giant shoulders effortlessly. "I told her I didn't know what we was gonna do," he said. "I told her it was gonna depend, on what kinda shit this private eye gonna ask us, and what he be like. You know, how he strikes me."

The younger man grinned, proudly. "I'm a careful man, right? I gotta have me some kinda respect for somebody, 'fore I up and decide to tell 'em all my homeboys' business, an' shit."

"This process take long?" Gunner asked him.

"What's that?"

"This respect thing you're talking about. How long's it take to get? An hour, a day, what? Should I go grab a pizza and a beer and come back, or see you again in a week?"

Smalltime grinned again, getting the joke. "Can't be rushed, man," he said.

Rucker and Mullens broke out laughing, clowning and stumbling all over themselves for Gunner's benefit. Smalltime tossed them a short glance, still grinning, then said to

Gunner, "But I like you. You like to fuck with people, same as me. Don't take no week to figure that out."

He turned his grin on Rucker, who was suddenly silent. "Cat thinks you're an asshole, but he brought you here, anyway. That tells me somethin' right there." He laughed as Rucker took his abuse quietly, answering only with the shifting of his feet and the closing of one open hand, his left. Mullens stepped farther from his side, gingerly, giving him room to boil.

"What kind of help you need?" Smalltime asked, turning back to Gunner.

"He lookin' for Rookie, same as the cops," Rucker said, making an accusation out of the statement. "He 'spects us to tell 'im where homeboy's at, an' shit."

"Did you tell him?" the giant Blue asked.

"Hell no," Mullens said, his eyes full of denial. "We didn't tell 'im nothin', 'Time."

"We told 'im we ain't sayin' shit 'bout nobody 'til we talked to you, man," Rucker said. "That's why we here, so you can tell 'im yourself, pers'nally, to go fuck 'imself."

Smalltime paused, as if the suggestion was something worth considering. He looked Gunner's way again after a brief period of rumination and said, "What you want with Rookie?"

"Same thing the authorities do. I want to talk to him."

"That's bullshit," Rucker snapped. "You wanna bust 'im!"

"Fuck busting him," Gunner said. "That's not what I was hired for. All I want is to find out who it was in the car with him the night he rolled on Darrel Lovejoy."

"How you know he did?" Smalltime asked. "How come everybody so goddamn sure it was us what wasted Dr. Love? Why couldn't it've been the Tees? Or the Troopers? Shit, the fuckin' Hoods be just as down on him as us, why they always wanna blame everything on a Cuz set?"

"I don't know," Gunner said, not wanting to get into that discussion. "All I can tell you is that your man Toby doesn't seem to have any doubts. He's just guessing, same as the police, but he told me he'd bet the farm that Rookie was involved in Lovejoy's murder."

"Toby said it was Rookie what rolled on Dr. Love?"

"He said the description of the car used in Lovejoy's killing fits Rookie's to a tee, and Rookie's a driver for the Blues, so who else could it have been?"

"Man, now you *know* he's lyin'," Rucker implored Smalltime, dismissing the validity of Gunner's testimony with a flip of the wrist. "Toby wouldn'ta said shit like that 'bout Rookie, not to him, not to nobody."

"The way Toby looks at it, Rookie screwed him first," Gunner said, eyeing Rucker, "so he figures he doesn't owe him much in the way of set loyalty."

"The Rook still a Blue," Rucker said. "No matter what he done. So what if he *was* drivin' when Dr. Love got rolled on? It's the cops what say Toby was the one rode with 'im done the shootin', not Rookie."

"Then Rookie *was* the driver that night?"

"No! I didn't say that. I just said, what if he did? So what?"

It was a lie told too late. He had already allowed Gunner to hear the ring of truth in his voice, and now the detective could easily tell the difference between the two.

A snow-haired black man with a dirty apron tied around his waist appeared at the open door of the liquor store behind Smalltime, and the three Blues all turned in his direction when Gunner glanced his way. The store was apparently his, and he had a pained look on his face that said he objected to the assembly taking place out in front of it, but he let the look speak for itself and said nothing, cognizant of who a trio of these trespassers were and the myriad ways in which such people often reacted to attempts to dislodge them. To save face, he rubbed his hands on his apron and nodded his head, saying hello, but there was no mistaking his shame as he ducked back inside immediately after, an old man choking on his own fear of children.

"Look," Gunner said to Smalltime, "you boys are going to have to make a choice here. You can't protect Rookie and help Toby at the same time. Something's gotta give."

The Blues were silent. Smalltime scratched his chin to kill time, then said, "What you want us to do?"

"I want you to quit messing around and start giving me some straight answers. Was Rookie driving the car when Lovejoy was killed or not?"

Smalltime produced another shrug. "Prob'ly."

"What does that mean?"

"It means don't nobody know for sure, but the way he was actin' that day, he must've had somethin' like that on his mind. And he *is* hidin' out, right?"

"When you say the way he was acting, what are you talking about? How was he acting?"

"Well, like . . . he talked a lot of shit that day, way I remember it. Tellin' guys what he was gonna do to 'em if they didn't shut up, an' shit like that. Cappin' on 'em, an' stuff. That what the Rook usually do when he nervous, talk smack, like when we about to go 'bangin' some Tees, or somethin'.

"And he stayed straight, wouldn't get high. Phi and Donnell an' Cube tried to get 'im to do some rock, but he wouldn't do none. Said he was cuttin' down, some shit like that. Ain't that right, Phi?"

Mullens nodded his head, leaving Gunner to guess the details.

"The Rock don't never turn down no rock, man," Smalltime said. "Never."

"Boy's a head," Mullens said, agreeing.

Meaning Rookie was into crack, and not casually.

"Then there's the thing with the crib," Smalltime went on. "We had—I mean we got a place where we keep all our shit—you know, our rods an' everything. It's a secret place, ain't nobody s'posed to know where it is but the homeboys, but somebody still ripped it off. Motherfucker just broke in one night an' took everything, didn't leave shit. That's how we figure whoever it was done Dr. Love got hold of Toby's piece."

"And you think Rookie was the one who stole it."

Smalltime just shrugged.

Gunner asked if any one of the three had an idea where Rookie could be holed up, watching Rucker's face, in particular.

Smalltime shook his head. "Not me."

"Uh-uh," Mullens said.

Rucker said nothing.

"Or seen him since the shooting?"

"I ain't," Smalltime said.

"No," Mullens said.

Which again brought all eyes to bear upon Rucker, who looked to be as committed to his oath of silence as ever, and not because the deal he and Mullens had struck with Gunner had simply slipped his mind.

"Quit fuckin' 'round, Cat," Smalltime said ominously.

Rucker appeared to be unmoved, until he said, "I ain't seen *him*. But I seen his car, once."

"The Maverick?" Gunner asked.

Rucker nodded. The guilt he was operating under was almost palpable. "The King was drivin' it. I seen 'im drive it into a junkyard and leave it, one of them junkyards down on San Pedro. You know, downtown."

"When was this?"

"'Bout a week ago. Last Tuesday, I think."

"You're sure it was Rookie's car?"

"Yeah, man. I'm sure."

"You talk to the King yet?" Smalltime asked Gunner. "That's Rookie's old man, the King."

The detective shook his head. "I tried his place once, early Saturday morning, but he wasn't home. I'll have to try him again eventually, I suppose, but I'd just as soon not. Toby tells me he's an asshole I'm not likely to get a lot out of, and suggested I talk to Rookie's brother Teddy instead."

"So? You talk to Teddy, then?"

"I saw him Saturday. He wasn't much help, either."

"No shit," Smalltime said, not surprised. "Teddy an' the Rook, they ain't been gettin' 'long too good lately. Rookie say they had another fight, an' Teddy told 'im not to come around no more."

"When?"

"Couple weeks ago. Three or four, somethin' like that."

"You know what the fight was about?"

"Same thing all they fights is about: Teddy don't like no little brother of his gangbangin'. He always talkin' to Rookie 'bout quittin', pressurin' 'im to leave 'is set, an' Rookie don't wanna hear that shit. So they fight."

"You don't think Teddy would put Rookie up somewhere anyway, under the circumstances?"

"I don't know. Maybe. But usually, Teddy gets pissed, he stay pissed."

"And the King?"

"The King? Man, I don't know 'bout him. I guess he might put Rookie up, Rookie made it worth 'is while. Why don't you go talk to the man? He the one Cat seen drivin' the Rook's car, right?"

Gunner nodded, conceding the point. He understood that aiming the investigator in the King's direction was an effort on Smalltime's part to terminate the interview, to dismiss Gunner gracefully, and he rather admired the approach.

"I was you, I'd go talk to 'im," the big kid repeated,

trying to be helpful. "'Less you got some more questions for us."

"No," Gunner said, deciding to fold his tent for the moment, letting Smalltime think his diversionary tactic had worked. "Not right now, anyway."

"Cool."

"But I do have a couple of favors to ask."

"Favors? Yeah? Like what?"

Gunner paused before answering, hoping to make the request sound as harmless as possible. "I need to see the crib you were talking about earlier. The Blues's old hiding place for weapons. I assume you aren't still using it?"

"Uh-uh. No way," Rucker said, infuriated. "Where we keepin' our shit ain't none of your fuckin' business!"

Smalltime appeared to agree. "What you wanna see that place for?"

Gunner said, "If Toby's gun was stolen like you and Toby say, we find the man who did the stealing and we're halfway home to finding out who used it on Darrel Lovejoy. Rookie may have just told the gunman where to look; he didn't have to be the one who actually pulled the theft off."

Following his logic, if ponderously, Smalltime nodded his head.

Rucker was not so easily enlightened. "He's full of shit, 'Time," he said. "No way we can show 'im our crib!"

"I'll think about it," the big kid told Gunner, in a way that was meant to warn both the detective and Rucker that the matter was closed to further discussion. "If you gotta do it, you gotta do it. But talk to the King first. Leave lookin' the crib over for last."

"Sure," Gunner said. He made it seem as if he was giving something up, when in fact he was getting exactly what he wanted.

"What's the other thing? You said you had a couple favors to ask."

"Yeah. I did. It's about Michael Clarke. Cube."

"What about him?"

"I hear he's got a nasty disposition, that he's a real ballbuster, and all that. He cut up Toby's lawyer, I understand."

Behind Smalltime, Rucker let a smirk slide onto his face. "Sho did," he said.

Smalltime shrugged again, not knowing what to say. "Lady said the wrong thing. He scratched her a little. That's Cube."

"Uh-huh. That's what I mean." Gunner met the big kid's eyes directly, reducing the conversation to a one-on-one exchange between them. "I want you to tell that little prick that if he ever tries anything like that with me, I'll kill him. Not loosen a few of his teeth or blacken his eye—I'll turn his head three hundred and sixty degrees and break his fucking neck. Do you understand what I'm saying?"

"I understand you even crazier than I thought, talkin' like that 'round us," Smalltime said, gesturing toward Rucker and Mullens as if they were an army of thousands. "Tellin' us how you gonna fuck up one of our homeboys, an' shit."

"I'm only telling you what I'll do if the little sonofabitch fucks with me first. I don't want any trouble with you or any Blue, but if somebody decides they want a piece of me, they'd better want it bad enough to die for it, because I'm not going to play. I've got a job to do, Harold, and I can't do it and watch my back, too. That's all I'm trying to tell you."

"Cube got a mind of his own, man. Don't matter what nobody say, he gonna do what he wants to do."

"Do me a favor and tell him anyway," Gunner said. "And if he doesn't care to listen, that's his privilege. And his funeral."

Mullens and Rucker stood at Smalltime's side while the big Blue thought it over. They were waiting for the word, any word, that would release them to take Gunner apart, like guard dogs straining at the leash.

Only the word never came. Instead, Smalltime shrugged one final time and said to Gunner, "I'll tell 'im. If I see 'im 'fore you do."

"Thanks," Gunner said. "You three have been a lot of help."

The kind of help, he thought to himself as he walked away, any sane man would have preferred to do without.

chapter **seven**

....

Gunner's cousin Del Curry was an electrician, not a Bible scholar, but he was known to attend 10:30 Mass at Transfiguration Catholic Church on Martin Luther King Boulevard and Third Avenue with something akin to regularity, and that made him the closest thing to an authority on Scripture Gunner could find in his address book. Del had had all of Sunday night and a good part of Monday morning to interpret Deuteronomy 19:18–19, the Bible verses Claudia Lovejoy had claimed her hot-tempered phone caller had used to make whatever point it was he was trying to make, and so Gunner called him from a dis-repaired, off-brand pay phone following his meeting with Smalltime Seivers and company feeling certain that his cousin had come up with something by now.

"Like I've got nothing better to do," Del said. The phone made him sound as if he were voicing his complaint from a lunar command module on the wrong side of the moon.

"Well?"

"You could have looked this up yourself, you know. All you had to do was read it; the verse is self-explanatory: 'And the judges shall make diligent inquisition: and, behold, if the witness be a false witness, and hath testified falsely against his brother; then shall ye do unto him, as he had thought to have done unto his brother; so shalt you put the evil away from among you.' Get it?"

Gunner didn't respond.

"Aaron, there's no mystery here, man. It means what it says. The punishment for offering up false testimony against your fellowman is exile. Removal from the fold. Tell a lie, get out of town. Okay?"

"What kind of false testimony?"

"In this context, any that would cast doubt on a man's faith or commitment to God. But you could apply it to any form of perjury, I suppose."

"And that's it? There's nothing more to it than that?"

"If there is, you're gonna need somebody smarter than me to find it. What were you expecting, the meaning of life, or something?"

"I don't know what I was expecting. Just some insight into what Claudia Lovejoy's friend could have been so worked up about, I guess. But 'false testimony' . . . hell, Del, that tells me nothing."

"If that's supposed to be your way of saying thank you, you're welcome. You through with the car yet?"

"No. You need it?"

"Need it? No. You want to buy it?"

Gunner laughed. "Thanks for the research, Del."

He hung up as Del started to laugh, too.

It was only four o'clock, but Gunner was ready to write Monday off. The unsettling formation of black rain clouds that had been dangling the threat of a merciless downpour over the head of Los Angeles all day seemed finally ready to ante up, and the freezing shadow it spread out over the city made everything outdoors look dingier and more depressing than it really was.

The depression Gunner could handle, but it was the trauma of commuting in bad weather that had him thinking of ducking for early cover. He didn't want to be around when the sky finally gave out and began to pave the streets of a million Porsches with water, glassy and slick and full of surprises.

Still, leaving the bad pay phones of the Imperial Blues's hunting grounds behind, he found himself risking the elements anyway, pressing his borrowed Korean two-door west on El Segundo toward Gardena, because Kelly DeCharme wasn't paying him to stay dry and he had a sneaking suspicion Royal Davidson, aka the King, might not be an easy man to pin down if Gunner didn't turn the trick fairly soon.

Davidson lived in a tiny two-bedroom, wood-frame house on 132nd Street between Western and Halldale, a dilapidated stack of salmon-colored kindling with shingled sides and a huge front porch. Yellowed shades were drawn closed at both of the windows facing the street but the sound of a TV being changed from channel to channel announced the presence of someone inside as Gunner, for the second time in three days, reached for the doorbell. He had just made it to the porch when the rain he had hoped to avoid began to fall.

Surprisingly, Gunner only had to ring the doorbell twice before the someone inside answered it. A middle-aged black woman with a head full of curlers in Day-Glo colors appeared on the other side of the locked screen door, holding a beltless green bathrobe closed around her.

"Yes?"

She had a bowling-pin figure and the kind of face that looked as if it was perpetually braced for bad news. Gunner squinted at it through the shredded mesh of the screen door and introduced himself, holding his license chin-high, where she could get a good look at it. She was nodding her head in recognition before he could finish telling her what it meant.

"Another cop," she said petulantly.

Gunner put the license away and said nothing, saving the denials for another day.

"I suppose you wanna see the King," she said.

"You're pretty sharp."

"He ain't here. And let me save you the trouble of askin' your next two questions: No, I don't know where he is, and I don't know when he'll be back."

"That just about covers it. Thanks."

"Why can't you goddamn people leave him alone? He's already told you a thousand times, he doesn't know where that little shit son of his is. Rookie ain't lived in this house for nine months!"

"So where's he been living?"

"With his older brother Teddy. Where else?"

She saw Gunner's face register mild surprise and said, "Don't you guys remember anything?"

Stuck for an answer, Gunner glanced over his shoulder at the rain now falling in earnest beyond the shelter of the porch, beating down on the earth with windblown fervor. The sky had turned fully black and the temperature outside was falling rapidly.

"I think you have this confused with another investigation," Gunner said when he looked back again, having made up his mind he was not going to come away from Davidson's door entirely empty-handed.

"What?"

"You're the King's latest live-in, is that right? His new girlfriend?"

"*New*? The King and I have been together a full year come June!"

"You ever hear him mention a woman by the name of Lucille Bennett? Or Aquanetta Long?"

"Lucille Bennett? He doesn't know any woman named Lucille Bennett. Or Juanita Long, either."

"Aquanetta," Gunner said.

"Whatever. What the hell does any of this have to do with Rookie?"

"For now, nothing," Gunner said. "Everything to this point suggests the King acted alone. Although we may have to talk to the boy eventually, I suppose."

"Acted alone in what? What the hell are you talking about?"

Gunner paused for effect before answering, to give her the impression the subject was a difficult one to broach. "I'm afraid we have reason to believe Mr. Davidson—the King— may have been responsible for the deaths of two former girlfriends, Ms. Bennett and Ms. Long. It seems both women died under mysterious circumstances while shacking up with him, Bennett in October of eighty-six, and Long last January."

"You must be crazy!"

"From what we've been able to ascertain, his M.O. is to live with a victim for a while, long enough to figure out where and how their money is put away, and then knock 'em off in a phony mugging once he's actually got his hands on the cash. I'd venture a guess he's been badgering you about money lately. Right? Trying to get access to your savings or checking accounts?"

"He's had a hard time finding work," Davidson's friend said, still angry, but with her righteous indignation noticeably slipping.

"Uh-huh. I'll bet he has. You've made life pretty easy for him, haven't you?"

The woman behind the screen door was silent.

"He's a lady-killer, sister. A regular Jack the Ripper. You don't help us get him now, you're gonna be next on his hit parade. One of these nights he'll send you out after a pack of cigarettes and you won't make it back home. Ever. Think about it."

She did. She'd finally received the bad news she was

expecting, if not actually hoping for, and now the rueful cast to her features had taken on a new dimension. She was trying to decide whether or not the personality profile of a psychopath fit the man with whom she was sharing a home, and the very fact that she had to ponder the question at all said a great deal about the kind of human being Royal Davidson was to live with.

"You've got to promise not to hurt him," she said after a while.

"I promise," Gunner said, smiling.

Lies were coming easily to him today.

A striped nine ball, tapped off the side to avoid a solid four making a nuisance of itself in the middle of the table, was just tumbling into a far corner pocket when Gunner stepped fully into the room. It was the kind of shot any fool could make look easy, but this one had been executed to appear lucky, to identify the man who had made it as a buffoon just clumsy enough to actually drop a ball or two, however inadvertently. Fresh blood had just shown itself at the door and the gap-toothed black man working the closest table to it wanted to make a game against him seem as risk-free a proposition as possible.

The name of the place was Boulevard Billiards, as the faded arrangement of blue block letters painted on the inside of one window facing Century Boulevard weakly declared, and it was supposed to be the Inglewood hot spot where the King was hanging his hat this night. It looked like a better place to go blind than play pool; the overhead lighting was just good enough to make out a mere ten tables arranged in two rows of five and an unmanned bar set against one wall. These appointments appeared to be less than a major hit with the general public, as Gunner was relieved to see that Rookie's father didn't have much company; there were only six men in the room altogether, the shyster near the door playing alone and five others milling about a pair of tables toward the back.

"I'm looking for the King," Gunner told the man with the hole in his grin.

He could have washed and waxed the Hyundai outside in the time it took to get an answer. "That's him in the yellow shirt," the toothless one said eventually, using the pool cue in his hands to gesture toward the group behind him, saying it as if being helpful came as hard for him as seeing a dentist twice a year.

The man in the yellow shirt looked like anything but a king. He was bushy-haired and out of shape, and was dressed more like a bowler on Friday night than a pool shark; the yellow shirt was the kind one usually found with the name of a service garage stenciled on the back, and his pants were oversized dungarees that fit him like a potato sack with belt loops. He had an unrestrained beer belly and a bald spot in the middle of his head, and a three-day-old growth of beard on a puffy face that had almost as much lint in it as gray hair.

His four friends were no more attractive than he.

He had heard Gunner drop his name and stood waiting for the detective to cross to his end of the room, interrupting the game he had been winning handily from a smaller, younger man in a security guard's uniform.

"I s'posed to know you?" he asked Gunner before any introductions could be attempted. His speech was only slightly off-kilter, the way a man's who drank religiously always was.

Gunner shook his head. "We've never met," he said. "My name is Gunner. Aaron Gunner. I'm a private investigator working for the attorney representing Toby Mills." He went through the ritual of displaying his license, well aware of how meaningless these people would find it.

"I don't know no Toby Mills," the King said.

"That's not too surprising. He's not a friend of yours. He's a friend of Rookie's. And I know you know Rookie."

"Yeah, I know him. I'm his father, so what?"

"So I'm looking for him. I'd like to talk to him."

"You and every other fuckin' cop in town. The little shit don't spend five minutes a month at home; why you assholes wanna ask me where he's hidin'?"

"Because some fathers would know," Gunner said flatly, with no small trace of disdain in his voice.

"Sounds to me like he don't think you're a good father to the Rook, King," one of the King's friends said, trying to liven up the evening. He was a big man with a boyish face and a weight lifter's body; there were muscles in his bare arms Gunner never used, if he even had them at all.

"Sounds that way to me, too," the King said, handing his pool cue over to the younger man in the guard's uniform without allowing his eyes to leave Gunner's.

"I'm not interested in what kind of father you are, or aren't, to the boy," Gunner said. "I just want to talk to Rookie. And if you can help me with that, I could possibly make it worth your while."

"You talkin' 'bout a bribe?" the King asked, pretending to be insulted.

"Man ain't gonna sell out his own son, mister," the big man interjected again, rising from the corner of the table on which he had been sitting. "Only a dog'd do that."

"You shouldn't oughta show the King such disrespect, man," another bystander said, this one as tall as he was frail and hairless. "'Specially not in here, 'round all his friends, and shit." He had a cigarette hanging limp from his mouth and a beer bottle in one hand, and he changed his grip on the latter as if to use it for something other than drinking.

They were all standing now, their green felt tables and little round balls forgotten, and one by one they were moving to the King's side, bringing pool cues and beer bottles with them. Even the man nearest the door came to join them, appearing to relish this opportunity to lose another tooth.

"Everybody just cool out," Gunner said, on the slim chance he still had time to recover from making a potentially fatal mistake. "Take a deep breath and relax."

"Relax, my ass," the King said, his confidence bolstered by the show of loyalty all around him. "I'm sick of you motherfuckers messin' with my boy! I don't care if he is a goddamn gangbanger, the kid ain't got a fuckin' chance in the world of flyin' right long as you assholes keep ridin' him!"

"Tell him, King," somebody said.

"The boy been havin' to deal with the goddamn cops for fourteen years. Now he's got private fuckin' investigators on his ass!"

"Let's jack 'im up, King," the small man in the guard's uniform suggested. "A private investigator ain't no cop!"

"I heard that," the man with the missing tooth agreed.

Gunner didn't move. He was finally willing to concede that nothing he could say was going to turn the tide rolling against him, but he had been too slow getting around to it. Any alternative he may have had to mixing it up with the six men before him went by the wayside when the King lunged forward to take him by the throat at the same instant that somebody's beer bottle glanced off the side of the detective's head.

Gunner managed to slow the King's dive with a short right hand to the older man's nose, but the bottle had hit him with the punch still in mid-flight and had taken most of the sting out of it. Unfazed, the King drove him backward down to the floor, and in seconds, all six men were upon him, arms and fists, some empty and some not, flailing wildly at his face. Gunner brought both hands up to shield himself, deflecting only a fraction of the blows raining down upon him, but the man in the guard's uniform took to kicking him in the ribs and he was forced to bring his hands back down again.

For his part, the King concentrated solely on strangling him, using both hands to reshape his windpipe, but one of the King's friends, possibly the big one, landed a solid left to Gunner's jaw and broke something loose inside his mouth; Gunner could feel the bloody tooth tumble about on his tongue like a stone in a clothes dryer.

The disfigurement enraged him, and that was fortunate, because in his rage he found the necessary incentive and strength to lift a stray knee from his chest with one hand and draw his new Ruger P-85 from its shoulder holster inside his coat with the other. He had the automatic pressed flush against the spot between the King's two eyes before a count of two, but by that time everyone else had figured out that it wasn't his wallet he was reaching for, and they were already backing off.

Way off.

Gunner pulled himself slowly to his feet as they watched, careful to keep the Ruger in constant contact with the King's forehead. His body felt like a six-foot open nerve ending, and his mouth was bleeding like hell. He used his free hand to take the broken tooth from his mouth and sadly inspected it: it was a right-side molar, capless and filling-free.

"I want to see five motherfuckers facedown on the floor, and I mean *yesterday*," Gunner told the King's motley crew of friends.

They hit the floor with the speed of a fast wink and the unity of a precision drill team. It was a beautiful thing to see.

"Please, man," the King said, staring cross-eyed at the Ruger's nose. "Don't kill me. Please don't kill me."

"Shut up," Gunner told him, probing around the bleeding hole in his gum with his tongue as he contemplated what to do next. A number of things came to mind right away, things that would add considerably to the King's pain while making the detective feel better about his own, but he was wise enough to give these no serious consideration. He felt lucky just to be alive; lucky to have a friend like Dee Holiday, who had let him take possession of the Ruger before he'd had a legal right to it, and lucky that he hadn't yet fired a round from it. He didn't want to press his good fortune playing payback; he just wanted to get what he had come for in the first place and get out.

"Get over there against the wall, hands at your sides," Gunner said, nodding toward a point in the room less than fifteen feet away. The King's eyes moved to the spot, but he made no effort to go there, not liking the sound of the order.

"Move your ass," Gunner warned him impatiently.

He had to step over the men on the floor to get there, but the King eventually retreated to the specified area and took the position he was told to take. He flattened his back against the barren wall and waited for further instructions, his eyes wide and full of terror.

"This isn't going to be very complicated," Gunner said, picking up a yellow-striped six ball from a nearby pool table with his free left hand. "I'm going to ask some questions, and you're going to answer them. Straight. Think you can do that?"

"What kind of questions?" the King asked.

Gunner threw the six ball as hard as he could, missing the King's head by a foot to the left. The sound it made when it hit the feeble wall was like a crack of thunder, to which every man in the room reacted.

"Jesus Christ!" the muscular big man on the floor said.

"You didn't hear what I said," Gunner told the King, who had lost the capacity to stand still; sweating profusely, he kept shifting his feet as if a trip to the men's room were in order. "You don't ask the questions. I do. Now can you handle that or not?"

He picked up another ball from the table.

"Yeah," the King said, nodding his head enthusiastically. "I can handle it."

"Good. We'll make the first question simple. Where's Rookie?"

The King hesitated before answering, knowing it was the last thing Gunner wanted to see him do. "I don't know," he said sheepishly. "I ain't seen the boy in three weeks, so help me God."

"That supposed to be your idea of a straight answer, King?"

"I'm tellin' you the truth, man! I swear it!"

"Then how'd you get hold of Rookie's car?"

Another pause. "His car? Who the hell said—"

The next ball struck the wall an inch from the King's right eye, exploding against the soft plaster like a cannon shot. It had stirred the air near his head as it sped by, and he could still feel its breath on his brow as he cringed, belatedly, to defend himself.

"Somebody saw you sell the Maverick for scrap, King," Gunner said, collecting a cue ball with his left hand while keeping the Ruger out where no one could possibly miss it with his right. "Don't try to tell me you didn't have it."

"He's fuckin' my place all up, King!" one of the men on the floor cried. He was a short, dark-skinned man with off-centered eyes and a bulbous nose, the last of the King's friends to speak. "Tell the motherfucker what he wants to know!"

"All right, all right," the King said, offering Gunner the palms of his hands as a solicitation of peace. "I had the goddamn car, yeah. So what?"

"The question was, How'd you get hold of it?"

"I bought it, man. That's how."

"You bought it?"

"Yeah, I bought it. Rookie sold it to me. Showed up at the house one day and said he needed money bad, that the cops were out lookin' for him and he had to get lost some-where. He's my kid, he was in trouble, so I gave him a few dollars for his car. What's wrong with that?"

"When was this, exactly?"

"Like I told you, 'bout three weeks ago." He straight-ened up again, gaining confidence. "It was on a Monday, I know that."

"How's that?"

"'Cause my ol' lady's off on Mondays, an' she was home when I borrowed the seventy-five bucks."

Gunner marveled at the man's paternal generosity. Sev-enty-five dollars for a '78 Ford Maverick in running condi-tion was a fire-sale price of laughable proportion; even sold as a junker, it had probably returned the King's investment three times over.

"Rookie tell you he and Toby Mills had murdered Dar-rel Lovejoy?" Gunner asked him.

The King shook his head. "Hell no. He didn't tell me nothin' like that. All he said was, he was in trouble and he needed money. I didn't know who they'd shot up 'til I heard it on the news."

"Who's 'they'?"

The King shrugged. "Rookie and whoever it was in the car with him. This Mills kid, I guess."

"You guess? You mean you don't *know* who it was?"

"No. Rookie never told me that. He never told me nothin', 'cept he was in trouble, like I said."

"Maybe he didn't have to tell you. Maybe you were there to see for yourself."

"Me?"

"Yeah, you. You sure as hell sound too sure of Rookie's involvement to have just heard about it on the evening news. Or is there some reason for that you haven't mentioned yet?"

Again, against his better wishes, the King delayed his answer, unsure of what to say. "I found some shells in the car," he said in time, with some regret. "Twenty-eight gauge, in the back, on the floor."

"Damn," somebody prone near his feet said.

Mill's gun was a 28-gauge shotgun, but that wasn't something the King could have picked up from the press.

"Where are the shells now?" Gunner asked.

"I tossed 'em," the King said. "What else could I do? They was evidence could've put the boy up for life. I wasn't gonna leave 'em lyin' 'round for the cops to get hold of."

Gunner grimaced. "What's the name of the yard you sold the car to?"

"Solid Gold. Place is called Solid Gold Junk, on San Pedro, downtown."

"You seen Rookie since you bought the car?"

"No."

"Or talk to him over the phone?"

"No. I ain't heard from him at all since then."

Gunner pitched the cue ball at the King's left leg, throwing it sidearm to take some speed off, and scored a direct hit on the pudgy man's kneecap, a blow that restored his dwindling fear of Gunner immediately.

"Goddammit, man, that ain't necessary! I'm tellin' you the truth!"

"I need to find him, King," Gunner said, retrieving yet another ball from the table at his side. "Rookie's the only one who knows if the cops have the right man in Mills or not."

"So what the hell you come to me for? Boy's an almighty Imperial Blue; go ask the fuckin' Blues where he's at!"

"I did that. They sent me to you."

"Shit," the King said, rubbing his knee vigorously, "they know the boy won't have nothin' to do with me! Boy's father's s'posed to be his friend, somebody he can talk to 'bout things, but Rookie ain't never taken me into his confidence 'bout nothin'. Like he don't trust my judgment, or somethin'. He needs advice, he don't come to me, he goes to them little sorry 'homeboys' of his, or that fuckin' rock dealer he's so goddamn tight with."

He stopped, struck by a sudden thought. "Yeah, that's right! That's who you need to be talkin' to, 'steada me! You wanna find Rookie, go talk to that fuckin' dealer he's always suckin' up to, one's got him so damn fucked up all the time!"

"What dealer is that?" Gunner asked.

"Whitey. Whitey Most. Kids live over there 'round the house get most of their shit from him, 'cludin' the Blues. He's Rookie's connection; man even uses the boy to make runs for 'im from time to time. Why don't you go ask him where Rookie's at?"

Because crack dealers can be inhospitable, Gunner wanted to reply, but didn't.

"Rookie's strung out pretty bad, is he?"

The King grunted. "You ever seen somebody wasted twenty-four hours a day? Or hurtin' so bad to get high they can't sit still for a goddamn minute? Gotta be movin' their hands or their feet, steadily, like they're in a big hurry to get someplace, or somethin'?

"Boy's brother always be gettin' on my case, talkin' 'bout how livin' with me must be so hard on the Rook, and shit. Hey, I tell you what. It's hard livin' with Rookie, too."

Gunner didn't openly commiserate. He was thinking about the King's last question, realizing to his surprise that he did indeed know someone who exhibited similar symptoms of restlessness. And now he knew to what malady those symptoms could possibly be attributed.

"Where would I find this Whitey Most?" he asked the King. "If I should decide to look for him?"

"Ask any kid from 'round there, they'll tell you where you can find 'im. Motherfucker's always on the street somewhere; you won't have to look too damn hard."

Gunner nodded his head and said, "Thanks." He tossed

the solid six ball in his hand back on the table and started to back out of the room, keeping the Ruger out and at the ready, strictly as a precautionary measure. Several of the men on the floor dared to raise their heads to watch him leave, but no one made any effort to rise.

"Don't you hurt my son, man," the King said with commendable backbone.

Gunner let him have the last word and disappeared into the driving rain outside.

chapter **eight**

....

Tamika Downs slipped out of her house at a few minutes past ten Monday evening, not long after the city was granted its first respite from the rain's watery onslaught in five hours, but the relief team for the pair of plainclothes police officers in the green Buick Le Sabre Gunner had pointed out to her earlier in the day never saw her leave. They were wide awake and alert, still parked on the opposite side of Croesus with a good view of the house, but Downs went out the back way and through the alley dissecting her block, and there was no way for them to know she was gone.

Unbeknownst to Downs, however, her exit did not go entirely unnoticed, because Gunner was there to see it. He had parked Del's Hyundai near the mouth of the alley where it opened up onto 105th Street, and had been waiting only four hours and eleven minutes when Downs made her devious escape. True to Gunner's faith in the car, she took no note of the Hyundai sitting there; its generic profile was the ultimate urban camouflage. Wearing a huge brown wig, a pair of skintight fake leather pants, and a matted fur coat, she skittered by on the rain-slick pavement and rushed off, heading west on 105th toward Wilmington.

Keeping the Hyundai at a safe distance, Gunner followed.

Downs reached Wilmington and kept going, crossing over to the 1800 block of 105th, picking up speed. Gunner deliberately missed the signal at Wilmington to give her room to roam, confident of his ability to catch up before she could deviate from her course. He was in no hurry; he had his window rolled down and the cold night air, purged of its usual impurities by the recent rain, was a welcome passenger in the car.

In most other Los Angeles neighborhoods, Downs would have been alone on the street at this hour, but here she was only one nightcrawler among many. This was an acreage of the City of Angels where need ran round the clock and vice never closed its doors. Here and there, men and women uninterested in sleep, perhaps because many of them routinely got as much of it during the day as they did at night, stood in small numbers on dimly lit porches and around parked cars, laughing, shouting, spilling malt liquor on their clothing. Some made lewd remarks as Downs hurried by, too busy even to rebuke them.

She turned right on Willowbrook Avenue and then made an immediate left on 104th Place, staying on the south side of the street until she came to the fenced perimeter of the junior high school on the next corner. Unlike 105th Street, 104th Place was deathly still, dark and unattended. Killing his lights, Gunner dropped back and parked his cousin's car in the middle of the block, where he watched Downs take a seat on the steps of the school's main building, settling in to wait for someone.

She had to kill a few minutes glancing nervously about her, freezing in the cold, but she wasn't made to wait long. The man she had come to see made his appearance shortly before 10:30, having arrived on foot just as she had, coming from the opposite direction. Because he was dressed for the weather, fortified from the chilly night by a fur-lined leather jacket with the collar turned up and a black wool ski cap, his sex and height—the latter somewhere in the neighborhood of six two, six three—were the only two things about him Gunner could read clearly, and with any confidence, from his vantage point.

Downs got to her feet as her ambiguous friend climbed the stairs of the school building to join her, and the two engaged in a succinct, dispassionate conversation that ended with Downs receiving something too small and too briefly visible for Gunner to identify. Moving with the telltale speed of desperation, Downs accepted the man's offering with her right hand, shoved both hands into the pockets of her coat, and, without another word, turned to leave 104th Place Junior High School behind, apparently headed for home again. The man in the wool cap stayed put and watched her go, waiting to be convinced that all was well before abandoning the comfort of the shadows for the street.

It was a transaction not uncommon to these environs, save for one glaring omission: the payoff. Downs's friend had received nothing in exchange for his gift.

Gunner quickly reclined the Hyundai's driver's seat and lay still, eyeing the little car's cloth headliner as Downs passed by, splashing through sidewalk puddles on the other side of the street as she went. It was a posture that made him feel uneasy and somewhat vulnerable, because Downs's friend was now out of view and it was not safe to assume that he, like Downs, would leave in the same direction from which he had come. If he chose to follow Downs's route instead, walking eastbound on the Hyundai's side of the street, Gunner would need a miracle to avoid being discovered and labeled as a spy. And perhaps, consequently shot.

Still, having no choice but to trust blind luck with his safety, the detective lay in the Hyundai's reclined bucket seat and, with nothing left to distract him but the lackluster roof of the car, tried not to think about the tooth that had been killing him since his scuffle with King Davidson's band of merry men that afternoon. The profuse bleeding had stopped but there was no ignoring the pain. By the time the sound of Downs's passage had diminished to his satisfaction, he was ready to call his long-standing moratorium on visits to his dentist off, at least for a day.

Gunner brought the Hyundai's seat up slowly and rose with it, his eyes on the school building ahead, and found it as it had been before Downs's arrival, fully deserted. All that he could see of 104th Place was equally lifeless.

He started the car as discreetly as possible and retraced his route only as far back as the intersection of Willowbrook and 105th. Staying southbound on Willowbrook, he paused at the curb and merely peered down 105th, picking up sight of Downs in the middle of the block. When he was reasonably assured of her destination, he continued on Willowbrook to Santa Ana Boulevard, turned east, and raced back to Downs's home on Croesus, taking the same parking space he had originally occupied on the northbound side of 105th, near the alley she had used for her escape.

He stayed upright in the driver's seat this time and waited for Downs's return, no longer caring whether she made him or not. Within minutes, he could see her off in the distance, approaching fast, eyes straight ahead like a colt wearing blinders, single-mindedly giving nothing to her left or right so much as a glance.

She was in a bad way.

By the time she reached the mouth of the alley, she was running more than walking, risking a broken neck on the slippery pavement. When she heard Gunner step out of his car and turned to see him standing there, her left foot came out from under her and she fell to one knee in the street.

"Shit! You scared the hell outta me!"

She was making a mess of getting up on her own, so Gunner did the gentlemanly thing and gave her a hand.

"You really should be more careful, on a night like this," he said.

"What the hell is it to you? What you doin' out here, anyway?"

Standing, she pushed his hand away and brushed herself off, eyeing him warily. Great drops of water were starting to fall from the sky, signaling the rain's return.

"I think maybe we'd better discuss that inside," Gunner said, reaching out to take her arm.

She pulled away. "We can't discuss nothin' right now. I gotta go look after my kids."

Gunner grabbed her right wrist, hard, and said, "Only person you're interested in looking out for right now is Number One. That shit in your pocket's for you, not your kids."

"What shit? What're you talkin' about?" She was trying to break her arm free, twisting and turning, but she was only a hundred pounds or so, too frail for the task.

"I don't want to make this any harder for you than I have to, Tamika," the detective said, "but if you don't shut the fuck up and talk to me like you've got some sense I'll walk your ass around the corner and empty your pockets in front of those nice police officers watching your house. That what you want?"

"No! Let go!"

She was fighting as hard as ever. Gunner, smiling, allowed her to struggle for a moment, then started toward Croesus, dragging her behind him.

"You called it, sister," he said as the rain began to come down in earnest.

"Wait! Don't!"

He stopped and looked at her, waiting to hear what she had to say. She chewed on her lower lip pensively, the wig on her head leaning to one side like a crooked wall painting, and said, "What do you wanna talk about?"

"Whatever comes to mind," Gunner told her, reminding her of his grip on her wrist with a slight squeeze.

It was an attempt to point out that she was in no position to negotiate, a fact Downs soon acknowledged with a tiny nod of her head.

"In the alley," she suggested.

Gunner didn't let her go until they were standing at the backyard gate to her home, sharing space in the alley with misshapen garbage cans and illegally parked cars. Thunder was making noises of discontent above their heads and the rain was beating down on the earth as if it had a score to settle with mankind.

"Let's see what's in the pocket," Gunner said.

"Why I got to show you? You already know what it is."

"Let's see it anyway. I'm not always as smart as I think I am."

Downs gave him a sour look but did as she was told. Inside her right-hand coat pocket were a pair of small glassine envelopes, each containing several tiny crystalline chips of white, the end result of a process that had started with the cooking of a mixture of baking soda, water, and cocaine. It was a drug of many names but was most commonly referred to as crack.

Or as Downs and Gunner had learned to call it, rock.

"That's not a bad score," Gunner said, making only a feeble effort to suppress his contempt. "Looks like a full day's supply, assuming you're as fucked up as I think you are. Must've hit you for what? Fifty, sixty bucks?"

Downs started not to answer but thought better of it and nodded her head.

Gunner snatched the plastic envelopes from her grasp before she could withdraw them, and said, "Bull*shit*. I saw you make the buy, Tamika; you didn't pay the man a dime for this."

Instinctively, Downs threw herself at him, reaching to retrieve her stolen instrument of vice, but Gunner caught her right wrist in his left hand again and closed down on it, using the grip to subdue her.

"Nobody gets this much rock on a layaway plan, lady," he said. "Your credit's not that good. Somebody's supplying you for free, and I'd like to know why."

"You're crazy! I paid fifty dollars for that shit!"

Gunner twisted her wrist once, pinching the fragile bones beneath her flesh in a merciless vise that buckled her knees. "I'm not going to stand in the rain and listen to lies. You want me to catch my death of cold or something?"

Downs let out a little cry of anguish and crumpled some more, tears streaming down her face.

"Please! He'll kill me if I talk to you!"

"Then we'd better make this fast, before he catches us out here shooting the breeze—don't you think?"

Gunner clamped down on her wrist again and Downs began to nod her head frantically, acquiescing. The rain was still falling like an anvil dropped from a high rise and she was soaked to the gills, the wig on her head filled with water and weighing her down. Gunner was in only slightly better shape.

"Toby Mills wasn't in Rookie Davidson's car the night Darrel Lovejoy was killed, was he?" Gunner asked.

Downs shook her head, eyes cast downward. "No. I mean, I don't know. I don't know if he was or not."

"How's that again?"

"I couldn't see who was in the car! I couldn't really see that good; it was dark."

She was chewing her lip again, head still down but eyes turned upward to steal a peek at him, checking his reaction. Gunner released her wrist, afraid of what he might do to it if he didn't. "Then somebody paid you to lie."

"Yeah."

"Who?"

"I can't tell you that. I told you."

"You're getting on my nerves, Tamika."

"Look, ask me anything else. Anything. Just don't ask me to give you the nigger's name!"

"All right. Forget his name, for now. Unless I miss my guess, I already know it, anyway. So tell me about the deal, instead. What was it? Free rock for a month to be at the bus stop when it happened, to say it was Mills and Davidson in the car? Something like that?"

"Something like that, yeah," Downs said, nodding.

"That was Whitey Most I saw you with earlier, wasn't it?" Gunner asked straightforwardly.

Downs didn't answer, but her eyes betrayed her surprise.

"Yes or no, Tamika. All I need's a simple yes or no."

She made her choice faster than he anticipated, and it wasn't among those he had listed for her. He had found it too easy to be physical with her, and had relaxed, confident that her will to fight had been sufficiently broken. It was a false assumption she brought to his attention by ripping the two packets of crack cocaine from his right hand while shoving him backward and off-balance against a row of trash cans directly behind him. He had no time to do anything but fly ass-backward over the cans and land in a soggy heap on his back, garnished liberally with garbage and fully relieved of his pride. By the time he recovered and reached her backyard gate, she was already clambering into the house.

She was trying to lock the door behind herself when he got there, but she panicked before completing the job and never threw the dead bolt, choosing to retreat farther into the house instead. With only the lower lock on the door to stop him, Gunner lowered a shoulder and broke into the house easily, catching a glimpse of the fleeing Downs up ahead as he dodged splinters from the doorjamb flying about his head.

Downs disappeared into the dark living room at the front of the house and Gunner ran like a madman through a small and untidy kitchen in pursuit, driven by fear to reduce her lead before she could pull a gun from a nearby dresser drawer and aim it at his face as he rounded the next corner. She was diving into the bathroom off a short hallway leading to the bedrooms in the back, perhaps with just such a scenario in mind, when the detective finally reached her, and this time she couldn't close the door fast enough to lock it behind her.

With only Downs's paltry weight behind the door to stop him, Gunner forced his way into the bathroom with little difficulty and dragged her back out into the hallway. She was kicking and screaming for all she was worth, doing little damage but making one hell of a racket, and yet no one appeared to come to her aid. Gunner guessed the children she had professed such concern for earlier were either very sound sleepers or absent from the premises.

Issuing no further ultimatums for her to ignore, the detective marched Downs into the living room and straight out the front door into the street, setting a course for the unmarked police car parked across the way. The two LAPD plainclothesmen formerly inside the car were already starting across the street toward him, one white man and one black, hands gravitating toward their holstered weapons. Downs was begging for a reprieve, but Gunner wasn't listening.

The officers were only halfway across Croesus, and Gunner and Downs were still on the latter's front lawn, when a single headlight out of the north washed over the men in the street, announcing the presence of an onrushing doom. A battered and rusted '67 Chevrolet Nova that once upon a time had been lime green screamed out of the blinding rain in the distance to speed past Downs's address, the driver inside strafing the front of Downs's home with a helter-skelter spray of automatic-weapon fire. Gunner threw his hostage facedown onto the lawn and hit the dirt himself, reacting well, but playing tag with an arbitrary hail of bullets was a tricky business and he knew either he or Downs, if not both, would manage to catch one or two slugs even before he kissed the ground.

He was right.

As he lay on the water logged grass, his nose buried in a pool of mud, he heard the sound of dissimilar gunfire join that of the automatic rifle, and then a hard *whump!* preceding the Nova's tire-squealing song of escape. Tentatively, he raised his head and turned his gaze to the street. A few brave residents had started to spill out of their homes and assemble at each curb, watching as one of the plainclothes officers assigned to Tamika Downs's surveillance—the black one—tended to his fallen comrade, who was sprawled out on his back on the tarmac with his limbs splayed in awkward, unnatural positions.

Feeling sick, Gunner turned his head again to check on Downs, and the news there was just as bad. She, too, lay in an extraordinary position, left arm up, right arm down, her stomach flat to the ground but her head bent to the side, toward him. She was bleeding profusely from a throat wound and her eyes were open, searching the night for that last instant of crack-induced euphoria of which Gunner had deprived her.

Foolishly, the detective started to get to his feet, but a voice behind him said, "I think you want to stay right where you are, mister," and that's exactly what he did.

Because the black cop with the dead partner getting rained on in the street had his gun drawn now, and he looked like he just might want to use it.

chapter nine
....

Angry cops and pissed off D.A.s were nothing new to Gunner.

Eleven years on the job had taught him that the sight of a private investigator was often all it took to send either form of public servant into a frothing, venomous rage; theirs was an adversarial relationship decades old and still going strong. The names changed and the threats varied from man to man, but for the most part, a cop or a district attorney's routine was always the same. Depending upon the nature of his offense, either real or imagined, Gunner could almost guess beforehand what would be said, and how.

But Assistant District Attorney James Booker was different.

Booker was the forty-one-year-old prosecuting attorney whose job it was to represent the state in the Darrel Lovejoy murder case, and he was not a man to whom one could immediately warm up, even on his better days. He was an angular-faced black man of medium height who prided himself on a body-fat ratio of less than 8 percent and a rapport with the LAPD to which few members of the District Attorney's office could lay claim. He was a snow-haired ex-navy man with a wife and three children, and he moved the way he spoke, with economy and precision.

In the first light of Tuesday morning, playing host to Gunner's reluctant guest in a small interrogation room at the LAPD's dilapidated Seventy-seventh Street Station, located in the heart of South-Central Los Angeles, Booker was facing an abundance of aggravations: the loss of both his prize witness in the Lovejoy case—Tamika Downs—and a six-year veteran of the LAPD's crack antigang unit known as CRASH (for Community Resources Against Street Hoodlums); the still-at-large status of the pair's drive-by killer; and Gunner, the unwitting idiot it seemed he had to thank for it all. He had every right to be distraught—even Gunner had to admit that—and yet only Rod Toon, the third man in the room and the head of the CRASH task force, could see that Booker was livid. To Gunner, seated on the opposite side of the barren desk that separated them, Booker appeared to be little more than *miffed*.

"I'm sure I don't have to tell you that that was the weakest damn story I have ever heard," the Assistant D.A. said to the investigator, using the same tone of voice to issue the critique that he might have used to read a bedtime story to one of his kids.

"Ditto for me," Toon said, smirking from a standing position behind him. "I think maybe you'd better reconsider and call your lawyer after all, Slick."

For a change, Gunner had a comfortable chair to sit on during an LAPD grilling, but he squirmed in it just the same. His tooth was bleeding again and someone was playing the inside of his skull like a kettledrum. The thought of having Ziggy, his attorney, around to offer Gunner his own special brand of professional mothering was beginning to look like a better idea all the time, but the detective wasn't ready to concede that such a measure was necessary. Besides, he was trying to convince his inquisitors of both his innocence and good intentions, and running for the shelter of a good lawyer was in his opinion no way to accomplish the feat.

"I'm afraid that's all the truth there is to tell, fellas," he said, shrugging.

"Or all the lies," Toon said.

Toon was three years Booker's junior but he wasn't likely to live as long; he was a prisoner to junk food and his body showed it, from the rubbery bulk of his clean-shaven cheeks to the massive thighs straining the seams of his polyester slacks.

"You ask me, Jim, we ought to yank this joker's papers and put him away for a couple of years. Take him off the street."

"Look, what do you want me to say? I was in the process of turning Downs over to your boys when the shooting started. How the hell is what happened my fault?"

"I think that's something you ought to be smart enough to figure out for yourself," Booker said, still talking like an insomnolent DJ pulling the graveyard shift on a beautiful-music station. "Or are you just too dense to see how deep you're in it this time?"

"Hell, Jim, he knows what he did," Toon piped in eagerly, stepping forward to look down his nose at Gunner from shorter range. "You should have let somebody know you were in the goddamn house, Gunner. Harper and Lewellen didn't know who the fuck you were; you come dragging Downs out into the street like you did, what the hell were they supposed to think?"

"What you did was, you made an asinine play," Booker said, declining to follow Toon's example of lost cool, "and it's cost us a great deal. One good cop and an irreplaceable witness in a homicide case. Now I'm glad to hear that you were trying to do the sensible thing by turning Downs in when the shit hit the fan, but I'm afraid that does little to alter the fact that there must have been a thousand better ways to go about it."

"You had no business being there in the first place, ass-hole," Toon added. "It was our fucking stakeout, not yours."

"In that case," Gunner said, "either Harper or Lewellen should have had their ass in position to watch the alley, just like I did. Or did they learn to cover only one entrance to a house from you?"

Toon started to go after him, but Booker said, "Take it easy, Rod. Mr. Gunner here's in enough trouble. He doesn't need any infirmary time to compound his misery." As Gun-ner watched, Toon took a moment to think about it, then heeled like a good watchdog, as always showing Booker more respect than he generally reserved for D.A.s.

"You could use some serious attitude adjustment, my friend," Booker said to Gunner, finally betraying a trace of emotion, albeit a slight one. "Our mutual associate in homi-cide, Matthew Poole, says you're okay, as far as private li-censes go, but you don't act okay to me. Doug Lewellen was a good friend of mine. Not to mention Rod's. I think we'd both feel a lot better about you if you'd show us some sign of remorse, and accept your fair share of responsibility for his death."

He gave Gunner a cold, hard stare and said nothing more, waiting for an answer.

Gunner let him look but would not be induced to offer a quick reply. He knew that Booker was right, of course; up to this point, Gunner had been making a complete jerk of himself, callously deflecting any and all blame for the deaths of Downs and Lewellen as if there were something or some-one else upon which to pin it. Booker and Toon could only assume that he was too ashamed of his ineptitude to admit to any wrongdoing, but Gunner knew there was more to his mode of denial than that.

In truth, his feigned insensitivity was designed to keep the pair from realizing that he was already shouldering all the guilt he could handle, and not merely because he had been the common denominator who had brought both Doug Lewellen and Tamika Downs to the spot where their killer eventually found them. There was also the matter of an earlier contribution to the tragedy of Monday evening to consider, and the undeniable probability that Downs's late-night trek to her candy man had only escaped Harper and Lewellen's attention because the detective had stupidly made her aware early Monday morning of the LAPD's interest in her home.

Considering the price of this momentary lack of discretion, and who had ultimately paid it, it was the kind of secret that could get a man shot in the back of the head some dark and lonely night somewhere down the road. Accidentally, of course.

Sixteen or seventeen times.

"Tell me what you'd like to hear, Booker," Gunner said, tiring of the charade. "You want to hear me say I fucked up? Okay. I fucked up. Badly."

"So far so good," Booker said dryly.

"You want apologies now, I imagine."

"You imagine correctly."

"Okay. Give me a number. Tell me how many it'll take to bring Lewellen and Downs back, and you've got it. Because I'll say I'm sorry as many times as you and Toon can stand to hear it if that's what it'll buy me. Otherwise, I fail to see the point."

"Please. Jim," Toon pleaded, "let me show this sonofabitch the 'point.' As a favor to me—go get yourself a cup of coffee or take five to call the missus. I won't leave a mark on the bastard, I swear to God."

"No," Booker said sharply.

"Look, Toon," Gunner said, "all I'm trying to say is, what's done is done. I zigged when I should have zagged, and making me feel like shit isn't going to change it. Instead of leaning on me to make yourselves feel better, I think we'd all be better off if you'd devote your energies to finding that Chevy Nova."

"Now he's giving advice," Toon said.

"We'll find the car, don't worry," Booker promised. "That's just a matter of time."

"You run a make on it?"

"Of course we ran a make on it," Toon said, still fuming. "But all we've got is a partial on the plate, so a positive I.D.'s going to be tough. Not that the name of the registered owner would mean much. No Blue drives a Nova, that we're aware of. Chances are good it was stolen, and only sometime tonight. It probably hasn't even been reported missing yet."

"Then you do figure it was the Blues again."

Booker nodded. "The only thing left to be decided is which one. Davidson has to be our first choice, obviously."

"Obviously?"

"It adds up, doesn't it? He does the driving for Mills on the Lovejoy drive-by, then tries to get himself and Mills off the hook by killing Downs."

Gunner shook his head. "I don't think it was Rookie. From what I've heard about the kid, he might have the stomach for one murder a month, but not two."

"You know somebody better qualified, do you?"

"I might. What about Whitey Most?"

"What about him?"

"You pick him up yet?"

"No. We see no need to talk to Mr. Most at this time," Booker said flatly.

"Do you mind if I ask why?"

"Because Most doesn't have a fucking thing to do with anything," Toon snapped, interjecting. He had taken the weight off his feet by sitting on a corner of the desk, and Gunner was mildly amazed that it could handle such an oversized load without doing cartwheels across the room. "The man in that car was an Imperial Blue; it shouldn't take a Rhodes scholar to figure that much out. What the hell do we want with Whitey Most?"

"I thought I already explained that. It was Most who put Downs up to fingering Toby Mills and Rookie Davidson for Darrel Lovejoy's murder."

"Downs said that?" Booker asked. "Verbatim?"

"Not verbatim, no. She said it in so many words."

"And what exactly does that mean?"

"It means she told me she hadn't really seen Mills or Davidson in the car that night, that it had been too dark on the corner to see *who* it was. She said she was only placing the Blues at the scene because someone was paying her to do so."

"And this someone was Most?"

"I think so, yes."

"Did she say what possible motive Most could have had for all this?"

"No."

"You have one in mind, then? Something maybe we've overlooked?"

Gunner didn't, of course. It was the one question they could hit him with all day and probably never get a sensible answer to.

"Sheeeiiit," Toon said disgustedly, "where the hell's he gonna get a motive for a dealer to frame his best goddamn runner for murder? Every day Mills spends in jail probably costs Most close to three grand!"

"What?"

"You read your client's rap sheet, didn't you, brother? He's a distributor. A runner. What his homies would call a roller. You ever saw him out of his prison uniform, you'd know: He bears all the signs. Turkish Ropes, rings, watches . . . more gold than losers like you or I will see in a lifetime."

"He's got 'snaps,'" Booker said almost appreciatively. "Money."

"Whitey Most's money," Toon said.

Gunner's silence made an open book of his surprise. He had noted Mills's lengthy drug-related arrest record, but had never given much thought to who his supplier might be.

"Still think we ought to talk to Most?" Booker asked.

"Look," Gunner said, "all I know is, anything Downs had to say about Mills and Davidson being involved in Lovejoy's murder isn't worth a shit. She lied about seeing them in the car that night and was getting free rock as a payoff, as the buy I saw her make indicated. Or didn't you guys know your star witness had a thing for crack?"

Booker was slow to respond. "Certainly we knew. But that hardly made her any less valuable to our case. The woman saw what she saw, and there was nothing to suggest she was under the influence of any controlled substance at the time. Why should we make an issue of something that was the woman's own personal business?"

"Coming from somebody in the District Attorney's office, I'd say that's a curious question."

"Look," Toon said, "what the hell were we supposed to do? Throw out her entire testimony just because she was nobody's Snow White?" He shook his head. "Beggars can't be choosers, brother. Eyewitnesses to drive-bys willing to cooperate with the authorities are rarer around these parts than an insured motorist, so when one turns up, voluntarily yet, we don't exactly bust our asses looking for reasons to disqualify 'em."

"Maybe your Ms. DeCharme would have trashed Downs on the stand, and maybe not," Booker said, "but it was a chance we felt we had to take. Your client's a bad egg, Gunner. Easily one of the worst. There are few kids out on the street we'd love to see out of circulation more."

"Even if all the evidence against him was thumped up by Most?"

"There's that name again. Whitey Most. Did Downs say it was Most she was allegedly working for, or not?"

"No."

"But she implied it?"

"Yes. She implied it."

"How?"

"By omission. When I suggested the man who hired her might be Most, she didn't correct me."

"Then you were the one who actually entered Most's name into the conversation."

"Yes."

"And you think it was Most she met with at the school on a Hundred Fourth Place last night?"

"Yes."

"Did Downs admit that much?"

"No."

"Have you ever seen Whitey Most?"

"No."

"Then you can't even say for sure whether it was Most you saw or not?"

"No. The light was lousy; I could barely see the guy."

"Come on, Jim," Toon said. "We're wasting time with this line of questioning. We're supposed to be talking about who killed Downs and Lewellen, not solving the Darrel Lovejoy murder all over again. The goddamn Blues killed all three of them, you know it and I know it, and this clown's just confusing the issue, bringing Most into the picture."

"Don't go away confused, Toon," Gunner said. "Just go away."

"He's right, Gunner," Booker said quickly, trying to defuse the growing threat of war between the two men. "This Whitey Most angle of yours sounds like a dead end to me. You dropped his name, Downs didn't."

"All I'm doing is putting two and two together, counselor. Downs was getting paid with free rock to frame the Blues for Lovejoy's murder, and Rookie Davidson's old man told me the kid is a one-man Whitey Most fan club. I work that around awhile and I come up with a man who had access to both a steady supply of rock and the supposed driver of the car in the Lovejoy drive-by: Whitey Most. You could do the same, if you cared to try. It's called deductive reasoning."

"You want deductive reasoning? I'll give you deductive reasoning: Nobody bribed Downs to say or do anything. There was no bribe and there was no frame. Because Downs was in a bad way when you talked to her, by your own admission. She was hurting. And any fool knows that an addict will say damn near anything when they find themselves backed into a corner. Especially what they think the person who has them there might most want to hear."

Gunner paused to consider that, putting his memory to the test. What had Downs actually said of her own volition, and in her own words? Merely that her testimony against Mills and Davidson was a lie, that she couldn't say one way or the other whether either man had been in Davidson's car the night Darrel Lovejoy was murdered. The bribe had been Gunner's idea, and she had simply gone along with it, perhaps only to hasten her exit from the rain.

In his mind, Gunner reconstructed the earlier conversation: "So tell me about the deal, instead. What was it? Free rock for a month to be at the bus stop when it happened, to say it was Mills and Davidson in the car? Something like that?"

"Something like that, yeah."

Downs's inability to differentiate between a green unmarked police Buick and a Ford of the same color parked a few cars behind it, when she had supposedly been a woman who could tell the difference between a Ford Maverick and a Mercury Comet, did tend to deflate her credibility as a witness even further, but how could Gunner share this observation with Toon and Booker without confessing to his biggest blunder of the day?

"This is bullshit," the investigator said abruptly, annoyed by the way Booker had deftly maneuvered him into doubting the validity of his own testimony. "The woman told me flat out, she didn't see who was in the car the night Lovejoy was killed. What difference does it make if she was climbing the walls when she said it? If you didn't give a damn about her condition when she was fingering the Blues, why the hell should you care about it now that she's vindicated them?"

"She hasn't vindicated shit," Toon said, getting to his feet again. "She's dead. That's why we called this little meeting, remember?"

"Face it, Gunner," Booker said. "We're digressing. All you've got to offer where Most is concerned is your own interpretation of what Downs had to say, and from what I've heard so far, she didn't say much. Furthermore, you're working the wrong homicide, as Rod here points out. The Lovejoy killing is a closed case; the drive-by we're trying to make heads or tails of this morning is the one that went down nine hours ago."

"And you don't think there could be a connection between the two, is that it?"

"Based on what you've given us to go on? No. I don't."

Gunner said, "Could be I'm being overly cynical, Booker, but I wonder if you're not just saying that because the case you've got against Mills, even without Downs, is too good to pass up."

Booker gave him a second hard look, this one accompanied by a fierce twiddling of his thumbs. It was beginning to look as if that was as close as the man could come to flying off the handle.

"I'll excuse you for that insult to my professional integrity because you've had a rough night," he said stiffly. "But if you make any more such baseless inferences of misconduct on my part, I promise you I'll make a personal project out of seeing you do the wrong end of fifteen-to-twenty for your part in last night's fiasco."

He sat back in his chair for the first time, daring to be seen in a relaxed state during working hours. "You're reaching, Gunner, that's all. You're way out in left field. What happened last night was exactly what we expected to happen, sooner or later. The Blues made a run at Tamika Downs, either to shut her up or to make an example of her. The kind of target she made of herself, we knew they'd have to go after her eventually."

"And we were ready for 'em, too," Toon said bitterly. "We had the woman covered like a blanket; there was no way they could have reached her if you hadn't fucked up the works."

"Look, get off that, Toon, all right?" Gunner said. "Lewellen I'll bite the bullet for, but Downs was dead with or without my help. Whoever it was in the Nova was parked down the street in the dark, for Christ's sake; the first time Downs showed her face, he was going to be on top of her before Harper and Lewellen could stop stirring the sugar in their coffees."

"According to you, she'd just fixed herself up for the night. Where the hell was she going to be going after that? To the beach?"

"All right, all right. Cool off, both of you," Booker said, raising his voice for the first time. He still had done little or nothing characteristic of an angry man, yet Gunner and Toon had no trouble recognizing the fact that he was through playing referee in their little on-again-off-again cockfight. He wanted the floor to himself now, and they were wise enough to let him have it.

"Did anybody know you had plans to tail Downs last night?" the Assistant D.A. asked Gunner.

"No. Nobody."

"You're sure about that."

"Yeah, I'm sure. I didn't know myself until I was damn near parking the car. I did it on a hunch; it was a spur of the moment thing."

"You didn't mention to any of the Blues you talked to that you might be looking her up eventually?"

"No. Hell, no."

"Did any of them say anything to you to give you reason to believe they might be out to get her? Did anyone threaten her in any way?"

Gunner shook his head. "Other than to refer to her in some rather unflattering terms, they had very little to say about the lady."

"What kind of terms?"

"Come on, Booker. You know the terms. 'Stupid,' 'bitch' . . . the usual endearments."

"But no one threatened to kill her?"

"No."

"That go for the Davidsons, too? Rookie's father and brother?"

"Yes."

"What Blues did you talk to, specifically? Besides Mills, of course."

Gunner ran the short list down for him: Rucker, Mullens, and Seivers.

Booker looked up and over at Toon, and the CRACK unit leader shook his head in a way that seemed to say, Not a chance.

"You don't approve of my choices?" Gunner asked Toon.

"On the contrary," Toon said, grinning. "I think you picked the perfect group of kids to hassle. They're harmless, all of 'em."

"Which is to say they're only interested in killing each other," Booker said. "Not overly inquisitive private investigators."

"If Davidson didn't do Downs and Lewellen last night, another Blue did," Toon said. "And it'll probably turn out to be a Blue of another breed altogether, like Mills. The kind a novice like you would've pissed off just by casting a shadow on his Nikes."

"You don't want to try and ask this class of gangbanger the time of day, Gunner," Booker said. "It wouldn't be healthy. You find yourself on the same side of the street as any one of them, you'd be smart to keep your questions to yourself and just go back the way you came."

"Take the kid they call Cube, for example," Toon said. "Real name's Michael Clarke, but they all call him Cube—"

"For 'Ice Cube,'" Gunner said, ending the sentence for him.

"For 'Ice Cube.' Right. You heard about him, huh?"

"There was no way not to. He's the talk of the town."

"Yeah. I'll bet he is. And there's good reason for that. Namely, that he and the gestapo would've had a lot in common. The Cube's that fucked up."

"I see."

"What I'm trying to tell you is, you give a kid like Cube half a chance, you're gonna wind up butt-naked on a gurney at the county morgue. And there's a lot of kids out there like him, make no mistake. Blues, Little Tees, you name it."

"Correct me if I'm wrong," Gunner said, "but I sense all this cautionary info leading up to something."

"Do you?" Booker asked.

"In a very roundabout way, I think you're advising me to quit. Pack up my bags and leave the big, bad juvenile delinquents to you professionals."

"I wouldn't exactly describe what we're doing as 'advising,'" Toon said. "Mr. Booker and I are *telling* you: You don't know what you're dealing with here. You're an amateur in a fucking war zone."

"I'm no more an amateur than Willie Raines," Gunner suggested.

"Shit. Willie Raines. That goddamn peace conference of his is going to be the biggest bust since the Edsel. He thinks he can just call the Blues and Tees together, get 'em to break some bread and shake hands, and a hundred years of programmed behavior is going to fly out the window, just like that. The man doesn't understand a fucking thing about the social and political underpinnings of gangbanging. And neither do you."

"But you're an expert, right?"

"Yeah, that's right. I'm an expert. It's my job to be an expert. While publicity hounds like Raines are dicking around under the pretense of trying to save these kids' souls, I have to try and save their *lives*. You tell me which is harder, when most of these poor sonsofbitches have as much to look forward to in death as they do in life.

"You live in this neighborhood. You know what I'm talking about. Take one kid, male. Put him in a fatherless family of eight that lives in a two-bedroom bungalow full of roaches and bad plumbing. Give his mother a problem with the bottle and a tenth-grade education, and send him to a school where the books are eleven years old and the teachers are too preoccupied with the prospect of getting shot to teach anybody anything. Give him a college-educated older brother who can't afford to buy a two-bedroom home in Lynwood and then move a gold-laden, Four-fifty SL–driving crack dealer into the house next door. What've you got, inevitably? Somebody that learns fast not to give a shit about tomorrow, that's what. A turned-off, tuned-out, full-fledged illiterate dying to take his dead-end future out on the whole goddamn world."

"Nobody has the time to sit here and tell you horror stories, Gunner," Booker said. "Toon and I just think you ought to have some kind of understanding of the dynamite you've been playing with. There are seventy thousand kids in this city affiliated with over four hundred and fifty different gangs, and last year they were responsible for the deaths of four hundred and seventeen people, an all-time high. These kids you've been talking to, they kill when they're loaded and they kill when they're straight, and at least half the time they kill somebody other than who they were out to get in the first place, simply because some poor bastard happened to look like somebody else, or was caught standing in the wrong place at the wrong time, wearing the wrong colored shoelaces or driving the wrong colored car."

"The kind of toys they play with, those kind of mistakes are gonna happen," Toon said matter-of-factly. "You take what they used on Downs, for example. Ballistics says it was an Uzi. A semi-automatic, nine-millimeter assault gun with a thirty-round clip. The Israeli Army trains a man for three weeks before they'll actually issue him one, and here we've got fourteen-year-old eighth graders firing them off in the street ten minutes after buying one."

"If you want to continue playing Twenty Questions with Mills's homeboys, we can't stop you," Booker said grudgingly. "You've been legally retained to do so, however unwisely. But what we can do is, we can make you two promises. One, if you come across the wrong gangbanger, you're not going to see any switchblade knives or single-round zip guns. Those days are history. You're going to see an Uzi or an AK-Forty-seven, a twelve-gauge sawed-off or an M-Sixteen. More sophisticated weaponry than that of half the countries in Western Europe."

"And number two?"

"Number two is, we're going to be watching you. Carefully. Because the first time you give us any reason to believe you really are as irresponsible an idiot as you appeared to be last night—any reason at all—we're going to put you out of action. For good."

"In other words, we don't wanna see any more fuckups," Toon said, translating the Assistant D.A.'s edict in more basic terms. "No more interference in police affairs.

No more dead witnesses. And, be sure you read me good on this last one: *no more dead cops.* You've just used up your lifetime quota. Just conduct your piddly-ass business and stay the fuck out of my unit's way. We've got enough to worry about without having you out there building a fire under the Blues."

Gunner waited for either man to dismiss him officially, but Booker and Toon had nothing left to offer him save for a pair of blank expressions that made the sudden silence in the room unbearable. Gunner stood up.

"Is that it?"

Booker nodded. Toon didn't do anything.

Still, Gunner wouldn't leave. He had an ace left to play, and he didn't want to be caught holding it later.

"Get out of here, Gunner," Toon said.

"You still looking for Davidson's car?"

"What the hell do you think?"

"If I could tell you where to find it, and Whitey Most's prints were to turn up on the upholstery somewhere, you'd have to bring him in, wouldn't you?"

Toon glared at him. "This better not be a hypothetical question."

"There's nothing hypothetical about it. I think I know where the car is. Or at least, where it was as of a few days ago."

He told them everything he knew about King Davidson's sale of Rookie's Ford Maverick to a downtown salvage yard, leaving out only the details of the clean-up job the King had done on the car before disposing of it. Booker took the name of the yard down on a note pad and handed it to Toon.

"Thanks," he said to Gunner grudgingly. "We find anything in or on the car to implicate Most, we'll pick him up and give you a call. Fair enough?"

Gunner nodded, only half-believing him. He turned away from Booker to watch Toon screw his face up even tighter, as if the sight of the investigator was getting harder to take by the second. Gunner knew his mind was on Doug Lewellen.

"For whatever it's worth, Toon, I'm sorry," Gunner told him.

The dead cop was still dead after he had said it, but he somehow felt relieved nevertheless.

It was crazy, but Gunner wasn't ready to go home. He had been up and on his feet for over twenty-four hours now, dodging rain and gunfire with dogged equanimity, but the last place he wanted to drag his weary bones to rest was home. The warm bed waiting there was an inviting thought, but it, like the rest of Gunner's bland little Stanford Avenue duplex, was empty, and the drone of loneliness was the kind of companionship the detective wanted no part of this morning.

The rain he had braved the night before was no longer falling, but it was clear that it was only taking a breather; the sky above was still black and bloated, making no attempt to hide its intentions. Unfazed, Gunner bought a five-dollar breakfast at Jack-in-the-Box and drove to Mickey Moore's Trueblood Barbershop on Wilmington and Century to eat it. Mickey was a forty-four-year-old veteran of the Korean War who collected original Motown 45s and still cut a black man's hair the old-fashioned way: *down to the bone.* Sooner or later, every head in South-Central Los Angeles turned up under Mickey's shears, and any ex-serviceman who had ever had the pleasure invariably left Mickey's chair as a friend. No one knew the painful ups and downs of the lonely war veteran's reentry to civilian life better, or tried as hard to help those that he could.

Gunner would have been the first to point this out about Mickey. He had often been the beneficiary of some of the barber's more selfless gestures, and Mickey was coming up with new ones every day. He had roughly two hundred square feet of unused storage space at the rear of his shop, and three weeks ago he had offered it to Gunner as a place from which to operate, rent-free. Gunner took two days to accept the gift, but only to give his pride some time to get used to the idea of falling even deeper into Mickey's debt than he already was.

The barber was in the process of giving Joe Worthy, one of his many regular customers, his once-a-month trim when Gunner arrived. Gunner promptly moved to the pay phone hanging on one wall inside and called Kelly DeCharme, briefly filling her in on the highlights of his long night.

"You've been a busy man," she said when he was through, no apparent sarcasm intended.

"I've been a stupid man," he said irritably. "But I plan to get smarter. Think you can make it over to County to see Mills sometime today? I'd like to hear what his feelings are for his boss Whitey Most these days. Maybe they don't get along as fabulously as Toon likes to think."

DeCharme made a small sound of concurrence and said, "I'll see what I can do."

After agreeing to check with the public defender again later in the day, Gunner left the phone and immediately sat down in a poorly upholstered chair near a stack of unreadable magazines to eat his breakfast and watch as Mickey brought Worthy's head around to the desired shape, that of a prizewinning, flat-topped garden hedge. The trio's banter was light and inconsequential until Worthy asked Gunner how his latest case was going, and Gunner endeavored to tell him, deleting some details here, embellishing others there.

Gunner did not confide in the pair with the thought in mind that either man could offer him any sage advice; he told his tale of woe merely to expunge it, to purge the good and bad of it from his memory while its details were still sharply drawn and within his reach. For him, the last sev-

enty-two hours had been a roller-coaster ride of mixed emotions, and he was anxious to learn whether or not he had
made it so merely by overreacting to certain stimuli.

"You makin' a mistake in the first place, messin' with
them damn gangbangers," Mickey said when Gunner's account was finished, shaking his head like a bad boy's weary
mother. He was as bald as a jaybird and everyone knew it,
but he insisted on wearing a ridiculous and totally uncon-
vincing rayon Afro wig because he was certain that no one in
their right mind would trust a man with no hair of his own to
take a pair of scissors to theirs.

"It was me," Joe Worthy said, "I wouldn't have nothin'
to do with none of 'em. They're crazy, all of 'em."

Gunner could do nothing but nod his head; it was as if
they had read his mind. He had gone into this thing despis-
ing Toby Mills and everything his homeboys and their ilk
represented, and nothing had happened so far to improve his
opinion of them. He had always made it his business to avoid
gangbangers like the plague, to look the other way whenever
they reared their ugly heads, and yet here he was, up to his
neck in their latest assault on his city, his home. He had
taken a job best suited to a man with three times more com-
passion and ten times less resentment than he had to offer his
client, and he couldn't figure out why.

"Think I should quit?" he asked Mickey and Joe Worthy, asking the question as if he might actually adhere to
their answer to it.

"Shit, too late for that," Mickey said. "You already went
and committed yourself."

"Man gotta finish what he starts," Worthy agreed, nodding emphatically. "No matter what it is."

"Uh-huh." Gunner stood up. "That's what I thought
you old geezers would say."

He tossed the waste of his breakfast into a trash can behind Mickey, then turned to leave them for the confines of

his little office in the rear. Only he never got there. The tiny
bell over the door to Mickey's shop sounded, signaling a new
arrival, and the woman standing there stopped him cold
when he looked up to see who it was, just as she had stopped
Mickey and Worthy dead in their tracks, too.

It was Claudia Lovejoy.

They sat in the cold, dimly lit blandness of Gunner's quarters
in the back and drank the only kind of coffee Mickey ever
kept around, a generic brand of instant with a bite like
Drano. Lovejoy had left home without her umbrella, and
looked it, but even wet and disheveled, dressed in running
shoes and sweats, she was spellbinding.

Gunner tried to offer her a seat on the unsightly, thrift-
shop couch that sat against one wall, hoping she would allow
him to join her there, but she opted for the chair in front of
his desk instead, forcing him to take his own chair on the
desk's other side. The formality of the arrangement discouraged him, but he resolved to make the best of it.

"I heard about what happened last night," Lovejoy said,
gamely trying to finish her cup of Mickey's godawful coffee.
"It was all over the news this morning. They said you were
being held by the police for questioning."

Gunner shrugged. "I was. They only let me go about an
hour ago."

"Are you all right?"

"Sure."

"I mean, I thought you might have been hurt in the
shooting. There was no mention of your condition in any of
the news reports."

"I'm fine," Gunner assured her, unable to keep a small
grin of self-satisfaction from his face.

The grin caught Lovejoy's attention and she bristled,
unamused. "You were lucky this time," she said. "You could

have ended up like the Downs woman very easily. You're not too fatheaded to see that, are you, Mr. Gunner?"

Gunner didn't know what to say. "I beg your pardon?"

"You're going to get yourself killed," Lovejoy said. "You're dealing with young people who are best left alone. Believe me."

"Now where have I heard that before?"

"Don't make light of this, Mr. Gunner. If you've been hearing the same kind of things from the police, it's probably because we both know what we're talking about. You keep playing around with Toby Mills and his friends, you're going to ask someone the wrong question, or say the wrong thing to someone, sooner or later."

"And wind up like Darrel?"

"Yes. Exactly. And wind up like Darrel!"

She tried to accentuate the point by harshly returning her coffee cup to the edge of Gunner's desk, but she came up short on the cup's landing and it shattered in her hand, instead. She leapt to her feet with obvious embarrassment, shaking. Her clothes and Gunner's desk were the only apparent casualties of the accident.

"I'm sorry." She had to struggle to say it as Gunner came around the desk to check on her.

Mickey Moore came flying through the curtains at the door like a den mother on the warpath, but Gunner caught his eye and waved him off, and the barber disappeared again without a word.

After watching in silence for a moment as Lovejoy wiped coffee from her clothes, Gunner asked if she was okay.

"Yes. I'm fine."

"Would you like me to get you a wet rag or something for your clothes? Mickey has some hot towels up front, if you think that would help."

"No, really. This is just an old sweatsuit of mine, it's not worth the bother." She finally looked at him directly again, her gaze discouraging him from questioning her further.

Gunner nodded, getting the message. "I shouldn't have brought Darrel's name into this," he said. "It was an insensitive thing to do."

"Yes. It was. But you were right. I did have Darrel in mind when I decided to come here like this, to warn you of things of which you're obviously already aware. I had no right to do it; I don't know what made me think I did."

"Would it be too much to hope that you did it because you've changed your mind about me? Or am I still just an unscrupulous worm without principles, as far as you're concerned?"

Lovejoy affected a light shrug, almost smiling. "Let's just say I've had some time to reevaluate you," she said, "and I'm not so sure my original impression was a fair one."

"Good."

"But that doesn't mean I understand you. Any more than I understood Darrel. This reluctance of yours to retreat—to admit you're in over your head and withdraw—baffles me completely. Men like you and Darrel, you forge ahead with your little war games, wisdom be damned, in pursuit of some nonexistent, macho concept of self-respect, and for what? What do you ever gain that's more valuable than all that you lose?"

For want of a decent answer, Gunner shook his head. "I don't know. But I think you're comparing apples to oranges with Darrel and me. My initiative can generally be chalked up to pig-headedness, not courage. I don't think you could safely say the same about Darrel's."

"No. I suppose not." She smiled forlornly. "Still, I do see a lot of Darrel in you. His self-righteous indifference to reason; the inability to take no for an answer. I noticed that about you right away. No wonder I treated you so badly."

"No harm done," Gunner said.

"Maybe that's what I thought I was doing coming here to ask you to quit: saving Darrel from the Blues; trying to keep that stubborn, stubborn man from dying all over again." Rainwater glistened on her brow, but she let it be. She just stood there and let her eyes fill slowly with tears, no longer caring to hold them back.

Gunner tried to approach her but she backed away, shaking her head. "No! Please!" She put an arm out to stop him and he heeded it, however reluctantly.

"You can't imagine what it's like, feeling so whole one minute and barren the next," she said, as infuriated by her tears now as she had been upon her first meeting with Gunner. "To have everything and then nothing—*so quickly*! So quickly . . ." She looked at him imploringly, as if hoping he *could* imagine it. "It doesn't seem fair, does it?"

"No. It doesn't."

Her voice barely above a whisper, she said, "I wasn't ready to be alone so soon. I pray for strength, but it doesn't come . . ."

Without thinking, Gunner started toward her again, and this time she offered him no resistance. He took her face in both hands and said, "I've been praying, too."

Then he showed her just what it was he'd been praying for.

chapter ten

....

He took her home and made love to her, taking her body into his hands like a glass bubble he was afraid to break.

Gunner's bedroom was a dungeon of pitch-black shadows, but the utter darkness they were operating in could do nothing to obscure the power of her beauty or the magnitude of her need. Her skin was as smooth as the finest silk and her flesh in the nude kept all the promises it had made to him clothed: Her legs were velvety cords of hard muscle and her breasts spilled out of his open palms in firm, resilient abundance.

From the beginning, it was she who manipulated Gunner to her liking, silently telling his hands what to do with her own, demanding and receiving his total compliance to her design. She handled her breasts for him, feeding her rose-colored nipples into his mouth like a nursing mother, and steered his tongue from the nape of her neck down to the tepid space between her legs, drawing a slow, meandering course across her torso in the process. On and on she went, directing him from one diverse pleasure to the next, undulating spasmodically but never making a sound, save for a low, feline rumble of contentment she occasionally failed to suppress.

Gunner was given no say in their lovemaking until Lovejoy had fully tortured him with waiting, and had brought her own mouth to bear upon him in all the ways she had taken satisfaction from his. Even then, as she finally took him inside of her, relinquishing the reins of control for good, she did so in accordance with her own rhythm, guiding his entry and every stroke so that each was a long, deliciously protracted affair.

It was a technique that neither of them had the strength or the will to endure for long; the blinding white rush of orgasm they'd been working up to came quickly for them both, glorious and debilitating, seemingly interminable.

They lay in each other's arms afterward and surprised themselves with silence. The bitter weeping Gunner had braced himself to hear never came, while he in turn failed to offer her any of the clumsy apologies she had feared he might. Neither was disappointed.

Hours later, when nothing remained of the love they had shared but a faint, benign glow, they resolved to start again—Gunner's way.

Late that afternoon, he drove Claudia Lovejoy back to Mickey's, where they had left her car many hours before. He had begged her to stay with him until Wednesday morning, knowing he was pressing but not giving a damn, but she had firmly declined his invitation.

The rain had continued its renewed assault all during their retreat, though it was falling now with only halfhearted enthusiasm, making a nuisance of itself and little more. Night, in the meantime, was coming on fast. Mickey's shop was dark behind its windows and traffic on Wilmington was light, tentative, as Gunner joined Lovejoy in the cold car to say his goodbyes.

"Are you all right?" he asked. She looked infinitely better than she had that morning, but still lost, preoccupied.

She smiled. "Yes. I'm fine."

"I have an idea this may not be the best time to look for any meaning in what we've just done."

"No. This isn't."

She let her eyes do her pleading for her, imploring him to leave well enough alone.

He nodded his head and turned away, searching the street in vain for something else to hold his attention.

"You ever hear of a man named Whitey Most?"

She was taken aback by his abrupt change of subject but eventually shook her head. "I don't believe so, no. Who is Whitey Most?"

Gunner shrugged. "Nobody special. Just a crack dealer I thought your husband might have had a run in with, once. But if the name doesn't mean anything to you . . ."

She gave it some more thought, only to shake her head again. "I'm sorry."

"Did Darrel have an office of any kind? A place where he kept papers and records, that sort of thing?"

She paused, surprised by the question. "He had an office at Peace Patrol headquarters. They have a suite in a medical building over on Hoover and a Hundred Twelfth. Why?"

"Is everything still there, or has it all been cleaned out?"

"It's all still there, as far as I know. I haven't gone by to take anything. Do you want to see it?"

Gunner nodded his head.

"Right now?"

"The sooner the better. Do you have a key?"

Lovejoy nodded, getting that faraway look in her eyes again. Gunner didn't know what to make of it at first, but when he finally understood, he felt foolish and dense for not having figured it out sooner.

"You haven't been there since he was killed, have you?"

"No." She tried to smile. "I haven't. I guess I've been putting it off."

"I can go alone, if you prefer."

"No. I want to come. Really."

He watched her try the smile again, and though a try was still all it was, it was good enough for him.

"Okay," he said.

She started the car.

The official home of the L.A. Peace Patrol was a four-story office building that dated back to the mid-1960s, when architects couldn't get enough of checkerboard facades of cheap plate glass set in unimaginative rows. Whatever had been holding it together all these years was losing its grip, and what must have looked like an Erector Set construction even when it was new, now looked like a death trap waiting for the next blip on the Richter scale to take a nose dive into the street.

Despite the apparent danger, there were tenants on every floor, mostly medical professionals who found the rent palatable if not the accommodations. Daring to test the building's willingness to support them, the Peace Patrol operated out of a third-floor suite of offices sandwiched between those of an orthodontist named Scott and an ear, nose, and throat man named Rheins. Roaming the empty hallways like a pair of midnight men, Gunner and Lovejoy came to the door they were looking for and stood beneath a stuttering overhead fluorescent lamp as Lovejoy used a noisy chain of keys to let them in.

When they finally made it inside to view the offices beyond the door, nothing about them suggested that the Peace Patrol was getting anything for their monthly rent they weren't paying for. The carpet throughout was worn and discolored, the walls were in need of paint and repair, and the panels of the acoustic-tile ceiling overhead were either spotted with old water stains or missing altogether. As if to remain true to the overall morose mood of the place, the receptionist's desk out front was also an abomination: Bearing a Styrofoam cup of cigarette ashes floating in a shallow wash of cold coffee, the tattered blotter pad atop it was tattooed with unintelligible names and phone numbers scribbled three layers deep, while the wastepaper basket on the floor beside it was overflowing with trash.

Seeing the look on Gunner's face after bringing up the lights, Lovejoy said, "Yes, I know. It is disgusting, isn't it?"

Gunner started to disagree, but she was already moving, leading the way into a short hallway off the receptionist's area. They passed four offices full of dated furniture and obsolete word-processing equipment—two on the left and two on the right—and went directly to the larger office at the hallway's end, where a placard on the door bore Darrel Lovejoy's name, sans one mutinous plastic *o*.

Here, the hand of a more orderly man was in evidence, though the same budgetary restraints were, as well. The huge oaken desk that served as the room's centerpiece was clean and uncluttered, and the wastepaper basket beside it was nearly empty, but it still looked like something the Salvation Army would snub its nose at, as did the high-backed swivel chair leaning to one side behind it, having as it did only three of four casters left on which to stand. An old wooden coatrack and a squat two-drawer metal file cabinet were the only other pieces of furniture in sight, but the walls were lined with photographs to offset this deficiency: Darrel Lovejoy shaking hands with the mayor; Darrel Lovejoy handing a football off to O. J. Simpson; Darrel Lovejoy accepting an award from the Big Brothers of America.

And Darrel Lovejoy in partnership with the Reverend Willie Raines, ad infinitum.

"Do you know what you're looking for?"

Gunner turned from his innocent inspection of her late husband's recorded past, to find Claudia Lovejoy still standing out in the hall, hugging herself in the open doorway as if the room were a cold ill wind she was afraid to brave.

Gunner shrugged. "Not really. Hate mail, maybe. Anything that could attach a name or a face to some of your husband's enemies."

"He wouldn't have kept any hate mail. He never read it."

"The anonymous stuff, no. I would think he'd just chuck that. But anything that might have come from someone he knew, he might have held on to."

"I don't understand. Are you talking about blackmail?"

"I'm not talking about anything, yet. I'm just saying, if someone other than the Blues had a motive to kill your husband, there might be something here that proves it."

"Someone like who? This dealer you asked me about before? This Whitey something-or-other?"

Gunner nodded, seeing no point in denying the obvious truth. He *was* hoping to find something that could connect Most to Lovejoy.

There was nothing, however. The room was free with its secrets—neither the desk nor the filing cabinet was locked—but none of the information it volunteered was of any real value to him. While Lovejoy's apparent skill in calligraphy lent an unusual old-world flair to many of the items Gunner pored over, nothing else about the documents left much of an impression. There were receipts and business cards, old newspaper clippings and a notebook full of handwritten gang-banger case studies, correspondence of every kind, and a wide selection of inspirational self-help books, including two leather-bound copies of the King James Bible. There were names among all of it, written on legal pads and listed in address books, taken down in pencil and ink with varying degrees of legibility and in a variety of different script styles that were a tribute to Lovejoy's chirographic virtuosity—but the name Whitey Most, or any other he might have considered noteworthy, never turned up.

The case studies, at least, made for some fascinating reading—the Imperial Blues were covered extensively and Gunner recognized many of those mentioned—but like the rest of what he had seen, nothing in any of the entries particularly enlightened or surprised him.

Sensing his disappointment from where she stood in the hall, refusing to cross the threshold of the room as she had throughout his gentle defilement of her late husband's personal effects, Claudia Lovejoy said, "Guess you didn't find anything, huh?"

The question had sounded innocent enough, but Gunner looked up at her and realized immediately that it had not been a question at all, innocent or otherwise. She was asking him to leave. He had rattled the bones of Darrel Lovejoy's ghost enough for one night, and her patience for playing his accomplice had run out.

Without a word, Gunner cleaned up after himself and left the room, taking only the notebook of gangbanger case studies with him.

"Mind if I borrow this for a few days?" he asked her out in the hall.

She took it from his hand and looked it over, weighing its significant worth. After a moment, she shrugged and handed it back.

"How will that help you?"

Gunner tossed her a shrug of his own. "I'm not sure. I only skimmed through it. That's why I'd like the extra time with it."

Lovejoy nodded and started out, taking for granted that he would follow.

The ride back to Gunner's car was an uneasy one. There was no small talk and no attempts to manufacture any. Even the car's wipers were silent; the rain had finally given up for good and the windshield was dry and clear. This was the way Lovejoy obviously wanted it and Gunner wasn't going to contribute to her unexpected mood change by forcing the issue. He had decided he had done all the trespassing he was going to do tonight.

They arrived at Mickey's and Lovejoy pulled up alongside Gunner's borrowed Hyundai, leaving the engine running as she waited for him to get out. Without warning, and before she could protest, he reached out to draw her near and kissed her, briefly but not entirely without conviction. She pulled away, but too late, too diffidently.

"Thank you," he said. "For everything."

He stepped out into the street and managed to close the door behind him before the Toyota sped off, spraying rainwater in a heavy, unrepentant gray mist behind it.

chapter eleven

....

The walls in Dr. Earvin Ashe's office were too thin. Sound passed through them like smoke through a screen door, and whoever it was presently howling in the Chair of Pain was scaring the bejesus out of everybody out in the waiting room.

"I think maybe we should postpone this conference until after you get out of here," Kelly DeCharme said, standing to leave.

Gunner shook his head and latched onto her hand. "We'd better do it now. I may not be capable later."

DeCharme nodded and sat down again, seeing his point. If Gunner's visits to the dentist were anything like hers generally were, the detective would be lucky to have use of his toes three hours after the Novocain set in, let alone his tongue.

"All right. So what are you going to do now?"

"Look up Whitey Most. What else?"

"Despite the fact Toby doesn't think he had anything to do with Lovejoy's murder."

"Despite that fact, yeah. I wasn't there when you saw Mills yesterday, but if you say he only seemed to halfway mean all the fine things he said about Most, that's good enough for me. Maybe he's thinking he can settle things with Most on his own."

"What about Rookie's car? Most's prints didn't turn up anywhere on it, you said."

"That's right. They didn't." Gunner had spoken to Rod Toon two hours ago and was told that Rookie's Maverick had been found exactly where Gunner had said it could be. "And if the cops want to assume a lack of prints means he never spent a night in the backseat, that's their business. Me, I can't afford to be so sure. Rookie's old man said he'd cleaned the car up before getting rid of it, maybe he did a real bang-up job. Besides, the way Toon described what was left of the car when they picked it up yesterday, there may not have been much of a backseat to dust."

DeCharme nodded again, trying hard to seem at ease. This wasn't where she had wanted to hold this meeting, but they weren't making very good connections by phone—Gunner had forgotten to call her as promised the day before—and the investigator's broken tooth had been put off long enough.

"You're not actually thinking about talking to Most directly?" DeCharme asked.

"You figure he might object?"

"Let's just say I've never met a dealer of illegal narcotics who could accurately be described as garrulous."

"Yeah. That's been my experience, too. So I thought I'd just follow him around for a while. Watch him make the rounds, get to know some of his friends. Maybe I'll learn something."

"You mean about Rookie, I hope."

Gunner shrugged, staunchly absorbing the discomfort of the movement. "If I'm lucky, yeah."

"Good."

"Good?"

"Yes, good. I'm all for pursuing this Whitey Most angle as long as finding Rookie Davidson remains the focus of your investigation. Otherwise, I'm not sure I see the point. You've managed to establish Rookie's participation in the Lovejoy murder, but Most's is strictly speculative. Were it up to me, I wouldn't spend a great deal of time worrying about Most when Rookie's still the only witness my client's case really needs."

"Nobody said I was giving up looking for Rookie," Gunner said. "I'm merely suggesting that it might be wise to start looking for alternative methods for getting your client off. If Most is connected in any way to Lovejoy's murder, it's possible he could tell us as much about it as Rookie. Maybe more. And if he's not, he's still Rookie's supplier, according to the King. How much imagination does it take to see Rookie seeking him out, sooner or later?"

DeCharme pondered the question as a little Hispanic girl with a swollen jaw, sitting in her mother's lap on the other side of the room, began to whimper, justifiably dismayed by the terror serenade still playing somewhere beyond Dr. Ashe's anteroom door.

"This dentist of yours does use some form of anesthesia?" the public defender asked.

"He does on me. I'm afraid I insist."

"You sure you wouldn't rather see my dentist? His name is Tate; he has an office in Inglewood. You never hear anybody screaming bloody murder in his waiting room."

"Gunner! Aaron Gunner!"

It was Ashe's overweight and implacable receptionist, a white-clad, two-legged mountain of pink flesh brandishing pen and clipboard like sword and shield. Gunner stood up, and DeCharme eagerly did the same, relieved to be on her way.

"Don't misunderstand," she said, getting back to business. "It's not that I'm convinced you're not on to something with Most. But we go to trial in two weeks. Whatever route you decide to take from here, you're going to have to make it pay off, one way or another. And fast."

Gunner nodded and said, "Naturally. No sense keeping a choirboy like Mills behind bars any longer than necessary."

The cries of Ashe's anguished patient finally died, abruptly. Gunner's turn to entertain the lions had arrived.

DeCharme walked out before he could ask her to wish him good luck.

"That's him there," Smalltime Seivers said. "The one with the fucked-up face. Looks like one of them ponies. I forget what you call 'em."

"Palominos," Gunner said.

"Yeah, that's it. Palominos."

Smalltime was pointing to one of three black men standing in a narrow alley behind the 1900 block of 114th Street in Watts, the trio conversing in the furtive but jocular manner inner-city drug sales always seemed to bring out in people. The man in question stood just over six feet tall and looked to be in his early thirties. He had a glistening jheri-curled mane of black hair that petered out at his shoulders, and ten fingers laden with more gold than the average jeweler's window dared display. His most distinctive feature, however, was the spotty coloring of his flesh; even from a distance, it was obvious that he suffered from the disfigurement of vitiligo, a degenerative epidermal condition that gradually bleached skin of its darker pigmentation, spreading ever-expanding patches of pink flesh across the body. There were signs of the disease on both of his hands and at the open throat of his blue silk shirt, but the greatest casualty of his affliction, as Smalltime had pointed out, was his face; were it not for a large island of dark skin on his left cheek and a smaller one encompassing his right eye, the man easily could have passed for an albino in a dark wig.

No wonder they called Most *Whitey*, Gunner thought.

He and Smalltime were standing about thirty yards farther east down the alley from Most and his customers, hunched over the raised hood of Gunner's borrowed silver and black Hyundai as if working to solve some debilitating automotive mystery of the Orient. Ordinarily, Smalltime might have been hard for

Most to miss, but the alley was a popular place for amateur grease monkeys to labor over their latest wrecks, and the two had plenty of camouflage behind which to work. If Most had taken note of them, he showed no signs of caring.

"He ain't gonna be here long," Smalltime observed, pretending to be checking for loose spark-plug wires. "Looks like we caught 'im 'bout to finish up."

Gunner nodded. Most's small gathering had been joined by one lone woman in an iridescent bathrobe and matching house slippers, but there was no one to be seen behind her, either waiting boldly in line or hanging back discreetly.

"You have any idea where he might go from here?"

The big man looked at him blankly; Gunner had spoken like somebody trying to talk through a mouthful of under-cooked mashed potatoes. Exactly as he had feared, his dentist had made a pincushion out of his lower jaw with his syringe of Novocain, and nearly a full two hours later, the lower half of Gunner's face was still just a useless, distant memory.

He asked the question again, enunciating deliberately: *You have any idea where he might go from here?*

Smalltime shrugged. "I know a few places he might go."

Gunner straightened up and made a show of wiping his hands on a dirty rag. "Let's get out of here," he said.

He slammed the hood shut on the little Hyundai and got in behind the wheel. Smalltime took the passenger seat and the car did a fast tilt to his side, groaning, its suspension being crushed and compressed like a watch spring under a dead rhino. Gunner started the engine and began to back slowly out of the alley, away from Most.

"Okay. Now you seen 'im," Smalltime said.

Gunner tried to play dumb, but the Blue wasn't buying. Their arrangement, after all, had been explicit: In exchange for pointing Most out, Smalltime would get to hear to what the dealer owed the detective's interest. Most was no great friend of his, Smalltime had said, but he was a close business associate of Toby Mills's, and the Blues did make regular use of his services, at least indirectly, so the Blue could not see how making an enemy of him would benefit anyone. Enemies came easily enough in the 'hood; there was no need to go out and make more.

Gunner thought of himself in the Hyundai's place, squashed under the big Blue's weight like an empty pie tin, and decided to tell him a fraction of the truth, at least—that his interest in Most stemmed from the suspicion that Rookie Davidson might be paying the dealer a visit sometime soon, either out of need or simply out of habit.

"Yeah. I can buy that," Smalltime said, nodding, satisfied that the investigator was playing it straight with him.

As the little Hyundai labored along beneath his weight, he let his eyes linger on Gunner with open curiosity, apparently trying to solve whatever riddle it was the man represented to him. "When you gonna ask me?" he asked at last, grinning.

"Ask you what?"

"Why I 'bang. You know, why I ain't doin' somethin' more 'constructive' with my life. Shit like that. You ain't asked me nothin' like that, yet."

Gunner kept his eyes on the road. "Maybe I'm not interested," he said.

"Shit. You're interested. Everybody's interested."

"Maybe I'm not like everybody. Maybe I've heard all the answers to that question before, and couldn't relate. I'm dense like that."

"You're sayin' 'bangin' don't make no sense to you."

"A lot of things don't make any sense to me."

"Man, you ain't even curious 'bout my reasons?"

Gunner finally glanced at him. "What difference would it make if I were? You don't want to hear my feeble pleas for reform and I don't want to hear your lame explanations. If I thought anything I could say would wise you up, I'd make the effort. But I don't. You're a big boy, 'Time. I can't talk you in to or out of anything, and I'm not going to lose any sleep trying. Sorry."

Smalltime just looked at him. He had either come to understand Gunner better, or was simply more amused by him, because soon he was grinning again, from ear to ear.

The notebook Gunner had taken from Darrel Lovejoy's office less than eighteen hours ago was sitting between the car's front seats, and Gunner asked the Blue to take a look at it as they made their way back to the corner of Avalon and Imperial, where the detective had picked Smalltime up that morning. He had glanced through it himself the night before, in bed, but could find nothing in the case histories within that seemed unusual or significant, either obvious or written between the lines.

"What the fuck is this?" Smalltime asked, leafing through the notebook's pages, amused.

"It belonged to Darrel Lovejoy. It's a book of gangbanger case histories, but I'm not sure what it means. If you can read it all right, I'd like you to tell me what you make of it."

Smalltime seemed inclined to object to the insinuation that he might not be able to "read it all right," but he merely nodded his head again and dug into the book, maintaining a heavy silence until they reached their destination.

The Hyundai was sitting idle by the curb, its engine running, when he handed the notebook back to Gunner, still without comment.

"Well? What does it mean to you?"

The Blue did a clean-and-jerk with his massive shoulders, shrugging, and said, "Don't mean nothin' to me. It's just a book full of 'bangers. Serious 'bangers. Kind like to jack people, just for fun. I used to know some of 'em."

"What do you mean, 'used to'? They don't 'bang anymore?"

"I mean they don't do *nothin'* anymore. They dead. Most

of the cats in that book are dead. You a serious 'banger, down
for anything, that's how you gen'rally gonna end up. Right?"
He grinned once more and got out of the car.

Following Most around for the next day and a half turned out
to be just as uninspiring an occupation as Gunner feared it
might be. Little separated the dealer's way of earning his
money from any other legitimate salesman's, and that never
spelled excitement; he spent all his time being sociable with
good clients and uncompromising with bad ones, negotiating
terms but never arguing over them, hopping like a speed
freak from one illicit point of sale to the next.

He drove a brand-new pearl white Nissan Maxima sitting on low-profile wheels and tires that made the car look
like a cat forever about to pounce. On foot and on the road,
Gunner watched him buy and sell, compare notes with a
number of his brethren, and seduce a few homely women,
but all it really taught him was that Most and the man with
whom he had seen Tamika Downs only hours before she died
were about the same general size and shape. Gunner never
once saw anything he had never seen before, or had not expected to see, at one point or another, from the very beginning of his surveillance effort.

Like the invariable destitution of his customer base,
Most's chosen locales of business were uniformly common
and predictable. Street corners and alleyways crowded with
the lifelong unemployed, parking lots and playgrounds, shop-
ping-mall eateries and abandoned residential buildings. In
such places, he made deals with preadolescents and the el-
derly, males and females and the lost souls in between, kids
on their way to school and adults on their way to nowhere.
No one was too young or too innocent, too old or too wise to
be denied his goods and services. Success in the drug trade
refused a dealer the liberty to be discriminating.

Gunner was not an expert tracker, as a past full of painful failures in the endeavor had pointed out, but he somehow never attracted Most's attention, even though Most was acting like a man thoroughly convinced he was being followed. He had a way of taking one last look around before departing that went beyond the usual wariness of his kind. Gunner had at first feared that he had tipped his hand in some way—not an unreasonable assumption considering his record—but it soon became obvious that Most was merely fearful of a tail, as opposed to being actually aware of one.

Still, he appeared to be conducting business as usual, making as many stops as was likely to be his norm. He kept Gunner hopping like the last ball in a pinball machine, and by late Thursday afternoon, Gunner was fed up. Most had offered him nothing. He had seen the spotty-complexioned dealer trade rock cocaine with hookers and mail carriers, mothers and grandmothers, runners and suppliers, cops in uniform and in plainclothes, Cuzzes and Hoods of every denomination, friends and even some competitors.

There had been no sign of Rookie Davidson, however.

In fact, there had been nothing worth a second thought in the twenty-nine hours he had invested in shadowing Most save for two mildly peculiar, seemingly unrelated occurrences.

The first was a pair of trips Most had made to a run-down bowling alley on Western near Imperial, early in the afternoon both Wednesday and Thursday. Gunner knew the establishment as a hotbed of inactivity, an empty-bellied pink elephant where anything actually moving stood out like a sore thumb, and so to avoid detection he had chosen to wait outside for Most each time, parking the Hyundai across the street rather than in the alley's desolate parking lot. He was left to guess what magic the place held for Most, but it was at least safe to say that the sport of bowling wasn't it; on each occasion, the dealer had gone in and come out in less than ten minutes.

The other oddity involved a meeting Most had taken during the last daylight hours of Thursday with what Gunner

figured for an Imperial Blue, only not the one he had been
hoping all along to see. Most had driven out to Venice Beach
and found the kid waiting for him in an all-but-empty public
parking lot, freezing his tail off in the cold and wet spring-
time gale blowing in off the Pacific. Dressed in only a Lakers
T-shirt and a denim ensemble of pants and jacket, he wore
Cuz colors in all the customary places—the laces and trim
on his basketball shoes, for example—and displayed them as
well in the fashion the Blues had made their trademark: A
blue wristband rolled up high on the right biceps. He didn't
look a day over fourteen, but he moved like an old man,
taking his time, daring the world and everyone in it to try and
rush him along. He had a small head crowned by a flat-top
haircut, with a twist: The top had been sheared off at an
angle, descending left to right. It made him look as if he was
wearing a hat he could not keep straight on his head.

There were a number of Blues Gunner had not yet
come to know, but he didn't feel like any introductions were
necessary to figure out which of these this one was. Whitey
Most's behavior around the Blue said it all. Up to now, he
had shown no apparent deference to any gangbanger, re-
gardless of set; his manner around them, in fact, had struck
Gunner as wantonly reckless and haughty.

This was a different Whitey Most, however.

As Gunner had watched from the vantage point of an
adjacent, more heavily populated parking lot, Most had left
his car to go to the Blue, giving himself up to the cold outside without complaint, a concession Gunner had seen him
make for no one in the past. Where before he had been all
too willing to stand toe to toe with anyone, with the Blue he
kept his distance, circling and sliding as they spoke, smoothly
frustrating any attempt on the kid's part to close the distance
between them. All of the forceful gesturing and finger pointing that usually accompanied a Most discourse was gone; his
was the body language of a man walking a tightrope—deliberate and controlled.

The Blue, meanwhile, remained motionless, hands in his jacket pockets, eyes fixed straight ahead, keeping his words, when he had something to say, to a minimum. His lips barely moved when he spoke.

There was no doubt in Gunner's mind that this was Cube Clarke.

Exactly what kind of business Most had with Clarke was impossible to ascertain, since their meeting was over quickly and nothing was passed between them. However, there had been something in the way they had said their goodbyes that seemed to suggest Most was buying information, and that Clarke had sold him precisely what he had wanted to hear.

Above the razor-sharp horizon line to the west, one of Los Angeles's patented burnt orange sunsets was in full swing when Most left Clarke—if it was Clarke—and Venice for the northbound San Diego Freeway, clearly not headed for home. Gunner played with the idea of letting him go and sticking with Clarke instead, but decided that would only be trading one blind hunch for another. He had gone out on a limb with Kelly DeCharme to come this far with Most, and he knew that to back off now would be as good as admitting that his professional instincts, such as they were, could not be safely trusted again.

So he followed Most's low-slung Nissan into the darkening bowels of the San Fernando Valley, with nothing more substantive than curiosity to claim as incentive.

It turned out to be the best move he had made in a week.

Exchanging the northbound San Diego Freeway for the westbound 118, Most led Gunner into the valley's answer for the L.A. barrios, the city of San Fernando, where he made two stops. The first was at a Chevron gas station on the corner of Glenoaks and Van Nuys, where he spoke briefly with the tall, gangly black man sitting inside the attendant's booth. Most parked his car beside one of the pumps but didn't buy any gas. Between the interruptions of other customers, the black man slid him a note of some kind and was repaid with an indeterminable amount of cash.

From there, Most drove directly north to an address less than three miles away, near the northeast end of the 900 block of Brand Boulevard, on the opposite side of the 118. Single-story tract homes from an era gone by lined the street, brave but disintegrating monuments to a dust-ridden, virtually all-Hispanic neighborhood trying desperately to hold on to the last vestiges of middle-class status. With nightfall a foregone conclusion, all was quiet and dark. Most pulled up in front of a canary yellow house with white window shutters and trim, but it would be five hours before he gave Gunner any indication that the place he really wanted was actually four houses down, though on the same side of the street.

He spent the entire five hours in the Maxima, waiting, leaving Gunner, parked almost a full block away, no alternative but to do the same. Whatever he did to help pass the time, he did alone; no one ever appeared on the street, to walk by or to join him in the car. Gunner had brought along a pair of infra-red field glasses, but there was only the back of Most's head to see, and he tired of using them quickly. Finally, sometime after midnight, Most stepped out of the Nissan to give his surroundings a cautionary once-over, displaying the paranoia Gunner had learned to expect from him.

When he was satisfied he still had the street to himself, Most walked the short distance to his eventual destination, a tan-colored wooden bungalow and a detached garage, the former sitting sideways on the lot, showing only a flat, windowed, nondescript end to the street. The house was dark, seemingly empty, but Most approached it with care nevertheless, loitering on the sidewalk before it, either trying to build his nerve or listening for sounds within, Gunner couldn't say which.

As a result of its transverse orientation, no direct entrance to the home was available from the street. Gunner couldn't be sure, but he guessed that the "front" door was positioned somewhere along its northeast wall, beyond a wooden fence and gate that joined the house to its forward-facing garage on the southwest half of the property. Most finally went to the gate, and his long, seemingly forlorn inspection of what lay on the other side lent credence to Gunner's theory. Most was only discouraged, however, not deterred. As Gunner took up his field glasses again and watched, the dealer reached over the gate with his right hand and unlatched it, the effort he put into silence impossible to miss, with or without field glasses. He babied the gate open and stepped into the backyard, out of Gunner's view.

Without hesitation, Gunner left the Hyundai and started toward the house, sensing that Most was actually on the verge of doing something worth witnessing for the first time in two days. He closed on the house slowly, trying to listen over the barking of a distant dog for some clue to the dealer's whereabouts, but he could hear nothing. He edged up to the garage to steal a quick glance over the fence Most had disappeared beyond and caught a glimpse of a barren, grassless backyard and Most, hunched over near the main door to the house, fingers working frantically to jimmy the lock.

It was an art he apparently had some skill in, because he was inside when Gunner next looked for him, mere seconds later. Again, Gunner didn't hesitate to follow, careful to handle the gate leading into the backyard as gingerly and silently as had Most. He had the Ruger out of its holster as he reached the door Most had forced open and left ajar; the small living room beyond was pitch-black, and empty. There was no sign of Most among its shadows.

The dealer did not turn up again until Gunner entered the house after him and spied him at the end of a short hallway off to the right of the living room, near what appeared to be an open bedroom door. Gunner's eyes were taking their time warming to the darkness, but he had no trouble discerning the fact that there was a revolver of some kind in Most's right hand as the dealer reached out with his left to bring the lights up in the bedroom and step inside.

"Well, well, well," Gunner heard Most say wryly.

The splotchy-faced black man had caught Rookie Davidson sleeping, half-naked and unarmed. The Blue had jumped up from the mattress on the floor he had been sleeping on with nothing but a handful of sheet with which to defend himself, and there he sat at Most's mercy, his back to the wall, looking like a wounded gazelle shivering beneath a salivating lion's gaze.

It was hard to imagine him as an accessory to murder.

It would have been Gunner's preference to keep his distance and just let Most make his play, to watch and hear how things were going to go down, but his better judgment ruled that option out. Most was behaving as if he had come here to do more than scare the pants off of Gunner's quarry, and there was no way to know how much time, if any, he would devote to conversation before actually getting around to what he really had in mind.

Gunner let the dealer get halfway into the room, advancing upon Rookie in small, catlike steps, before the investigator showed himself at the bedroom doorway and said, "That's far enough, Whitey."

Most turned, startled, and now both he and Davidson had the same comical mask of dread contorting their faces. He started to swing his body around, but his eyes caught sight of the Ruger and he terminated the movement immediately, though he made no effort to lower the gun in his own hand.

"Who the hell are you?" he asked.

"It's not important that we get to know each other," Gunner said. "We don't attend the same dinner parties. Drop the gun on the floor and step back, hands behind your head. Slowly."

Most looked at Rookie, disdaining Gunner's order. "You know this motherfucker?"

Davidson shook his head. He had the same pitiable expression on his face the police photographer had captured in his mug shot, only worse.

The dealer looked at Gunner again. "Who the fuck are you? You ain't no cop. You woulda said so by now, if you was."

Gunner took a single step into the room and said, "I'm the man who's going to drop your polka-dot ass like a ton of bricks if you don't do what I say and lose the gun. What else do you want to know?"

Most's eyes darted from Gunner to the Ruger and back again, weighing the power and potential of both the weapon and the man wielding it. Reaching an unspoken conclusion, he finally dropped his revolver at his feet and retreated from it, following Gunner's instructions to the letter.

"You the motherfucker tried to kill me the other day?" he asked.

The question took Gunner completely by surprise.

Most grinned and said, "You ain't too good with that thing, are you? Man's payin' you to do me, and all you end up doin' is fuckin' up the windows on my ride."

Gunner said nothing, adding an attempt on the dealer's life to everything else he already knew about him, and realized how well it all fit. Most's inclination toward driving the white Maxima around in all types of inclement weather with the driver's side window down could suddenly be seen as more than a mere peculiarity, as could his symptoms of borderline paranoia.

"I know who you workin' for, man. Don't think I don't fuckin' know," he said.

"Turn around and shut up," Gunner said, hoping Most would take the initiative to elaborate further on his own. "And put your hands behind your head, like I said."

Lackadaisically, the dealer complied, his back now to the gun he had left on the floor.

Gunner used the lull in their interchange to look the room over, concluding quickly that there wasn't much to see. Outside of the room's source of light—a rotund, shaded ceramic table lamp sitting on the floor—the mattress Davidson was sitting on had nothing to keep it company but an empty carton of milk and the clothes the Blue had liberally scattered about it. From the investigator's position near the door, there was a large window to the left, near Davidson, and a closet with sliding doors to the right, in front of Most.

While he was anxious to hear more of what the dealer had to say about his near assassination, his professional curiosity piqued, it occurred to Gunner abruptly that his only real objective had already been met, and that this victory could hardly be improved upon, no matter what wondrous tales Most had to tell. Davidson was in hand, and Most was the reason; if he never said another word about anything, he had served his purpose, after all.

Keeping his eyes on the dealer, Gunner said, "Get some clothes on, Rookie. You're coming with me."

"Where we goin'?"

"I'll tell you when we get there. Move it."

Reluctantly, Davidson started putting on his pants.

"Now wait just a goddamn minute," Most said, fighting the urge to turn around. "What you want with him? I thought your business was with me!"

"You've got the right to think whatever you want to think, Whitey. They don't call this a free country for nothing."

"Somebody put up a reward, right? You after the reward."

"What I'm after's none of your business."

"Look. You just tryin' to make a dollar, I understand that. You thinkin' you can get paid for doin' me an' make a little somethin' on the side with Rookie here. But let me tell you somethin'. If it's money you want, I'm the man you wanna see. Whatever you gettin' to do me, plus whatever they offerin' for the boy, I'll double it. How's that sound to you?"

"No! Don't listen to 'im, man!" Davidson said.

"Shut the fuck up!" Most demanded, his voice splitting the night like a crash of thunder. *"You shut the fuck up!"*

The power of the order struck Davidson like a closed fist. He stopped in the middle of what he was doing—pulling a filthy white sock onto his left foot—and froze, rigid with fear. It was as if Most had somehow pulled the plug on a remote-control doll.

"The kid wants to talk, he can talk," Gunner said, feeling his blood begin to boil.

"He ain't got nothin' to say can help either one of us," Most said. "He's a rock head, an' he's all messed up. Probably ain't had no shit to do for 'bout a week now."

"So what's your interest in him?"

Most shrugged, composed again, and said, "He runs for me. I'm a friend. I came here to fix 'im up."

"You needed the gun for that?"

"I brought the gun 'cause he didn't know I was comin', an' I know how he likes surprises. Boy's scared shitless, cops out everywhere lookin' for 'im, and I figure he's carryin' somethin' of his own. You don't get the drop on 'im first, show 'im what's what 'fore he can go off, don't matter who you are. The Rook gonna start shootin'. That's just how he is."

"How'd you know he was here?"

"Man, what's the difference? A friend of a friend told me. Somebody seen 'im out here and the word got around. You know how it is. Why you askin' all these questions? We got a deal, or not?"

"Fuck no," Davidson said.

Gunner didn't have to look at the Blue to know that something ageless had changed him, in the way it had of always changing a man, cowards most especially. He looked, anyway, unable to do anything else.

This time, courage had been found in a .38-caliber Taurus revolver, probably a Model 85, snub-nosed and gripless. It had been hidden under Davidson's shirt on the floor, inaccessible until this moment. Gunner felt like an idiot for not having checked the kid for weapons earlier.

The Blue had the revolver pointed at Gunner's waist, one finger dancing on its trigger nervously, holding it out with both hands like something foul he detested handling. "Put the gun down, man. Right now."

He got to his feet and Most turned around, catching the drift of what was happening. Gunner was doubtful that the Blue could actually bring himself to shoot a man deliberately, but he seemed fully capable of shooting one by accident, and that made him only five times more dangerous. Gunner let the Ruger go limp in his hand and set the automatic gently down on the floor at his feet.

"Over here, man!" Davidson told him. "Push it over here!"

Gunner used his right foot to pass the gun across the hardwood floor toward him.

As Davidson bent down to retrieve it, Most, laughing, said, "Way to go, little home! Put this smartass, interferin' motherfucker in his place!"

Most started to move forward, as if to join Davidson on the other side of the room, but the teenager shifted the unblinking eye of the .38 to gaze in his direction and said, "Stay where you are, motherfucker! I'll pop you, man, I'll pop you!"

Most froze, frowning. "What kind of shit is this, Rook? I come all this way to give you what you need, and this is how you gonna act?"

Sliding sideways over to the window, reaching out with one hand to open it, Davidson shook his head, so hard that Gunner feared it might come off. "Don't bullshit me, Whitey, man," he said. "I ain't that stupid. You didn't come here 'cept to do one motherfuckin' thing!"

He tossed Gunner's Ruger out the window, then picked up Most's revolver and did the same with it, never taking his eyes from the pair of men in front of him for very long. He used the

.38 to move them where he wanted them, keeping his distance, eventually positioning himself by the door and a ready escape.

"Why *did* he come, Rookie?" Gunner asked the Blue straightforwardly.

It was an inquiry Most tried to punish Gunner for asking with a big-league glower, one he had to soften before turning back to Davidson to see what his response would be. For the first time, the kid named Rookie grinned, just a little boy's smirk with a twist of adult sadism at the corners.

"Go on ahead, Whitey. Tell me again to shut the fuck up," he said.

Wisely, Most declined the invitation.

"Gimme the keys to the ride, man," Davidson told him, motioning with the open palm of his left hand. "Right here. Real slow."

"Shit. You *must* be crazy," Most said defiantly.

The kid turned his revolver's nose downward and fired a single round into the floor at Most's feet, blowing a hole in the hardwood and missing the inside of the dealer's left shoe by only fractions of an inch.

"Gimme the goddamn keys, man! Don't fuck with me!"

Both amazed and infuriated, Most turned over the keys as directed, putting more on his toss than he had to. Davidson slipped them into a pants pocket and said to Gunner, "Okay. You. Get down on the floor. 'Less you want some of this, too."

"I asked you a question," Gunner said, staying put.

"Man, I ain't got time for no questions! Who the fuck are you, anyway, all you wanna do is ask questions?"

"I'm a private investigator. My name is Aaron Gunner."

"What?" Most said, incredulous.

"I'm working for Toby Mills. I was hired by his lawyer to find you."

"Toby?" Davidson asked.

"That's right. Mills is sitting on the hot seat for the Darrel Lovejoy murder, but he insists the cops have the wrong man. He says you were driving for somebody else the night Lovejoy was killed, that he was at the movies at the time."

"You ain't got to tell 'im nothin'!" Most barked. "He's just tryin' to get you to admit it was you what did the drivin'!"

"Nobody needs you to admit anything," Gunner said to Davidson. "The cops have your car, they know you were driving. All they need from you—all *I* need from you—is the name of the man who put you up to it. The trigger man in the backseat. You come up with that, and you just might be able to do yourself and Mills a big favor."

"He's just tryin' to burn you, boy! Listen to me!" Most insisted. He was having a hard time keeping still.

"Shut up! I know what he's doin'!"

Davidson had the gun fixed between both hands again, trained almost exclusively on Most. He had been holding it for a long time now, and every minute it spent in his sweaty, excitable possession brought the two men before him that much closer to a bullet.

"Just like I know what *you're* doin'," the Blue told Most, shaking his head sadly, riding the fine line between rage and utter despair. "You shouldn't oughta've dissed me like that, Whitey. That was fucked up."

He steadied his hands to shoot, just as Most kicked out with his right foot and pitched the room into total darkness. What Gunner had taken for a doomed man's fidgeting had actually been inspired maneuvering; Most had edged his way over to the cord of the table lamp sitting on the floor and had yanked it free from the wall. Davidson fired the .38 three times into the blackness before making good his escape, pausing to verify neither hits nor misses. Gunner, at least, went unscathed; he saw the last two muzzle flashes from a face-down position on the floor, having done some inspired maneuvering of his own to get there.

If the same thought had struck Most at all, it had not come

quickly enough. He had hit the floor with a different sound than Gunner, and now was making all the muffled noises of a man in considerable pain. When Gunner's groping hands found him, working in the dark, he offered no resistance, and there was plenty of something wet and sticky on his clothes. How badly he had been hit, Gunner couldn't tell, and didn't really care. The fact that he was incapacitated, as far as the investigator was concerned, was a stroke of incredible luck.

Gunner jumped up off the floor and went after Davidson, confident that Most would be waiting for him upon his return.

The Blue was trying to turn the Maxima's engine over when Gunner arrived on the street, the latter cursing Most for having parked the car four houses farther down the block. Gunner reached the white Nissan only seconds after its big V-6 came to life, but all he had time to do was try the handle on the passenger-side door before Davidson stood on the gas and pulled off, painting the asphalt by the curb with burnt rubber. He watched Davidson bounce the flying Maxima off several parked cars en route to running the signal on Brand, and then the detective actually sprinted halfway to his cousin Del's Hyundai before realizing how futile it would be to press the gutless little car into pursuit.

He turned and went back to the house.

Including the time it took to retrieve the two handguns Davidson had tossed out the bedroom window, Gunner had been away less than ten minutes, but that proved to be long enough. Most was nowhere to be found when the investigator returned to the bedroom to look for him. All the dealer had left behind was a messy pool of blood on the floor that Gunner had no intention of cleaning up.

Like the two in the bush, clipped wings and all, the bird in the hand had flown the coop.

chapter **twelve**

....

Friday morning was for losers. In the wake of Thursday night, both Gunner and the LAPD had to start their weekends off lamenting about the ones that had gotten away.

For his part, Gunner had cruised about the San Fernando neighborhood where both Whitey Most and Rookie Davidson had slipped through his fingers as long as he dared, searching primarily for the former, but the cry of advancing police sirens had finally forced him into a hasty, empty-handed retreat. Not long afterward, the police contingent that reached the 900 block of Brand Boulevard, where Gunner's little adventure had begun, achieved similar results in their attempts to find Davidson and the white sedan that had allegedly torn up half the parked cars in the entire east valley.

Gunner didn't have to be told that the smart thing to do with his Friday would have been to voluntarily offer Rod Toon and the authorities his own account of the previous evening's events, preferably before they came around to demand one, but Kelly DeCharme told him as much, anyway. She did it to ease her conscience more than anything else. She had come to understand that the smart thing to do and Gunner's eventual course of action only rarely coincided—as they failed miserably to coincide here.

Having spent his first waking hours looking in vain for Most in all the obvious places with which he had become familiar in the last few days, Gunner decided to follow his own contrary navigational inclinations and let Toon and the police fend for themselves, hoping for the best. Had he thought his story would compel Toon and James Booker to pursue Whitey Most in earnest, he would have made De-Charme happy and gone in to let them hear it, but he knew his story wasn't that persuasive. It seemed to further imply that Most had been involved in Darrel Lovejoy's murder, to be sure, but it was nothing about which a hardened cop or D.A. was likely to get excited; all he'd really be doing by coming clean now would be adding more holes to a puzzle already full of them, and he didn't feel up to taking Toon and Booker's abuse when they demanded he do better than that.

If he was lucky, they would never know the difference. But he would have to be *very* lucky. Holding his tongue was a calculated risk that merely required him first to dismiss the possibility that the officers on the scene in San Fernando had traced Thursday night's disturbance to the bloody bedroom where Most had been shot, and then assume that in their ignorance they had written the whole thing off as some kind of bizarre drunken-driver scenario, to which the investigator was not likely ever to be connected.

All in all, this made for a perilously thin web of conjecture upon which to base an argument, but it was one in which he had to profess some faith in order to convince himself—not to mention DeCharme—that his most logical next step was to drop in not on Toon and Booker but on the Reverend Willie Raines, instead.

DeCharme, of course, disagreed, but there was little she could say, as it had been she, at Gunner's request, who had spent the early part of her Friday morning determining that the title holder to the house where Most and Gunner had found Rookie Davidson in hiding was none other than the Children of God Ministries, Raines's ever-diversifying religious and political enterprise. DeCharme tried lamely to sell Gunner on the idea that simple coincidence explained this revelation, but Gunner wouldn't buy it. Compared to all the disjointed scraps of intelligence the investigator had managed to accumulate so far—ranging from a drug dealer's fascination with bowling alleys to a notebook full of dead gangbangers—Raines's connection to Rookie Davidson's hiding place was the closest thing to hard evidence he had come across yet, and he wasn't about to dismiss it as anything but.

As he had the day before, Gunner tried all morning to reach Claudia Lovejoy by phone. Today, at least, he had an excuse for making the call—he was going to take her up on her offer to set the table for a conference with Raines—but an excuse was all it was, and he knew it. What he really was doing was what he had attempted to do Thursday—start his workday off by meeting a need he could not explain—but again, the gesture was fruitless. Not one to buck a technological trend, Lovejoy had turned the drudgery of answering her phone calls over to a machine, and all Gunner could do was leave her a second message identical to his first, a succinct "please call me" ditty that was as vague as his reasons for leaving it.

Unlike Lovejoy, Willie Raines personally answered Gunner's phone calls from his offices at the First Children of God Church in Inglewood, though he arranged for their two o'clock meeting to take place at the Reverend's Baldwin Hills home. He had sounded cordial and gracious, more than willing to help, and yet not terribly surprised to be called upon in relation to Rookie Davidson.

Gunner wondered what that meant.

Inching his cousin's Hyundai up the steep, winding incline of Punta Alta Drive toward its scenic culmination among the crests of Baldwin Hills, it struck Gunner that the West Los Angeles hillside community wasn't what it used to be, as few communities that had undergone the transition from an all-white neighborhood to an all-black one, seemingly overnight, ever were. Peeling paint and shedding tile roofs were an intermittent sight along both sides of the street, as were unkempt shrubs and lawns, turned brown and brittle by benign neglect. Here and there, a pedestrian Chevrolet or Plymouth sat in a driveway, instead of a BMW or a Mercedes-Benz. Still, from its unequaled vantage point high above the city, where a clear day often rewarded its residents with a panoramic relief that stretched from the beaches of Santa Monica to the high rises of downtown Los Angeles, this remained the kind of real estate that demanded a sizable entry fee, and Raines's home turned out to be one few self-respecting CEOs would be ashamed to call their own.

Waiting at the end of Punta Alta's seemingly endless climb skyward, only yards from the tremendous earthen crater that had once been the Baldwin Hills Reservoir before the calamitous rupture of its southern wall had precipitated the community's infamous flood of 1963, a cobblestone driveway described a brief arc before a two-story brick Colonial replete with white-on-white four-column portico and trim. The landscaping was immaculate, as was the car complementing it, parked at the apex of the driveway: an emerald green Jaguar XJ6 that someone had waxed and polished to its light-refracting limit.

Neither the car nor the home surprised Gunner in the least. Anyone who had ever tuned into one of the Reverend's weekly televised Sunday services would have realized, as Gunner did, that such fixings of opulence were in no way contradictory to the man or his teachings. The Gospel of Jesus Christ as Raines had always disseminated it was one of many rewards, and he liked to use himself as an example of what a self-made man or woman could accomplish, both financially and spiritually, once they saw fit to place their fate squarely in the Good Lord's hands. While most evangelists of the electronic age chose to shy away from the subject of their own personal wealth, Raines freely advertised his, using it as the perfect validation, as opposed to a repudiation, of his doctrine.

Gunner parked the Hyundai in the driveway behind the Jaguar and rang the front doorbell, feeling not unlike a vacuum-cleaner salesman well out of his territory. When the door swung open, it was Raines himself Gunner found standing behind it, though the Reverend was not entirely alone. Dressed casually and comfortably in a powder blue polo shirt and a pair of navy cotton twill pants, he had as his escort a matching set of male rottweilers, one at his left hand, the other at his right, both watching Gunner like something better tasted than trusted. Massive, rock-solid, and brooding, they were the kind of animals a man kept around the house to do anything but turn the other cheek.

"Let me guess," Gunner said. "Cain and Abel."

Raines shook his head and laughed. "I'm afraid I didn't go quite that far back for inspiration," he said. "Though their names do hold some historical significance of one sort, I suppose. Perhaps if you tried thinking Stax records. 'Soul Man' and Isaac Hayes."

Gunner understood immediately. "Sam and Dave?"

Raines nodded, grinning. "Sam here is the friendly one," he said, reaching out to scratch the dog on his right behind one ear. "Dave, on the other hand, is a mite antisocial, I'm afraid. Not dangerous, of course; just antisocial." His grin widened. "But he's in my prayers daily. He'll come around."

Gunner didn't appear to be encouraged.

"Forgive me if I've put you ill at ease, Mr. Gunner," the Reverend said, reaching forward to shake Gunner's hand, "but they're both perfectly safe, I assure you. Come in, please."

Gunner braved a mauling to step inside, and Raines

closed the door behind him. The twin rottweilers just stood
there, biding their time, in no hurry to feed. His eyes on the
dogs, Gunner could catch only glimpses of the foyer, but
they were sufficient to impress him: pinewood flooring oiled
and gleaming, eighteenth-century furnishings of pecan and
oak, and seamless, textured wall coverings in cool and lazy
colors.

Raines was supposed to be a married man, but it appeared that the missus was out; the house was silent and
Raines made no reference to her. Left alone to play gracious
host, he allowed Gunner to appraise the foyer for only a moment before leading him past a similarly well-decorated,
high-ceilinged living room into a large wood-paneled study
that took its name quite literally: Dominated by an immeasurable collection of books that lined every inch of the four
walls an empty, dormant fireplace failed to claim, the softly
lit room looked like a small university library. Reading tables
were conspicuously missing, but the mahogany desk standing
in the middle of the bare floor was large enough to pass for
one. Arranged around its considerable breadth were a mere
three chairs, all upholstered in sumptuous black leather: a
high-backed executive on casters to the rear, and two smaller
chairs on fixed legs in front.

Raines struck a relaxed pose beside the majestic executive and suggested with a flip of his right hand that Gunner choose between the two chairs facing him. "Make
yourself comfortable, Mr. Gunner. Please."

His rottweilers, now standing alongside each other at
their master's left hand, seemed determined to wait for Gunner's acceptance of Raines's invitation before sitting down
themselves. Sam looked as if no amount of waiting would
particularly annoy him, but Dave was already showing signs
of restlessness. He kept baring the teeth on the right side of
his mouth intermittently, spasmodically, apparently unable
to control the bizarre grin.

Gunner chose the chair on Raines's right and both dogs sank slowly to the floor, mollified.

"Nice trick," Gunner said to Raines.

Raines glanced at the dogs and merely smiled. "Can I get you something to drink?"

"With or without a lecture on temperance?"

"Without. Of course."

Gunner ordered Wild Turkey on the rocks and watched as Raines moved to the wall directly behind him, folded back a fake segment of the bookcase there, and exposed a well-stocked wet bar hidden behind it. Keeping his back to Gunner as he worked on their drinks, Raines said, "So tell me. What makes you think I can help you find Rookie Davidson?"

Pleased to see Raines get right to the point, Gunner shrugged, wasting the movement on a man whose eyes were turned elsewhere. "He's a gangbanger on the run. A lost lamb in search of a shepherd. Who better than you to take him in?"

"You think I'm hiding him?"

"I didn't say that."

"Then why the visit?"

Opting to say nothing about his night in San Fernando for the moment, Gunner said, "Because I'm down to the end of my dance card, and frankly, there aren't many other names left on it. The category I'm sifting through now is 'Rookie's Acquaintances'—no matter how remote—and that deals you in. Or wouldn't you call Rookie an acquaintance?"

Raines brought Gunner his drink and carried one for himself back to his chair on the other side of the desk, finally sitting down himself. His smooth handsome face was set in a doll-like expression of uncanny placidity. "I know the boy, of course. We've talked many times."

"About what?"

"I'm an ordained minister, Mr. Gunner. What would you suspect we talked about?"

"I wouldn't presume to guess. For all I know, Reverend, you're a sports nut who liked to lecture the kid on the immorality of the NFL draft."

Raines let the unflappable cast of neutrality on his face speak for his appreciation of Gunner's wit, and he said matter-of-factly, "We talked about God. About the power of Jesus Christ to change lives, no matter how dark or unsavory. We talked about love and forgiveness, and about the true meaning of manhood and brotherhood.

"Would it help you to know what specific passages of Scripture I referred to? Romans Ten, thirteen; Psalm One Hundred and Three, eight; Second Corinthians Five, seventeen. Are you familiar with any of these readings, Mr. Gunner?"

Gunner shook his head. "Not very, no."

"Are you a Christian?"

"Depending on how loosely you use the term, I suppose I am. Fundamentally speaking, anyway."

"But not in practice."

"The nature of my work inhibits my practice of a great number of things, Reverend. Golf. Tennis. Sex. My faith, such as it is, is no exception." Gunner sampled his drink, raised the glass in his hand slightly, and said, "But I thought the booze was supposed to come with no strings attached."

Raines grinned. "Sorry. I did promise not to badger you, didn't I?"

Gunner ignored the rhetorical question and asked Raines when he had seen Rookie Davidson last.

The Reverend paused to taste his own drink, as if he had to think about it. "Three weeks ago. Four, at the most."

"Where?"

"At our church. In my office. It was in the evening, late. Around ten, I think. I'd told him he could come see me whenever the Spirit moved him, and that was usually about the time he'd drop by. He had to sneak away from his 'homies' to talk to me, you understand, so evening visits during the week were about the best he could do."

"Why was he seeing you and not Darrel Lovejoy? Wasn't Lovejoy the Patrol figure gangbangers usually dealt with?"

"Usually, yes. But that was only because most of the kids we deal with want little or nothing to do with religion, at least initially. Those kids, I generally let Darrel have first crack at. 'Bangers he thought would be totally unresponsive to what I have to say, he worked with alone; the ones he felt I might be able to reach, he passed on to me. That was the Patrol's way. I think I should tell you, however, that Rookie was brought to me not by Darrel but by someone outside of the Peace Patrol altogether."

"And who was that?"

"A former member of the church. A relative."

Gunner remembered his brief meeting with Teddy Davidson, and how concerned the retread tire magnate had professed to be about doing the "Christian thing."

"You talking about the brother? Teddy Davidson?"

Raines nodded. The admission seemed to make him uncomfortable, somehow.

"You know Davidson very well?"

"Not very. He'd shake my hand after Sunday services, and I'd see him from time to time at one church service group meeting or another, but that was about it. I don't see him at all, anymore."

"Why is that?"

"As I stated earlier, he's a *former* member of the church. My understanding is, he's an excitable young man who has trouble getting along with people. Apparently, words between himself and several others were exchanged one evening at a Christian Youth Fellowship meeting, and a scuffle broke out. He left that night and never came back. I haven't seen him since."

Somehow, the story fit Teddy Davidson to a tee.

"Fortunately for Rookie, he brought his little brother to my attention before all this happened," Raines said, continuing without being prompted. "Given another week to work with him, I'd have sold the boy on the Lord, lock, stock, and barrel. I'm certain of it."

"You must have been quite surprised, then, when you heard he was wanted in connection with Lovejoy's murder."

"Yes. I was. His Imperial Blue credentials aside, Mr. Gunner, this is still just a fifteen-year-old boy we're talking about."

"With a rap sheet six pages long."

"Yes. Maybe so. But take it from someone who knows him: Like the vast majority of children involved in gangs, Rookie's really nothing more than a frightened little boy with murderers for friends. Does that in itself make him as ruthless and unrepentant as they? I don't think so."

"Then that leads us to ask an obvious question, doesn't it?"

"Why he would participate in Darrel's murder."

"Yes."

"Are you absolutely certain he did?"

"Absolutely, no. Reasonably, yes." Raines appeared to take the news badly; he actually blinked twice. "At least, when I spoke to him last night, I didn't hear any vehement denials."

The look on Raines's face was one of surprise, nothing more and nothing less. "You spoke to him?"

Gunner sipped lightly at his Wild Turkey and nodded. "I saw him. He was holed up in an empty house out in the San Fernando Valley. An odd-shaped single-story tract job at"—he consulted his pocket notebook—"Nine thirty-nine Brand Boulevard in the city of San Fernando. Maybe you know the place."

Raines actually reacted fully this time, though his frown

wasn't much to see; you had to be looking for it even to know it was there. "San Fernando, you say?"

"That's right."

The minister put his unfinished drink down and said, "I believe you're talking about our house. The church's house." It was not a confession, just a statement of fact. "But you already knew that, didn't you?"

"As a matter of fact, I did."

"And you say Rookie was there last night?"

"Yes."

"Alone?"

"More or less. Wasn't he permitted to have guests?"

"He wasn't permitted to be there at all, Mr. Gunner. At least, not by me." His anger seemed genuine. "Where is Rookie now?"

"I'd like to know that myself. To make a long story short, he left without saying goodbye."

"Was he actually inside the house?"

Gunner nodded.

"Then he must have broken in. He certainly didn't have a key." He saw the dull look on Gunner's face and understood that their discussion had shifted from casual conversation to formal interrogation, and that from here on in, nothing he had to say was going to go unquestioned as the Gospel truth. What the investigator wanted now was to be *convinced* that he had known nothing of Rookie's presence in San Fernando—not merely assured of it.

"If I interpret that funny look you're giving me correctly, Mr. Gunner, you don't believe me."

Gunner wouldn't say, one way or the other.

"You think I put Rookie up in the house, is that it?"

Gunner shrugged and said, "I've been wrong before, Reverend. But what would you think? Any other explanation for his being there involves more coincidences than I'd care to count."

Raines shook his head. "Not really. The boy knew the house was there and empty. Why wouldn't he take advantage of it eventually?"

"How's that again?"

"That's right. Rookie knew the house was there because he'd been there before. Last month sometime. I could be mistaken, but I believe Rookie was part of a group Darrel took up to the house one weekend to do some work on the place. Painting and minor repairs, that sort of thing. We bought the property to convert it into a shelter for homeless mothers, and it was Darrel's idea to let gangbangers help get it into shape, to make sort of a youth work program out of the project. To tell you the truth, it should have occurred to me sooner that Rookie might be there. I don't know why it didn't."

"And if it had? Had you gone out to take a look and found him there, what then?"

"I would have done the sensible thing, of course. I'd have tried everything in my power to convince Rookie to turn himself over to the authorities. What else could I do?"

"As a preacher," Gunner said, "probably nothing. But as the kid's friend, you might have felt there were some other options available to you. You might have agreed to let him stay, for instance."

Raines shook his head confidently, smiling at the absurdity of the suggestion. "No. I wouldn't have made that grave a mistake."

A grave mistake for whom? Gunner wondered. For Rookie—or for *him*?

"You don't believe he's innocent?"

"I hope and pray that he is . . . but I have no way of knowing for certain, one way or the other. My advice to him in any case would be the same: Give yourself up. Allow God and the judicial system to decide your fate."

"You wouldn't have any idea where he might be now, would you?"

"The assumption being, if I put him up once, I'd put him up again, somewhere else. No, Mr. Gunner. I have no idea."

His annoyance was visible but not intrusive. Something stirred on the floor beside him and Gunner looked down, to find the rottweiler named Dave getting antsy again, glaring at him with renewed discontent, as if his master's pique was something they shared equally.

"He thinks I'm angry," Raines said, tipping his head toward the dog. He was trying to dilute the scowl on his face with a smile but was having only mixed results. "He has a keen sense of emotions, especially mine, but the more complex ones seem to give him trouble. Abject frustration, for example."

Gunner waited for him to explain.

"You see, you've misjudged me, Mr. Gunner. Like the police who came before you, you obviously assume that, because I am a man of God committed to the task of delivering young people from the ravages of Satan, I see them all through rose-colored glasses, as supreme innocents the world has defiled but whom God can make right again. You think I'm incapable of or unwilling to separate the wheat from the chaff, to differentiate between those who can be saved and those who will never be. You are wrong. My vision of Cuzzes and Hoods, Troopers and Rollers and Blues and Tees, couldn't be clearer.

"It may appall some people to hear me say it, but there are many children in our community I would not waste my breath trying to save. It's a small minority, certainly, but one that's nevertheless beyond my reach, just too far gone. Considering the forces I'm up against, I feel blessed to have the power to touch any of them.

"Gangbangers are children who are born lost, Mr. Gunner. From the very beginning, they're given nothing to build upon, nothing to hope for. Vermin-infested living quarters, mothers and fathers on crack or booze, run-down schools and indifferent teachers . . . they leave their mother's womb not long for this world.

"And yet many of them can be saved. With Darrel's help, and with experience, I've learned to know these children when I see them . . . just as I've learned to know the others, whose bond with Satan is too great for my mortal abilities to ever compromise. In other words, I am not so great a fool as to treat all gangbangers equally. If I treated Rookie like someone who had the potential to turn away from sin and toward a life in Christ, it is only because that potential was there, and not because I imagined it.

"None of this is to say, however, that I assisted Rookie in any way in his flight from the authorities. The fact of the matter is, he never came to me to ask for help. Perhaps that seems odd to you."

Gunner remained noncommittal. "Perhaps."

"It shouldn't. Were you half as well versed in the beliefs of Willie Raines as Rookie, you would understand, as he must have, that I could not possibly have helped him run from the police without violating everything I and the Peace Patrol have ever stood for. Ask anyone who knows me what my feelings are about those who refuse to accept responsibility for their own actions; they'll tell you. They'll tell you I have only one word for such people: *cowards*. If a man is willing to reap the rewards of the next world, Mr. Gunner, he has to be willing to bear the just punishments of this one when he falters. Many of the lessons gangbangers need to learn can only be learned through Christ; but the lessons that pertain to consequence—to the concept of paying a fair price to society for one's assaults against it—are better taught by man."

He took up his drink again and sat back to enjoy it.

"Quite a philosophy," Gunner said. "Was it Lovejoy's as well?"

Raines shrugged. "For the most part."

"What were the points of dissension?"

"It was more a matter of degrees than actual points of dissension. Darrel's approach to 'bangers was just softer overall than mine. Perhaps being closer to them on a day-to-day basis had something to do with that, I don't know."

"You two never had any real problems getting along, then."

"No. Never. I loved Darrel like a son, and he never gave me any reason to believe he didn't feel as warmly about me." He paused, as if catching himself about to take a bad fall. "But how did we come to be talking about him?"

Gunner shrugged and finished his drink. "Would you rather talk about Whitey Most?"

The Reverend's face said no—not now, not ever.

"The name does mean something to you, then," Gunner said.

"He's a crack dealer," Raines said.

"Rookie's crack dealer."

"Yes."

"How well do you know him?"

"I don't know him at all. I've simply buried enough of the children he preys upon to know of him. And Rookie's mentioned his name once or twice, of course. What about him?"

"I was wondering if he and the Patrol had ever had any serious differences of opinion you might be aware of."

"By the Patrol, whom do you mean? Darrel? Or me?"

"Let's start with Darrel."

"First, define 'differences of opinion.'"

Gunner shrugged again. "Anything that might have led to bad blood between the two. They were two men who worked the same side of the street but had wholly conflicting merchandise to sell. I would think they must have locked horns at one time or another."

Raines got up to freshen his drink and said, "Darrel was not in the habit of confronting drug pushers directly, Mr. Gunner. He was too smart for that. But there were occasions when he had to exchange words with one, certainly. As you point out, his influence upon the children in this community was constantly at odds with that of men like Most; they used to threaten him all the time.

"Whether Most himself ever did so, however, I can't say. At least, I don't recall Darrel ever mentioning it if he did." He came back to his seat. "As for me, the only experience I've ever had with Most, good or bad, was at a public rally the Southern California Alliance of Christian Churches held at George Washington Carver Park last July. I said a few words to the crowd and Most tried to shout me down, created quite a disturbance. The police cited him and he went away. That's all there was to it."

"And you never heard from him afterward?"

"No."

Raines thought he was being helpful, but he was really only making Gunner's life that much harder to bear. For all his magnanimous cooperation, he had managed neither to shed new light on Darrel Lovejoy's murder nor implicate himself in it, a rare double play that to all extents and purposes transported Gunner back in time to the moment of his introduction to a pair of imposing rottweilers named Sam and Dave: a moment otherwise known as Square One.

On the outside chance that Raines might slip up and contradict himself in time, assuming he knew more about Rookie Davidson's whereabouts than he was telling, for instance, Gunner could have asked for a fresh drink of his own and run the minister through a second, more grueling round of inane questions. However, he chose not to do so for one simple reason: He believed every word Raines had said.

Whether it was the power of the truth or just the power of the man to whom he was surrendering, Gunner declared his interview of Raines officially over and agreed to let his three hosts escort him out.

At the door, Raines shook his hand again and said, "You didn't come here prepared to like me very much, did you, Mr. Gunner?"

His insight took Gunner aback a little. "No. I must confess that I didn't."

"Do you mind if I ask why?"

"For all the usual reasons I'm sure you've heard before. The way you've managed to mix success and piety so seamlessly, for one. Your love of overexposure, for another."

"The word and will of God can never be overexposed, Mr. Gunner. That is a fallacy. But your mistake is a common one. You've confused a need to draw attention to my message with a need to draw attention to myself. I seek a certain amount of fame, certainly. But there's a reason for that. Who is a sinner most likely to listen to . . . a poor man shouting from a cardboard pulpit or a rich man speaking into a dozen microphones on the six o'clock news?"

He grinned broadly at the unavoidability of the answer.

It was a grin Gunner might have detested only a short hour ago—but now he wasn't so sure that it didn't have a certain, down-to-earth appeal. He decided he had better leave while he still had an ounce of skepticism for the man left.

"I'm sorry we never got around to talking about the upcoming peace summit," he said. "I'd wanted to ask you how it was going."

Raines threw another log onto the fire of his grin and said, "It's going magnificently. Thank you."

"I don't suppose I have to tell you that there are a lot of people out there in need of a miracle who will be expecting nothing less."

"I know," Raines said, nodding. "I know. They won't be disappointed."

"How can you be so sure?"

It was a stupid question to ask a Baptist minister, and they both realized it. Raines just smiled and said, "The secret is *faith*, Mr. Gunner. Faith in the Lord's almighty power to heal the hearts of men. These 'bangers attending the summit will all be young men who have accepted Christ Jesus as their Lord and Savior, kids who are committed to making peace with one another, and through prayer and open discussion of their grievances, that's exactly what they're going to do. For Proverbs Sixteen, seven says, 'When a man's ways are pleasing to the Lord, he makes even his enemies live at peace with him.' Amen!"

"Amen," Gunner heard himself say.

Choosing not to chime in, Sam and Dave just stood there.

chapter **thirteen**

. . . .

The voice on the phone said, "Somebody seen Rookie."

It was Smalltime Seivers.

Gunner had just sat down with a cold one an hour after seeing Willie Raines when the phone rang. "Where?"

"I gotta show you. You busy?"

Gunner said, "I'll pick you up in ten minutes," and put his beer back in the refrigerator.

"You sure you gotta go in? Donnell and I could prob'ly go in an' get 'im, if you want."

It was the third time in fifteen minutes that Smalltime Seivers had made the same offer, and the third time Gunner had just shaken his head no. Once again, the big Blue was playing navigator from the passenger seat of Gunner's Hyundai, this time directing the detective to the Blues's former place of hiding for weapons and other assorted items of vice gangbangers always preferred held from prying eyes. Donnell Henderson, the latest Blue to make Gunner's acquaintance, was in the backseat, keeping quiet.

Henderson looked as if keeping quiet was something he did a lot of. He was a short sixteen-year-old with a headful of hair and an expressionless, cherubic face. Kelly DeCharme's dossier described him as the Blue with the least impressive police record, a highly intelligent kid who did surprisingly well in school and who liked to talk about being an auto-motive designer someday.

He was a classic example of the ultimate inner-city trag-edy: a gangbanger with both potential *and* ambition.

Though this trip had been Smalltime's idea in the first place, he was nevertheless squirming around in his seat like somebody sitting on a live eel, clearly regretting ever having agreed to come along for the ride. Invading the Blues's pri-vate domain—abandoned or otherwise—was supposed to be Gunner's last resort, Smalltime had reminded him. Abso-lutely the final request he could make of the Blues after all his other options had run out.

Gunner had assured him that such was indeed the case, thinking to himself that the big Blue didn't know the half of it. Henderson's tip regarding Rookie's whereabouts hadn't come a moment too soon.

This was desperation time.

For what DeCharme had predicted eight days ago, Gun-ner had only managed to prove in the time since: Rookie was the key to everything. Everyone else the investigator had seen fit to talk to in reference to Darrel Lovejoy's murder was ca-pable of providing only mere fragments of the truth, or so it seemed. The total picture of Lovejoy's death—the names, faces, and myriad motives involved—was apparently Rookie's alone to know, and Gunner was finally ready to concede that he had to turn the fugitive Blue up again, alive and con-versant, if he ever hoped to share the boy's invaluable in-sight.

He had let Rookie slip through his fingers once; he wasn't going to let it happen again.

The site Smalltime had in mind turned out to be the skeletal husk of a small abandoned house sitting along what used to be the 1700 block of 117th Street, just south of Imperial, before construction of the new 105 Freeway had advanced this far east to flatten everything in its path. The house was the only one of nine on the block still standing, a final tribute to the impoverished men and women who had held on to the only real estate they were ever likely to own right up to the last, but it was easy to see that it wouldn't be standing much longer. A chain-link fence surrounding the block kept Gunner and the Hyundai a full seventy yards away, but even from that distance, with the late afternoon sky going dark overhead, the house looked like something held together with spit and a handful of nails.

"We used to use the garage," Smalltime said. "The house is all fucked up; it wouldn'ta been safe to put nothin' in there, but the garage is cool. Cube put a lock on it and everything. We'd probably still be usin' it, 'cept whoever it was broke in and took our shit, they fucked up the door bustin' the lock off. Ain't no way to lock nothin' up in there now."

They were still sitting in the car, pulled over at the curb on Holmes Avenue. Gunner killed the engine and looked back at Donnell Henderson, who still hadn't said a word to anyone since they'd stopped to pick him up.

"This where you saw Rookie?" Gunner asked him.

Henderson nodded. "Yeah."

"Was he alone?"

Another nod. The kid had a definite gift for gab.

Gunner turned around again, thinking he was finished, but Henderson surprised him by elaborating.

"He called me up. Said he had to talk to somebody."

Gunner looked at him again.

"One of the homeboys, I mean. He called me this mornin', 'fore I went to school, an' said if he didn't talk to one of his homies, man, he was gonna go crazy." He shrugged. "So I asked him where he was at, an' he told me he was chillin' out here, an' asked me to come see 'im, an' shit. You know. To bring 'im a taste." Apparently, *rock* was a word he was not going to use in front of Gunner. "So I did."

"When?"

"When what?"

"When did you see him?"

"I don't know. 'Bout three o'clock, I guess. Soon as I got outta school."

"And?"

"And what?"

"Did you talk to him?"

He gave Gunner another nod, identical to the first two. "Yeah. I talked to 'im."

"What did he say, Donnell?"

The Blue held on to his answer for a long time, as if the fate of the entire world depended upon his silence. "He said somebody's tryin' to kill him. And, like, he don't know who to trust no more."

"Man, who'd be tryin' to kill Rookie?" Smalltime asked skeptically.

"Whitey Most," Gunner said flatly, watching Henderson's face for confirmation.

And confirmation came in another Henderson nod, slow and deliberate.

Gunner turned to Smalltime. "How do we get in there?" he asked, gesturing toward the house on 117th Street. He could grill Henderson later if he had to, but better to get the details from Rookie Davidson himself now, while the opportunity still appeared to present itself.

"There's a hole in the fence, 'round the other side," Smalltime said, referring to the south end of the block.

Gunner pulled a flashlight out of the glove compartment and opened his door to get out of the car.

"Show me," he said.

• • •

Somebody had done a surprisingly neat and clever job cutting the hole in the chain-link fence. Rather than tear a jagged segment out of the mesh as Gunner might have expected, the unnamed Blue with the wire cutters had sliced a large, almost perfectly symmetrical flap into it instead, creating an inconspicuous opening that was not likely to be easily detected by anyone looking for such things.

With what was now total darkness as an ally, Gunner and his small raiding party slipped through the opening and started toward the house in the distance. There was no security to be concerned about; there was nothing here to steal. Piles of rubble and unlevel earth made up the entire block, save for nine hollow rattraps waiting their turn to go beneath the bulldozer, the ghosts of ghettos past.

The little two-bedroom house they were interested in looked no better up close than it had from a distance, and all was quiet inside. Despite all the effort its new owners had put into boarding up its windows and doors, it was as Smalltime had described it: a clapboard sieve unsuitable for anything. Gunner imagined it had always been so, even in life.

True to Smalltime's word, however, the garage was in better shape. Its walls were filthy and discolored, but seemingly whole and intact.

"See?" Smalltime said, voluntarily playing tour guide. "This is where they busted the lock off."

He was moving toward the garage door when a figure stepped out of the shadows beside the building and said, "Get the fuck away from there, 'Time."

The night was pitch-black, making the man before them nothing more than a three-dimensional silhouette, but this particular silhouette Gunner knew he had seen before, standing in a cold Venice Beach parking lot with Whitey Most.

"Cube!" Smalltime Seivers said. It was the first time

Gunner had ever heard him sound like anything other than the giant he was.

Cube Clarke stepped farther out of the shadows toward the big man, and Smalltime's change in demeanor was suddenly even easier to understand. Clarke had an automatic rifle in his right hand. He was resting it barrel-up on his right shoulder, using it in contrast to the Texas Rangers baseball cap on his head to strike the sadistic, casual pose of a battle-mad soldier of fortune.

It was hard to be sure in the darkness, but Gunner thought the gun looked like an Uzi.

"Who the fuck is this?" Clarke demanded, giving Smalltime little notice and ignoring Henderson altogether, his attention fixed solely on the investigator.

"You know who it is, Cube," Smalltime said, trying to sound like himself again. "Gunner. The cat I told you about, one's workin' for Toby's lawyer."

Clarke moved in for a closer look, still holding the automatic rifle's barrel up near his ear, finger at the ready on the trigger. Darkness or no, there was no doubt: He was wasted. Fucked up. The eyes were dead behind a glistening layer of crack-induced haze.

Gunner knew how zombies like this could be, how easily they could kill a man if something, *any*thing brushed them the wrong way. He let Clarke look him over and said nothing, thinking about the Ruger under his coat and how long it would take him to draw it if the Blue decided to cap his evening with an act that could only enhance his reputation as a psychopath.

"This is him, huh? The pussy said he was gonna jack me if I ever fucked with 'im, right?"

He slapped Gunner full on the face with his left hand, hard. Stupidly, Gunner had been watching his right almost exclusively, thinking he'd go for the rifle first, and never saw the blow coming.

"Well, I just fucked with him."

Too dazed to speak, Gunner blinked back tears and instinctively reached for the Ruger, but caught himself before he could complete the movement. He didn't need to see Clarke clearly to know what such a maneuver would buy him now, this late in the game.

"I'm waitin', man. What's the problem?"

"Hey, Cube, man, chill out," Gunner heard Smalltime say.

"Fuck chillin' out. Man say he gonna jack me an' he don't do shit! He's a pussy! A motherfuckin' pussy!"

His eyes still watering badly, Gunner looked up, to find that the weapon Clarke had so proudly displayed up on his shoulder was now being held only inches from the investigator's face, barrel-first. Seen from this perspective, and at this range, it could no longer be mistaken for anything but an Uzi.

"Don't do it, Cube," Smalltime said, making the plea sound as much like an order as he dared. "Man didn't come here to fuck with you, he come here to look for Rookie!"

"Rookie ain't here," Clarke said sharply.

"He was here before," Donnell Henderson said, finally contributing to the conversation.

"Nobody asked you, Donnell. Did they?"

Nobody had, but Henderson didn't say so; he just shut up all over again.

"You ain't got no business bringin' 'im here, 'Time," Clarke said, holding the Uzi up defiantly, swaying slightly in his drugged-up stupor, never letting his eyes stray very far from Gunner's. "Wasn't nobody but the Blues s'posed to ever know 'bout this place."

"I told you, man. We was lookin' for Rookie," Smalltime said.

"I don't give a fuck what you was lookin' for. This is the Blues's crib, home. You s'posed to have some kinda respect for that."

He was questioning the big Blue's loyalty to his set, and Smalltime let him, falling silent. For a gangbanger of his rank—Smalltime was what was commonly referred to as an O.G., or Original Gangster—it was as good as an admission of guilt, if not an outright apology.

"Get the fuck outta here, pussy," Clarke said to Gunner, still aiming the Uzi at the investigator's left eye.

Gunner hesitated, looking for Smalltime to speak, as if Clarke wasn't standing here holding a gun to his head and giving all the orders.

"I said get the fuck outta here!"

"Do what homeboy say, man," Smalltime said, serving final notice.

Gunner glanced at Henderson, then at Clarke again. He knew there was nothing short of dying he could do that would make his loss of face any less real for Smalltime and Henderson, as he had just committed the cardinal sin of reneging on a prideful, unrealistic oath of war in their presence, but he wasn't so sure about himself.

"If you don't already sleep with that thing," he told Clarke before retreating into the darkness, back the way he came, "I think you'd better start."

It was just another empty threat, of course, but it took some guts to say it.

At least, he liked to think so.

Gunner found the Hyundai where he had left it and got in behind the wheel. His eyes were still watering profusely and the whole right side of his face was on fire. Half-blind, he put the key in the ignition and noticed with some annoyance that Smalltime had left the window on his side down. Gunner reached across the passenger seat to roll the window up and finally realized he wasn't alone in the car.

Rookie Davidson was sprawled out on the backseat, staying low.

"I can't run no more, man," he said, crying.

• • •

A few minutes past nine that evening, Kelly DeCharme entered the dim confines of the Acey Deuce—a marginally popular nightclub/bar on the corner of 109th and Vermont in the heart of South-Central Los Angeles—and headed straight for the bar. Following Gunner's instructions, seemingly oblivious to the reaction some among the light, early-hour crowd were having to her pale-skinned presence here, she introduced herself to Lilly Tennell—the giant black woman working the bar and the owner of the establishment—and was promptly shown to the storeroom in back, where Gunner and Rookie Davidson were waiting for her.

She was a nervous wreck. All she'd had time to do was throw some rumpled clothes on and flip a comb through her hair half a dozen times, and she felt like the "before" picture in a *Glamour* magazine makeover article.

The Deuce's storeroom was short on amenities, but it was warm and well lit, and Gunner could think of no better place to hold this delicate meeting. He had no reason to believe that his home on Stanford Avenue would not have been equally safe and secure, but he was intent on taking no chances that someone might see him with Davidson before he was ready to release him to the police. Rookie had a lot of explaining to do, and Gunner was determined to hear what he had to say first, under his own conditions.

He was fresh out of favors owed him by Lilly, but she agreed to let him use the room, anyway. He had brought the boy in through the back door, used Lilly's office phone to call DeCharme at home, then sat among the Deuce's countless crates of Jim Beam and Michelob Light to await the public defender's arrival.

Now she was here.

Davidson looked terrified but otherwise all right. He was wearing the same outfit Gunner had seen him in the night before. Lilly had given him a tall glass of Coke on ice, and

. . . .

he sat on an aluminum folding chair nursing it like a wine taster sampling a fine Cabernet.

"Have you talked to him yet?"

Gunner shook his head.

DeCharme sat down. "Do you want to start, or should I?"

"If you don't mind," Gunner said, "I think I'd better."

DeCharme agreed, nodding.

Gunner turned his attention to Davidson and said, "Rookie, this is Kelly DeCharme . . . Toby's lawyer, the one I told you about last night."

Davidson glanced at her, but didn't say anything.

"We're going to ask you some questions and we want you to answer them as truthfully as you can. All right?"

Out of a long stretch of nothing, a nod emerged.

"Toby Mills didn't kill Darrel Lovejoy, did he?"

Another long stretch of nothing. Then a shrug. "No."

"Who did?"

"You know who it was, man. You know the motherfucker."

"Tell me, anyway."

"Whitey. It was Whitey."

"Whitey Most?"

"Yeah. Whitey Most. How many cats name' Whitey you know?"

Gunner and DeCharme glanced at each other, exchanging a common, unspoken sense of relief.

"You drove, and Whitey did the shooting, is that it?" Gunner asked Davidson, turning around to face him again.

"Yeah. That's right."

"With Toby's gun."

"Right. That's it." He was starting to cry again. "I didn't wanna roll on Dr. Love, man. Me an' Dr. Love, we topped it off, we was cool. Cube an' some of the other homeboys, they was always talkin' 'bout jackin' 'im an' shit, but I never had no problem with Love. Never."

"But Whitey did."

Davidson nodded his head again. "One day, he just say he gotta roll on somebody, an' me, I gotta drive. *Me.* He say if I don't do it, he gonna say it was me what told him 'bout Toby doin' bus'ness on the side, talkin' 'bout how he gonna open a car wash with Whitey's money, an' shit. He say I know if Toby hears that, I'm as good as got. The homies'd jump me out, like a fuckin' perpetrator, or somethin'."

"Toby Mills was doing business on the side?"

"Yeah, you know." He shrugged again. "Holdin' back. Keepin' a little somethin' to sell to 'is friends, shit like that."

Gunner shared another knowing glance with De-Charme.

There was Whitey Most's motive for framing his best runner for murder.

"So then you stole Toby's gun for him."

Davidson sipped his drink, trying to delay his answer as long as possible. "I stole *all* the homeboys' guns. 'Cause Whitey, he didn't say, 'Go get Toby's gun.' He just say he needed one—a *Blue's* gun—an' told me to go get one. Snatch everything outta the crib so's it'll look like somebody just ripped us off. You know, another set, like the Tees or the Deuce-Nines, somebody like that."

"It didn't occur to you what he might have in mind, using you and another Blue's gun in a drive-by? Couldn't you guess he was setting you up?"

"Yeah. I could guess. But what could I do 'bout it? I done told you what he said, right? I don't do what the man say, he gonna jack me up with my homeboys, get me jumped outta the set. What the fuck could I do?"

The numerous answers to that question seemed obvious to Gunner, but he didn't bother to advance any of them. Clearly, it would have been a waste of his time.

Sensing a rift between the two about to rear its ugly head, DeCharme leaned forward toward the gangbanger, resting her elbows on her knees, and said, "Rookie, when did you first find out you'd be rolling on Darrel Lovejoy?"

"The night we done it," Davidson said. "I didn't know it was Dr. Love we was rollin' on 'til that night, when I seen 'im comin' out of 'is house an' Whitey says, 'Let's go, that's him.'"

"Then you'd have no idea why Whitey would have wanted to kill him."

"No." Shaking his head prodigiously. "I ain't got no idea." He paused for a moment of reflection, then said, "I was thinkin' maybe this note had somethin' to do with it, but I don't know. The note, it didn't make no sense to me really."

"What note?" Gunner asked, taking over again.

Davidson showed them another one of his limp, lifeless shrugs. "It was like, you know. Just a note. With some names on it."

"What kind of names?"

"Gangbanger names. Cuzzes an' Hoods, homeboys from all kinda diff'rent sets, an' shit. Tees, Seven-an'-Sevens, Wall Streeters, like that. Even Toby's name was on it."

"Can you remember any of the others?"

"Some of 'em. Most of them cats I ain't never heard of, but some of 'em I knew, yeah. Late-Train, Li'l Ajax, Def-Mike. Casper-Gee, his name was on it. The Tee. 'Casper-Gee, the Tee,' they use' to call the motherfucker. Shit. Them was some serious 'bangers, man. Them cats, they was loc-ed *out*."

Late-Train, Li'l Ajax, Def-Mike, Casper-Gee. Gunner recognized the names, too.

They were all in Darrel Lovejoy's notebook, the one he had borrowed from Lovejoy's office and shown to Smalltime Seivers two days ago.

"These 'bangers you're talking about—with the exception of Toby, of course—they're all dead now?" Gunner asked, just for the record.

"Yeah. Hell, yes."

Gunner could see that they had lost DeCharme some time ago, but he pretended not to notice, unwilling to break the present rhythm of his thinking long enough to eliminate her confusion.

"Where's this note now? Does Most have it?"

Another perfectly bland shrug. "I guess so."

"Where did he get it?"

Davidson looked at him as if he had suddenly starting asking his questions in German. "Huh? Where did he get it?"

"Yeah. That's what I said. Where did he get it?"

The Blue drank some more of his Coke, lowered his glass, drank a little more, lowered his glass again, drank a little more. . . .

"Goddamnit, Rookie, answer the question! Where the fuck did Most get the note?"

Out of nowhere, tears again. Lots of them.

"Oh, shit," Gunner said, exasperated. He stood up to take a walk.

DeCharme gave Davidson a moment to rest, then picked up where Gunner had left off, taking the soft-spoken, motherly tack again. "Rookie, we have to know," she said. "And you're the only one we can ask. You're the only one who *knows*." She let that sink in. "Where did Whitey get the note?"

"From Teddy," Davidson said.

He had spoken so quietly, half-whining, that she asked him to say it again, louder."

"From Teddy. We got it from Teddy."

"Your brother?"

"Yeah. My brother." He said the word *brother* as if it

was a supreme joke, Teddy being his brother, somebody who was supposed to actually give a damn what happened to him. "We busted into his office an' stole it."

"When?" Gunner asked, rushing back to his seat.

"Man, I don't know. A long time ago."

"How long? Weeks? Months? What?"

"Months. Coupla months ago, all right?"

"Then it was Teddy's note."

"I don't know. I guess so. He had it, right? Who the fuck's note's it gonna be?"

"And it was you and Whitey who stole it?"

"Yeah."

"Whose idea was that?"

"Whitey. It was Whitey's idea. He say, 'You gotta get me into Teddy's office,' just like that, don't say why or nothin'. I say, 'What the fuck you want in Teddy's office; Teddy don't keep shit in there?' But he just say never mind what he wants, just get him inside.

"So we go in there one night. Turn off the alarm, open the door, cool. I got the keys. Teddy don't even know they missin'. He leave the house at night, he don't never take nothin' but the keys to the house, leaves the keys to the garage an' shit in the kitchen, on a hook. Stupid. So we in his office, got a flashlight, just lookin' around. Whitey be lookin' though all of 'is papers an' shit, tearin' the place up. I say, 'Man, what you lookin' for?' But he don't say nothin'. He just say, 'I'll know when I find it,' an' keep on goin'. Then I found the note."

"You found it?"

"Yeah. I was just, you know, pickin' shit up. I find the note an' say, 'Wow, check this out. What the fuck Teddy be doin' with this?'"

"And that was what Whitey was looking for."

"Had to be. He look over, check it out, an' snatches the shit right outta my hand. Acted like it was gold, or somethin'. I say, 'What the hell is it?' But he wouldn't tell me. He just laugh, put the note in 'is pocket an' say let's go. Like that." He downed the last of his drink and shoved the empty glass at them. "Can I have another Coke?"

"In a minute," Gunner said. "What happened after that? What'd Whitey do with the note?"

Davidson shook his head and shrugged simultaneously. "Shit, I don't know. He just took me home, give me a little rock an' say if he ever find out I told Teddy shit—you know, 'bout us bein' the ones took the note—he was gonna kill me. So I never did. I never said nothin' 'bout nothin' to nobody."

"Until now."

"Yeah. 'Til now."

"He doesn't scare you anymore?"

Davidson flashed him a look of anger for the first time that evening. "Fuck him," he said bluntly. "Motherfucker tried to off me *twice*. Night we rolled on Dr. Love, after we done it, he say go out by the airport an' park the car. Ain't nothin' out by the airport. I say what for? He just say, 'Do it.' Then I figure it out. He was gonna try an' jack me. Jack me an' leave me in the fuckin' car for the cops."

"You talking about the Compton airport?"

"Yeah. Ain't nothin' over there. So I got the jump on 'im. Faked 'is ass out. I stop the car sudden like, grab the keys, an' run. Just left 'im there, in the middle of the fuckin' street, with 'is mouth hangin' open, an' shit. He in the backseat, what the fuck can he do?"

"Then you went back for the car later."

"Right. There you go. He gotta leave it, right? I got the keys. I wait 'til he takes off, then I slip back in. Cool."

"And he leaves Toby's gun where the cops could find it later."

"I dunno. I guess so."

"The King know any of this?"

"Hell, no. I wouldn't tell the King shit. He don't *wanna* know nothin' 'bout nothin'."

"But you sold him the Maverick."

Davidson dispensed shrug number six. "So?"

"How the hell have you been getting around?"

"Mavis."

"Who?"

"Mavis. The King's ol' lady. We click up. I call 'er up, she take me where I wanna go."

Well, well, well, Gunner thought to himself. The Wicked Witch of the North had a heart, after all.

"Can I have that Coke now?" Davidson asked.

Gunner stood up to find Lilly and said, "Yeah. You can have that Coke now."

chapter fourteen

....

Rod Toon thought it all sounded like a load of crap, but he started the manhunt for Whitey Most rolling, anyway.

Gunner and Kelly DeCharme had turned Rookie Davidson over into Toon's and the LAPD's custody only a few minutes after midnight Friday, not wanting to be responsible for him any longer than they had to, and like every cop Gunner had ever known, Toon had insisted on hearing Davidson's story three times. Once all by himself, and twice with Assistant D.A. James Booker in attendance, sharing the question-asking duties. Gunner was dead tired and sick of hearing the sound of Toon's voice by the middle of the third go-round, but the one he really felt bad for was Davidson. Listening to the same convoluted tale of woe four times in eight hours was one thing, but *telling* it that many times had to be something altogether worse.

To his credit, Davidson never faltered; somehow, someway, his answers to all of Toon's monotonous questions remained consistent and uncontradictory. DeCharme had called in a colleague at the Public Defender's office to represent the Blue, still committed as she herself was to Toby Mills, but the lawyer played a very small part in the proceedings. A red-faced white man with a long neck and a hideous tie, he briefly conferred with DeCharme upon his arrival, then followed her advice and let his client go the cooperative route and come clean, while he himself stayed silent and in the background.

Just after dawn Saturday morning, when all was said and done, Toon was fully informed but not necessarily happy. For his money, all Davidson had really managed to do was complicate matters, just as Toon had accused Gunner of doing earlier, by firmly establishing Most as a principal player in the Darrel Lovejoy murder case. Two hopped-up Imperial Blues gunning the often-despised leader of the L.A. Peace Patrol down, now that was a scenario where the motive was a given, a black-and-white, no-questions-asked, clear-as-the-nose-on-your-face proposition. However, the same could not be said for Whitey Most, all of Davidson and Gunner's talk about a list and notebook full of dead gangbangers notwithstanding. No. The case Toon and Booker had built before, that was a case; this one starring Most, and allegedly featuring Rookie's brother Teddy in a costarring role, for Christsake, this was just an enigma, a giant enigma, which was just another way of saying it was a pain in the ass Rod Toon didn't need.

There was more to Toon's discontent than that, however.

The business in San Fernando, at Willie Raines's would-be home for unwed mothers, had, of course, come out in the wash, and by the police detective's reckoning, he was hearing about it all a day late and from the wrong man. Gunner's oversight earned him a long, ugly stare and yet another recitation of the LAPD's most popular allocution: "Fuck with me again, and I'll yank your private license."

And still Toon wasn't satisfied.

The marathon, multiple-subject interrogation session

was over and everybody was filing out of the room when he said it: "There's somethin' you're not telling me, Gunner. I know it."

Gunner tried several different methods of denial, but nothing worked. Toon's faith in his integrity—not that he had ever really had any—was destroyed, and he seemed willing to bet the farm that Gunner was holding out on him again.

Gunner couldn't figure out how he knew.

It was a small thing, this secret of his. Sharing it with Toon and Booker would have been harmless, and possibly even rewarding. However, there was such a thing as one-upmanship in the law-enforcement profession—being the first to make sense out of the gibberish a complex case so often appeared to be—and Gunner was not beyond admitting it. After all the crap he'd been through to bring Rookie Davidson in—from the near-miss drive-bys to the humiliating slaps in the face administered by kids half his age—he felt entitled to know, before anyone else, what the *whole picture* looked like, Whitey Most, note, and all.

So he hadn't said a word about the bowling alley.

Toon and his band of merry men in black, they could look for Most elsewhere. For Gunner, the bowling alley on Western near Imperial was it, the place to be. He didn't know why. He paused at home to muss the sheets on his bed for a paltry three hours, knowing the establishment would be closed at least until eleven, then showered, dressed, and drove over.

This time, he waited inside, shooting pool with his shadow to kill time. His shadow and three people throwing lopsided balls down the lanes were the only other customers in the place. He had only seen the dealer come here two days in a row, and maybe that wasn't long enough to judge an obsession accurately, but he nevertheless felt safe assuming that Most had been here yesterday, and would show up again today, sooner or later.

....

Most didn't let him down.

Gunner had run up a three-hour, $5.70 tab at the pool table when the dealer walked in, his eyes on the move and his right arm strapped tightly to his chest in a heavy sling. He was wary, but in a hurry, and that helped Gunner's cause as he ducked for cover, farther into the poolroom, relatively out of sight. He still couldn't imagine what Most's fascination with the place could be, but he found out soon enough, and it was like a light coming on over his head, illuminating a thought that should have been obvious to him from the beginning: The lockers.

Bowling alleys always had lockers, lockers you could rent for an entire winter or summer season, if you wanted to, and this dump was no exception. They were designed to hold bags and balls, shoes and purses, anything a league bowler might want to stash away between games down on the lanes—but there was no law that said they couldn't be used for other purposes. They were locked by combination and nearly as sturdy as a safe, and they were the last place anybody inclined to steal would be likely to look for something worth stealing. A twelve-ounce lime green bowling ball and a pair of Brunswick shoes wouldn't bring a thief five dollars on the street, if that. And in a place like this—a veritable graveyard for the living, a parking lot waiting to happen—a man could load one of the things up with a wheelbarrow full of gold bullion and never be noticed.

It was genius.

Most was spinning the dial on a locker now, before a wall lined with them near the door. He had sized the place up upon entering, missing the flash of Gunner in the poolroom he might have caught sight of out of the corner of his eye had he not been so intent on getting in and getting out, and ruled it business as usual, the same old piece of shit, safe and sound and empty as a church on Thursday. He got the door open and started sorting through the locker's contents with the only free hand he had to use, his left. He was focused on what he was doing, incapable of being distracted. He never saw Gunner coming.

"Bet I can guess what you've got in there, Whitey," Gunner said.

Most spun, his feet rising up off the ground, at the sound of the voice. The vast expanses of pink flesh taking over his face were flushed with red and his eyes were like two puddles of white acrylic paint, each marred only by a nucleus of black ink.

"Bring your hand out of the locker and put it down at your side," Gunner told him, holding the Ruger P-85 waist-high, its muzzle pointed downward for the sake of discretion, but not so low as to give Most any foolish ideas. "And make sure it's *just* your hand. Leave the baubles—or the hardware—inside."

Most didn't want to comply, but the Ruger *was* compelling, so he did as he was told, suddenly in no hurry at all.

"Where the fuck you come from?" he asked.

"I have a part-time job here. I paint the stripes on the pins. Do me a favor and step back some, will you? Give me some room."

Gunner used the Ruger to say "please."

Most backed up. "So I was right about your ass. You just after the buck. You just in this for the motherfuckin' dollar!"

"And you're not, right?" Gunner peered into the locker, keeping Most in his peripheral vision. What he saw didn't make him drop the gun, but it did make him forget for a moment why he was holding it. It made him forget about a lot of things.

He had never seen so much cash in his life.

It wasn't the kind you saw in banks, or in those all-star-cast, million-dollar-heist movies that were always turning up on TV. It wasn't crisp and flat, freshly inked and bound in precise, uniform packets. This was *street* money. Stacks of it.

Off-colored tens, twenties, and fifties; folded, spindled, and mutilated. *Real* money. The kind of which *real dreams* were made.

The note nestled among it—the lined sheet of paper somebody had ripped from a yellow legal pad that Gunner had fully expected to see—was just a blip on the radar screen of his mind, a once-critical piece of evidence reduced to relative insignificance.

"Jesus Christ," Gunner said.

"How much you want?" Most was ever the practical negotiator. "There's almost fifty G's in there. You tell me what you want, it's yours. All you gotta do is gimme the rest and let me be on my way."

Gunner took a minute to make sure they had no new, inquisitive friends anywhere, finding the old man working the cash register still absorbed in "Wide World of Sports" and the three men out on the lanes still throwing gutter balls, then took the note from the locker and pushed the door to just enough to put its remaining contents out of sight and out of mind.

"And what about this?" the investigator asked, directing Most's attention to the yellow sheet of paper in his hand.

"That comes with me," the dealer said, not outlining a condition of the deal but stating a fact, irrefutable and nonnegotiable. Then he caught himself, realizing he had made too much of something he wanted Gunner to think was unimportant, and tried to play it off by grinning and shrugging, saying, "Ain't nothin' any good to you, right?"

"I don't know," Gunner said. "Let's see."

He looked at the note for the first time. Exactly as Rookie Davidson had promised, it was a handwritten list of names and gang affiliations, nine in all:

"Top Cat" Collingsworth, Seven-and-Sevens.
"Li'l Ajax" Brown, Stormtroopers.

"Def-Mike" Page, Wall Streeters.
Russell Meadows, Rockin' 90s.
"Late-Train" Anderson, Doom Patrollers.
"Casper-Gee" Brown, Little Tees.
"Two-Jay" Williams, Gravediggers.
Toby Mills, Imperial Blues.
"Nite-Train" Brooks, Double-K Gangsters.

All the names looked familiar; all had no doubt come
from Darrel Lovejoy's notebook. The list was precisely what
Gunner had hoped for, and just as he had envisioned it, with
one surprising, notable exception: it hadn't been written by
Teddy Davidson.

The inimitable calligraphic style displayed here, Gunner
had seen before, on flyers and in ledgers, memo books and
calendar pages, check stubs and business cards, all scattered
about a cluttered office on the third floor of a crumbling
medical building on Hoover and 112th. It was the very same
handwriting that filled the book whence the names in question had been taken: Darrel Lovejoy's.

"Shit," Gunner said angrily. Another wrench had been
thrown into the machine, and his precious one-upmanship
was now just that much further out of reach.

He slammed the locker door shut all the way, sealing
the money inside, and spun the dial on its face a few times to
secure it. Most didn't know what this meant, but he knew he
didn't like the looks of it.

"All right, all right, what's happenin'?" he asked.

"Outside," Gunner said. "Right now."

"Where we goin'? What about your money?"

"I'm not worried about the money. It's not going anywhere."

"Shit, neither am I 'til I find out where we goin'."

"We need to talk, Whitey. Just you and me. I know a

nice quiet place where the drinks are free and the conversation comes easy. How's that sound to you?"

"Like a ripoff," Most said, but he started for the door all the same.

The first thing Mickey Moore said when he saw them was, "Now there's a man needs a haircut!"

He was talking about Whitey Most, thinking the dealer was just some new business Gunner had drummed up for him, but then he saw the Ruger pinned hard against Most's ribs and the "Cut the shit" look on Gunner's face, and he knew that wasn't the case. Naturally, the place was packed with the usual Saturday-afternoon crowd, much to Gunner's chagrin: They had to weave their way through seven men, not counting Mickey, to get to Gunner's work space in the back. Everybody noticed the gun, of course, despite the detective's efforts to hurry Most along, but that couldn't be helped. Mickey had a back door, too, just like Lilly Tennell's Acey Deuce, only his was locked and boarded up, in deference to the thieves who had used it to break into the shop five times in the past two years.

Moore put down his scissors and stuck his head through the curtain after them, as Gunner had figured he would, but Gunner just said, "It's okay, Mickey," and the barber went away, a snoop who knew how to take a hint. He and his small army of customers created a dull roar debating the possible meanings of what they had just seen, but there were no more interruptions.

A desk, a couch, two chairs, a desktop reading lamp, and a wastepaper basket—that was still the extent of Gunner's office. It all looked pretty feeble in the dark, and turning on the reading lamp did little to improve it. Still, Most took the chair in front of the desk, Gunner took the chair behind it, and they both made the best of it.

"You said somethin' 'bout drinks," Most said, slightly

agitated. He was still looking down the unfortunate end of a German-made 9-millimeter automatic, yet his first priority was getting something to drink. He was as bad as Rookie Davidson.

"When we're finished," Gunner said. He could have explained that when he had made Most the promise of "free drinks," he had had the Acey Deuce on his mind, but he felt like Most should have figured that out. He had been right there when Lilly had turned them away, less than ten minutes ago, closing the Deuce's back door in their faces, saying, "Not two days in a row, no, no, no, no! This ain't no goddamn speakeasy!"

"Finished what?" Most asked.

"Filling in the blanks. What else?"

"Man, make some sense."

"I'm talking about the list, Whitey. I want you to tell me about it."

"The list?"

"The list of gangbangers. Dead gangbangers. The one I just took out of your locker at the bowling alley. That list."

Most said nothing. Recognition did not register on his mottled face.

Gunner shook his head and said, "You tell me you want to make a deal, and then you don't talk to me. What kind of shit is that?"

"Look, man, why you gotta know 'bout the list? What the hell do you care 'bout it?"

"Because it's mine now, Whitey. It doesn't belong to you anymore, it belongs to *me*. Assess the situation at hand and I think you'll see what I mean. All the options are mine. I can turn you over to the cops right now and make myself fifty thousand dollars richer, or I can listen to you tell me what I want to know and maybe forget the fifty grand is even there."

. . . .

"Forget it?"

"Yeah, that's right. Forget it."

"Shit. I'm s'posed to believe you're gonna forget about fifty motherfuckin' grand?"

"Look at it this way: The money's there for me to take no matter what you do. You decide to cooperate and clear some things up for me, maybe the money'll be there the next time you go to look for it, and maybe it won't. On the other hand, you waste another five minutes of my time with this deaf, dumb, and blind routine, and you can kiss your money goodbye. Guaranteed. I'll go into the Fox Hills Mall tomorrow and make like I just hit the big six in Lotto."

Most still had to think about it. Watching him sit there, bitterly ruminating, it occurred to Gunner that he looked not unlike a man trying to decide whether he wanted his left arm lopped off at the shoulder, or his right.

Finally, with much reluctance, he said, "What about the list?"

Gunner smiled. Now you're being smart, the smile said. "Let's start with why the people on it, with one or two notable exceptions, are all dead."

Most shrugged, as if the answer to his question was self-evident. "They're 'bangers. What else do 'bangers do 'cept die?"

"You mean they were murdered."

"Yeah."

"By Teddy Davidson, maybe?"

"Who the fuck tol' you that?"

Gunner shrugged himself. "Nobody keeps a list of dead people unless they're an undertaker or a murderer. Davidson's in the retread business."

"Who says it was his note?"

"Somebody making a lot more friends downtown than you are here. Somebody who knows the value of a good rapport with his local law-enforcement professionals. Somebody who was with you the night you broke into Davidson's garage and got your hands on the note in the first place."

"Rookie? You gonna believe *him*?"

"I'm going to believe whoever tells the most complete story. One with a beginning, middle, and end. Just like the cops. You think this is the last time you're going to have to cope with all these asinine questions? Get real. In the next couple of days, you're going to be answering them in your sleep. May as well get a little practice in now."

"Okay, so it was Davidson's note. So?"

"So how did you know to look for it?"

"Look for it? Shit, I wasn't 'lookin'' for it. I was just *lookin'*. Lookin' for *somethin'*. Somethin' like, you know, incriminatin'. Somethin' to prove what I seen."

"And just what did you see?"

The dealer shrugged yet again, smiling at his good fortune. "I seen the Rook's big brother waste a homeboy. That's what I seen. Little cat name' Casper-Gee. Casper-Gee, the Tee." He chuckled. "Over on Colden Avenue, by Avalon. Man made it look like a drive-by, thought there wasn't nobody 'round to see it, but I seen the whole goddamn thing."

"When was this?"

He paused to think about it. "Two, three months ago."

"If it was a drive-by, how did you know it was Teddy Davidson?"

"I seen the motherfucker's face. I was in the ride 'cross the street, doin' a little taste, an' I looked right at 'im. Right at 'im. Him, though, he never seen *me*. He wasn't thinkin' 'bout me. It's like I'm tellin' you, man had everything scoped, planned real nice. 'Gee, he was just standing on the corner, alone, like he was waitin' for a fuckin' bus or somethin'. Davidson come down the street, stop, *boom! boom! boom!*, then takes off. Gone. Perfect. He's thinkin' the coast is clear. 'Cept I seen the fool's face. The jig was up."

"You knew Davidson at the time?"

"Yeah, I knew him. 'Fore I got my Maxima—" The thought of his pearl white Nissan Maxima—the low-slung, wide-tracked, powerful beauty that was now, after Rookie Davidson's bumpercarlike pummeling, probably nothing more than a four-wheeled slab of twisted metal rotting away in some LAPD impound yard in the San Fernando Valley— stopped him cold. He had to squint—biting the bullet—before he could go on. "'Fore I got my Maxima, I use' to buy all my tires over at his place. Ted's Tires. He was always in there, servicin' with a smile. You couldn't miss his ass."

"So what happened after the drive-by?"

"Didn't nothin' happen. I lay back. I think about it. I ask myself how I can make this fresh information I got pay off. You know. Make it profitable. And I think, if I go to the man and just say, 'I seen what you did, ante up,' he's gonna laugh in my face. He's gonna say, 'Your word against mine, blood,' and there you go. There it is. My word against his, that's all it'd be, and why the Man gonna wanna believe me? So I think about it, I keep thinkin' 'bout it, and I re'lize I got to wait. I got to wait 'til I got more than my word 'fore I go to the man and give it up, tell him what I know, tell him what I seen. Wait 'til I got somethin' he gotta deal with, somethin' he gotta take *serious*."

"So you talked Rookie into letting you into his office to look around."

"Yeah. I thought, maybe the gun'd be in there, or somethin'. I was just *lookin'*. Hopin'. Then, I seen the list. I see homeboy's name on it: Casper-Gee. My man Toby's, too. And I figure, this gotta be it. I don't know what the fuck it means, but this gotta be it, right? Gotta be. So we book up, right there. Just like that. Now I got the list. Now I got somethin'. 'Cept I don't know *what* I got! It's a list, yeah, got homeboy's name on it, and shit, but what the fuck's that prove? First thing the cops gonna ask me, right? 'What the fuck's that prove, Whitey?'

"So I wait again. I wait. Every day, I'm lookin' at the list, readin' it over and over, trying to find somethin' in there, somethin' I can use. And then it hits me: Russell Meadows, that boy's *dead, too*! Right? Russell Meadows, he used to run for a partner of mine; cat talked about Russell for a week when homeboy got killed. Somebody rolled on him, the cat say. *Rolled on him!*

"Okay. Now, see, I think I'm finally catchin' on. Now, I think I'm finally gettin' the *picture*. So I do *me* some 'investigatin'.' I start askin' around a little. Droppin' names. Very discreet, like. *Top Cat. Def-Mike. Late-Train. Li'l Ajax . . .*"

"And you find out they're all dead."

Most nodded his head. "All of 'em. All dead, all rolled on. 'Cept for the last three. Toby and a couple other homeboys. Them, the man ain't got to yet, I figure. So now I understand. Now I see what I'm dealin' with. Everything Rookie ever said 'bout his brother, 'bout his temper and his hard-on for gangbangers, it all fits, way I look at it. He's crazy. *Crazy*. Motherfucker's jackin' *Cuzzes*! Cuzzes, Hoods, Tees, Troopers, goddamn *Rockin'* 90s! Any of them sets found out what he's doin', he wasn't gonna live to fuckin' *regret* it!

"So there it is. I got what I need, now. I got a motherfuckin' *ballbreaker*. I come down on Teddy with this, I know he's gonna shit in his pants."

"And 'ante up.'"

"Yeah. And ante up."

"That where the fifty grand came from?"

Most pondered not answering that one, then decided it wasn't worth quibbling about. "Most of it."

Gunner took a deep breath and said, "So when did you find out that it wasn't Davidson's list that you had? That somebody other than Davidson had written it for him?"

"Somebody other than him? Like who?"

"Like Darrel Lovejoy, Whitey. Remember him?"

Most didn't want to remember. They were getting around to the more damaging elements of his story and he was losing his enthusiasm to tell it.

Gunner was unsympathetic. "Ever hear of Sears, Whitey? 'Where America Shops.' Everything you could ever want in life is right there, and all at very reasonable prices. Clothes, furniture, the works. Can you imagine how much shit I could buy at Sears with fifty thousand dollars? Do you know what a vacant *wasteland* I could make out of the appliance department alone with that kind of money to spend?"

"I seen one of them flyers of Love's one day," Most said abruptly, almost regretfully. "The ones he be nailin' all over the goddamn place, talkin' 'bout the Peace Patrol this, and the Peace Patrol that . . . and somethin' just . . . *clicked*. I don't know what else to call it. Million times I seen those flyers, and I didn't never make the connection. I knew there was somethin' familiar 'bout the letterin' on the list, but I couldn't never put my finger on it. Then, one day, I see this flyer, I see the letterin', and I got it. I *got it*. Like, there it is."

"You figure Davidson's doing the killing, but Lovejoy's the man who put him up to it."

"Yeah. He's the one gotta deal with them hardheads every day, right? I figure, man's just tryin' to make his job a little easier. Gettin' some flunky like Teddy Davidson to take some of the most crazier motherfuckers off the street, out of his way."

"So you looked him up, just as you did with Davidson, even though Davidson was already paying you to keep quiet."

Most didn't answer.

"And that's where it all went wrong. You saw a second fat calf in Lovejoy and went for it. You got greedy. Only this time, it didn't pay off. It wouldn't have figured to. Lovejoy was a hard nut; he couldn't have done the kind of work he did and be anything less. You thought he'd roll over as easily as Davidson had, but he wasn't that gullible. Chances are good he told you to take your list of names and shove it up your ass."

Most laughed now, finding something incredibly amusing in the memory. "He tried to treat me like one of his homeboys. One of them runny-nose little suckers he could just say 'boo' to and get 'em to jump, give it all up an' go home. He wasn't thinkin' straight. Man would've been thinkin' straight, he'd've known I couldn't just let it go at that. 'He don't wanna pay, forget it.' How the hell was I gonna forget it? How the hell was I gonna keep his partner Teddy flyin' right if he ever found out I let Love slide, just let 'im tell me to go fuck myself and walked off? Shit. What'd the man *think* I was gonna do?"

"Maybe he didn't care. Maybe he figured all you *could* do was take whatever you'd gotten out of Davidson and consider yourself lucky. He would have been smart enough to know you couldn't go to the police without blowing even that."

"Smart? He was a goddamn fool! Shit I had on him and Teddy was worth more than some jive-ass fifty thousand dollars! They was killin' *gangbangers*, man! Homeboys off the streets! Wasn't no way I was gonna just walk away! Take fifty thousand sorry-ass dollars and make myself happy with it."

"So you rolled on him. You took a page right out of Teddy Davidson's book and faked a drive-by."

"Yeah, that's right." Most was angry now, pumped up by the recollection of how Lovejoy had just tried to shrug him off like a minor annoyance, and in his rage was ready to admit to—or boast about—anything pertaining to his revenge.

"Your boy Toby was playing games with your rock, and Rookie was always a little spaced-out errand boy close at hand, so you let the Blues play scapegoat."

"Shit, why not the Blues? Cops had to think *somebody*'s

set did it, right? The Rook, that boy's always fucked up, anyway. I figure him, I just be puttin' him outta his misery. But
Toby . . ." He shook his head sadly, like a mother talking
about a stray son. "That boy, he just pissed me off. *Off.* I set
the boy up, give 'im a piece, a real *piece,* and what does he
do? He disses me, that's what. Uses my own shit to try and
ace me out, like he's some kinda fuckin' entrepreneur, or
somethin'. So I say, cool. That's the way he wants it, fine. I
deal him into the drive-by. I tell Rookie to get me homeboy's
gun, one got his prints all on it and shit, and I give him some
piddly errand to run when we're gonna do it, so he won't
have no kind of alibi when the Man picks him up. I *fix* his
ass, you understand? I got another man can run in his place;
I don't need no goddamn backstabbers workin' for me."

"You're talking about Cube Clarke," Gunner said.

"Yeah, that's right. The Cube."

"He was the one who tipped you to where Rookie was
hiding in San Fernando."

"Yeah. He heard it from a friend of a friend, like I told
you the other night. See, the Cube, he ain't like most gangbangers. That's what I like about 'im. The Cube, you tell 'im
what to do, what you need, and it's done. No questions
asked."

"Especially when you can give him something fun to do
like roll on Tamika Downs, no doubt."

Most tried to make his face look apologetic, but it came
off as something far less. "Tamika, she brought that on herself. I was gonna trust the bitch to keep her mouth shut, but
she seen a couple cops sittin' outside her house an' went to
pieces, made me lose all faith in her ass. So, I put the Cube
to work, yeah. An' it's just like you say: He got off on it.
Didn't give me no shit, just went. The Cube, that motherfucker workin' for you, *you're* his homeboy. You understand
what I'm sayin'? 'Fuck the set, gimme my *money.*'"

He laughed again, obviously admiring such mercenary wisdom.

Gunner watched him cackle, the Ruger feeling somehow heavier in his hand, and decided he had heard enough. He stood up from his chair and started to circle the desk, toward Most, moving like he had something other than a short walk in mind.

"Do me a favor, Whitey," he said, waiting until he was right on top of the dealer to speak. "Don't laugh. I don't like the sound of it."

Most grinned, eager to please, and said, "Whatever you say, my man."

And then the last thing Gunner thought possible happened: Most used his right arm.

His right arm was supposed to be useless, he had taken a bullet, possibly even three, somewhere in his upper torso only two nights ago, and the sling he was wearing made a powerful argument that his right arm had paid the price. Gunner had even been compensating accordingly, favoring Most's right side, thinking himself wise, using the man's handicap to remain out of harm's way. But no. Most had brought the appendage up out of the sling like the head of a cobra, just a blur that had knocked the Ruger aside long enough for its owner to let loose with a straight left hand that caught the startled, stupefied investigator flush on the jaw.

That was twice now Gunner had been caught watching someone's "wrong" hand.

It was an error to be ashamed of, certainly, but Gunner didn't have time to feel ashamed. Most had knocked the Ruger from his grasp and was diving to the floor after it, with lousy form and decidedly bad intentions. The dealer's left hand hadn't had much behind it, but it had served its purpose all the same: Gunner couldn't get to Most, or the Ruger, in time.

Most had the gun aimed at his face before he could join

the dealer on the floor. Gunner froze in place, holding the pose of a cat about to pounce, but he could see by the gleam in Most's eye that it was a wasted effort. Unconditional surrender was not what Most had in mind. The dealer had the upper hand now, and he wasn't going to do anything with it but put a hole in Gunner's forehead and go back for his fifty grand.

A flash of white lightning lit the walls of the room, and a cruel, guttural thunderclap accompanied it—but Gunner did not go down. Most did. Something made a bloody mess of his left collarbone, separating him from the Ruger, and sent him sprawling, limbs akimbo, over Gunner's desk and down to the floor on the other side. His awkward landing alone suggested he would not be getting up again.

Gunner turned to find Rod Toon standing in the doorway, his chrome-plated .38 Special smoking in his right hand like a fat cigar. Behind him, fighting with the curtains hanging in the doorway, Mickey Moore and his seven customers were trying to look past Toon into the room, jostling for position, muttering excitedly among themselves.

Without saying a word to Gunner, Toon crossed the room to where Most lay and felt for a pulse.

To no one's great disappointment, he never found one.

chapter **fifteen**

··

The thing that had saved Gunner's life was that Rod Toon believed in one-upmanship, too.

His suspicion that the investigator was holding out on him, keeping secrets, had inspired him to assign a pair of plainclothes officers to the task of following Gunner around, but he had done so in the hope of getting something more out of it than a stranglehold on Gunner's P.I. license. No one had been more frustrated by the gaping holes in Rookie Davidson's wild story than Toon, nor more anxious to solve them, and he had made up his mind that when the time came to fill them, to lay the whole thing down for Assistant District Attorney James Booker with every who, what, where, and when perfectly in place, *he* would be the man with all the answers, not Gunner.

One-upmanship.

Gunner's shadows had been placed on his tail only hours after his release from police headquarters early Saturday morning, but they had missed him at home and did not actually pick him up until he and Whitey Most showed up at Mickey Moore's Trueblood Barbershop at a few minutes before three that afternoon. They recognized Most at once but made no move to apprehend him; Toon had given them specific orders to just sit tight and notify the CRASH unit detective directly if anything worth reporting developed, and that was what they did. Toon slapped the red dome light to the roof of his car and raced over as fast as he could.

Had he stepped through the curtained doorway leading to Gunner's office five minutes sooner than he had, things might have worked out exactly as he had planned. He could have handcuffed Gunner to a water pipe, grilled Whitey Most himself, and handed the completed tale of Darrel Lovejoy's murder to James Booker on a silver platter. Instead, despite all the precautions he had taken to avoid such an eventuality, he ended up yet again at the mercy of Gunner's sense of recall.

He was not a happy camper.

So this time, when his three-round verbal sparring session with Toon and Booker was finished, Gunner was not sent home with a stern warning and a stinging slap on the wrist. This time, they made reservations for him at the Black Bar Saloon, aka city jail, and advised him to get used to the decor of the place. The official charges pressed against him were "obstruction of justice" and "aiding and abetting a known fugitive," and they earned him, at least to start, two nights of bad sleep in a crowded cell and the use of a toilet bowl that looked like a plumber's worst nightmare.

It was mid-afternoon Monday when Ziggy, his fifty-two-year-old Jewish lawyer and a triathlon-running health freak, finally managed to get him released on bail. During the ride home, Ziggy didn't have many kind things to say about the way Gunner had handled things, but he did have some interesting news: One, the coroner's autopsy on Whitey Most's body had revealed that Most had suffered little more than a bloody and painful, though nondebilitating, flesh wound the previous Thursday night in San Fernando, hence his unexpected use of his bandaged right arm Saturday afternoon; two, the case against Toby Mills had been dropped, and Mills was on the street; and three, most significantly, Teddy Davidson had taken it on the lam. He had killed one cop and wounded another when they tried to pick him up for questioning early Saturday night, and apparently did not reappear again until the following day. It was only "apparent" that he had reappeared Sunday because the Reverend Willie Raines was the only one who claimed to have seen him. Raines had called the police late Sunday afternoon to say that Davidson was in his custody and was ready to give himself up, but when the squad cars arrived at the minister's Baldwin Hills home, Davidson was nowhere to be found. According to Raines, he had changed his mind about surrendering and had run off again, without giving Raines any idea where he might go.

In his absence, the police had gone through Davidson's home and come up with more reasons for Davidson to keep running than he would ever need: a dozen or so assorted rifles and handguns, a closet full of gangbanger attire in all the colors of the rainbow, and a key chain strung with car keys, over thirty in all. The guns and the clothes seemed to need no explanation, in light of the fact that ballistics had identified several of the weapons as those used in the murders of some of the deceased gangbangers on Darrel Lovejoy's list, but the keys were a source of confusion until somebody remembered what kind of business Davidson was in and who made up a good part of his customer base. Evidently, Davidson had been duplicating the keys to cars gangbangers were bringing into his shop, then "borrowing" the cars just long enough to use them on his faked drive-bys.

It was a brilliant setup.

In searching for Davidson's motives for his crimes, the police and the local press, for whom the "tire salesman gone mad" story was a big one, uncovered only a few, though one stood out from the others like a sore thumb: On the afternoon of September 7, 1988, three teenage gangbangers from the Rockin' 90s Hood set walked into a laundromat at 9116 Central Avenue and opened fire on the six people inside with two sawed-off shotguns and an automatic rifle, killing three and wounding three. Two of the dead were members of a rival Hood set, the Central Club Players, mere wannabes at twelve and fourteen, respectively; the third was a twenty-seven-year-old day-care-center teacher named Jennifer Wilkes. Wilkes had been six months pregnant at the time of her—and her unborn baby's—untimely death.

She also had been engaged to marry Teddy Davidson in October of that same year.

In the wake of the unsettling news that Darrel Lovejoy, his trusted and beloved cofounder of the L.A. Peace Patrol, had in fact been, at the very least, a conspirator in the murder of the very children the organization was supposedly dedicated to assist, the Reverend Willie Raines was holding up admirably well. He, of course, claimed complete ignorance of his partner's wrongdoings, vowed to make restitution in any way possible, and assured both the members of his immediate church and his vast following among the general public that both the Peace Patrol and his Children of God Ministries were capable of withstanding any amount of close scrutiny the authorities might care to bring to bear upon them. He was determined to diffuse any talk whatsoever that his one-year-in-the-making, precedent-setting youth gang peace summit—scheduled to take place that very Wednesday—could not proceed as planned.

The police, who had never been too crazy about the idea of the summit in the first place, weren't too happy with the timing of it—but they were willing to try anything that might keep the lid on what was now a highly unpredictable, possibly even explosive, L.A. gang scene. If he could get the 'bangers scheduled to participate to go through with the peacemaking process, they told Raines—despite everything the 'bangers had learned about Darrel Lovejoy and the true fate of some of their deceased homeboys—then he had their blessings. And their respect.

Toon, for one, didn't think the minister would be able to pull it off, but he hardly had the time to argue about it. There was still the matter of Tamika Downs and Officer Doug Lewellen's murders to attend to. It helped to finally know that Cube Clarke had been the Blue responsible for the double murder, as Gunner's latest statement to the police indicated, but it was beginning to look as if finding Clarke to extract a confession to that effect was going to be as big a headache as finding Rookie Davidson had proven to be. Cube had gone underground, apparently taking the green-of-sorts Chevy Nova with the missing headlight with him. And Toon's people were fast getting tired of searching for them both.

Still, Toon was not complaining. There was something new to be thankful for these days, and it made his load lighter just to remind himself of it. Sometimes, the thought even put a smile on his face. Aaron Gunner was off the street, and out of his hair.

He had won the game of one-upmanship, after all.

"It's a lie. Something that vile, disgusting man made up just to slander Darrel and make himself look less deplorable."

"I don't think so, Claudia."

"Then you're a *fool*. Anyone who knew Darrel—*anyone*—would know that it's not true. That it's just not possible. Darrel could never have murdered anyone."

Gunner thought to point out that no one had accused Claudia Lovejoy's late husband of committing murder, per se—all the evidence available to date merely indicated that he had commissioned someone else to actually commit several—but he figured the distinction would be no consolation to the woman, whatsoever. Less than two months ago, she had been forced to watch as the people of Los Angeles gently lowered Darrel Lovejoy into his grave—and now she was having to watch them dig him right back up again, for another pass through the muck and the slime of the living.

"What about the note? It was Darrel's handwriting. Even you admitted that."

"So what if it was his handwriting? That note could have meant anything! Just because a sick man made a death list out of it doesn't mean that's what it really was!"

She was beautiful. No amount of righteous indignation could change that. It was Tuesday, early evening, and he had finally caught up to her at home, having grown tired of leaving messages that were only going ignored on her telephone answering machine. She let him in reluctantly, resentfully, and they settled in the living room to do what he said he had come to do: say goodbye.

However, now that she was sitting here before him, the very picture of casual voluptuousness in a slate gray knitted sweater with a scalloped neck and a pair of pale blue hip-hugging denim trousers—her radiant face flushed with color and her green eyes dancing with light—there was no way he could do it. Saying goodbye was the last thing on his mind. For all the belated regrets she might be feeling for the night they had shared together, he had none, and he was not going to dismiss outright the magic of it as something that could never be duplicated or sustained.

"When they catch Teddy Davidson, you'll see," she said. "He'll tell you. He did what he did on his own; Darrel had nothing to do with it."

Davidson still hadn't turned up, and the police had all but stopped looking for him in Los Angeles. Investigators had learned that he had rented a car in Phoenix, Arizona, late Monday afternoon, and the search for him had moved eastward accordingly. He and Rookie had relatives in Houston, Texas, and that was where it was widely assumed he was headed.

"I'd like to take you to dinner," Gunner said, tired of being a participant in an argument he didn't really need to win. "Tonight."

Lovejoy shook her head adamantly. "No. I'm sorry."

"Don't be sorry. Be fair. To yourself and to me. Please."

She was still shaking her head.

It took Gunner close to forty minutes to make her stop, but for a long time afterward he would regard it as time well spent.

Wednesday morning, his eyes finally opened to the truth, and it was like getting hit by a train and a sudden awareness of his own stupidity all at once.

He was a private investigator; it was his *job* to look beyond the obvious, and yet he had had to lie down with a magnificent woman to see the light. Whether it was the sheer power of the sex alone, or the realization that this time her reasons for being with him had had more to do with conscious want than unconscious need, he awoke in Claudia Lovejoy's bed at exactly eleven-twenty-five with a new, frighteningly feasible outlook on her husband's murder, an outlook he wasted no time in testing for validity.

He turned to her and found that she, too, was awake, her head propped up in her left hand, watching the odd expressions roll over his face as the revelation established itself firmly in his mind. There was nothing on the bed with which to mask her nudity except for a single sheet in pastel blue, but she wasn't making much use of it. It was drawn up only to her navel and her breasts were playing peekaboo with his eyes. If he wanted to, he could draw up the memory of the things he had done to Lovejoy—and the things she had done to him—only mere hours ago. . . .

"You get the paper?"

"Pardon me?"

"Do you get a paper? A newspaper. Is there one outside right now?"

She yawned deliciously. "The *Times*. But why . . . ?"

He pulled his pants on and ran to the front door. As promised, the Wednesday morning *Los Angeles Times* was waiting for him atop the tattered welcome mat on the porch.

He returned to the bed and immediately leafed through the first section, but he should have known better. The local press had shown the Reverend Willie Raines's street-gang peace summit nearly as much unapologetic skepticism as the LAPD, and there was no way the *Times* was going to waste any part of its first twenty-eight pages telling people about it. It ran its story on the summit on the first page of the Metro section—the place where all poor-sister stories of only local import could be found—and it probably thought itself being generous just doing that.

The gist of the article was predictable: Raines had pulled it off. In the wake of a scandal that had rocked his church and embarrassed him personally—one that authorities claimed had exposed his close confederate in all of his ministry's antigangbanging activities as the mastermind behind a systematic assassination of L.A. street-gang members—he had found a way to make his greatest dream come true. The summit was on. Despite all the reasons their betrayal by Darrel Lovejoy—and, by association, the Peace Patrol itself—seemed to give them for declaring the conference a farce and backing out, six gangbangers representing six individual South-Central Cuz and Hood sets had succumbed to Raines's spiritual and oratorical sleight of hand and agreed to attend it as planned. According to the *Times*, the sets that would convene at twelve noon Wednesday to huddle with Raines and each other in the tiny meeting hall of the Reverend's First Children of God church in Inglewood were:

The Wall Streeters, Hood.
The Rockin' 90s, Hood.
The Seven-and-Sevens, Cuz.
The Little Tees, Hood.

The Doom Patrollers, Cuz.
The Stormtroopers, Cuz.

Gunner tossed the paper down and started to throw the
rest of his clothes on. The clock on Claudia Lovejoy's night
table said it was thirty-seven minutes past eleven.

"What is it?" Lovejoy asked apprehensively.

Gunner didn't stop moving, just said, "Look at the sets
who are going to show up at Raines's peace summit today.
Look at the *names*, then count how many there are."

She picked up the paper and quickly scanned it. "Six.
There are six."

"That's right. Six. *Only* six. You want to know why
there are only six? Because the other three sets Raines had
wanted to be there aren't coming. The 'bangers he would
have had to invite to see their sets represented—'bangers who
would have told him to take his peace summit and stick it
where the sun doesn't shine—are still *alive*."

Lovejoy watched him pull on his shoes with a dull look
on her face and said, "Oh, my God."

"That wasn't Darrel's list Teddy Davidson was working
from, it was Raines's. Davidson was weeding out the hard
cases, all right, but he was doing it for Raines, not your husband. He was paving the way for the summit, altering the
gangs' chains of command so that Raines's invitations to participate wouldn't fall on deaf ears."

Lovejoy nodded her head, seeing how clearly it made
sense. Gunner started for the door.

"Where are you going?"

He stopped and looked at her, realizing what a lousy
thank-you he had almost left her with. "To the church. I
can't prove a damn thing, but maybe I won't have to. Good
as Raines is at saving others, maybe he can still find a way to
save himself."

"Please, God, yes," Lovejoy said.

* * *

It wasn't until he hit the street that Gunner remembered what he was driving. The Hyundai had completely slipped his mind. He had intended to return the car to his cousin Del this morning, after having retrieved his own—a fire-engine-red Ford Shelby Cobra perfectly suited to such urgent missions as this—from the downtown parking garage it had been stored in for nearly two months. But now . . . now he had less than twenty minutes to get from Lovejoy's Palm Avenue Lynwood home to Willie Raines's First Children of God Church in Inglewood—a distance of roughly eight miles—before the gangbanger peace summit was scheduled to begin, and he was going to have to do it in a Korean-made windup toy too slow to be accurately described as "lethargic."

Were it possible to move the clock forward a good ten years, he could have taken what by then would be the newly completed 105 Freeway directly to his destination, as the freeway's proposed route practically drew a straight line between Lovejoy's home in the east and Raines's church in the west, but as there was little more to the 105 today than an oft-broken swath of destruction and a handful of overpasses that led to nothing in all directions, he had to blaze another trail along existing surface streets. Naturally, the route he was forced to settle for only pointed out one of the primary reasons the new freeway was being built in the first place: There was no easy way to reach Inglewood from Lynwood, and vice versa. An eight-mile stretch on the map was going to be an eleven-mile trip in practice, all shortcuts considered.

Also, it was nearing the city's lunch hour.

South on Burris Road to Rosecrans Boulevard, then west on Rosecrans toward Van Ness Avenue, Gunner pushed the little Hyundai along as hard as he dared, the whine of its overtaxed four-banger and anemic automatic transmission pleading with him to stop every inch of the way. The car, which hadn't turned a single head in five weeks, was now making quite a spectacle of itself: Pedestrians and motorists alike were stopping dead in their tracks to watch it speed by, their faces alight with either amazement, amusement, or a combination of the two.

Gunner just let them look. This was no life-and-death matter he was rushing like a madman to resolve, he knew, at least not on the surface—being late for Raines's peace conference was not likely to prove a "fatal" misfortune, by any means—and yet lives *did* hang in the balance, as far as he was concerned. For the *course* of six lives alone—*Cuz* and *Hood* lives—would almost certainly take a destructive turn for the worse if the gangbangers about to pass the peace pipe among themselves and Willie Raines were to discover—*after* the fact, and not *before* it—that they had played a crucial role in the holy man's second, and perhaps even more hypocritical, great deception of their brethren. Their humiliation was the disaster Gunner was racing to avert, and he could only hope that by doing so he could diffuse—or at the very least *limit*—the violent repercussions that were likely to follow their inevitable awakening to Raines's true colors.

If the Hyundai threw a rod through the windshield, it would die for a good cause.

The Hyundai didn't die, however. It just lost the race. It sang all the songs of death, engine pealing on the straightaways, suspension groaning on the curves, until its tortuous journey through the occluded arteries of Rosecrans and Van Ness was over, and Gunner's precious deadline had come and gone. The noontime peace summit had been underway a full four minutes when Gunner pulled the car into the large outdoor parking lot of the First Children of God Church. Any thoughts he might yet have entertained about crashing Raines's party in mid-swing without causing too much of a stir were now lost forever, as he had to vie for a parking space with an incalculable fleet of television- and radio-news vehicles. Though the news conference scheduled to follow the closed-door main event was a good three hours away, the media had apparently descended upon the site early, smelling blood. If any part of Willie Raines's well-intended little get-together was going to go awry, it was not going to go unreported.

Strangely, the LAPD did not appear to share the press's unabashed interest in the affair. Making his way through the church's grounds in search of the administration building, where the peace talks were reportedly taking place, Gunner failed to encounter the police in any of their myriad forms: no plainclothes detectives, no street cops in uniform, no black-and-white Chevys or Plymouths. Knowing Rod Toon as well as he did, Gunner assumed his CRASH unit's conspicuous absence here had to be the result of some demand that Raines's guests had made upon the Reverend, some condition they had placed upon their agreement to attend with which Raines had felt compelled to comply.

Gunner hoped to hell the Reverend knew what he was doing.

The mob of news people he had been hoping to avoid were assembled in the church's meeting hall when Gunner came upon them. The *Times* story had said Raines's news conference would convene in the church itself, but everyone appeared to be waiting here, instead. It wasn't hard to figure out why. Unlike the church, the small, white, windowless geodesic dome that was the hall was on the same side of the complex's grounds as the administration building, for one thing. And from here, no one—including Gunner—was going to get in or out of the critical conference room within the administration building without being seen. Secondly, also unlike the church, the hall was where the *food* was. As Gunner watched from a safe distance, the media types were swarming around a large buffet table with vigor and vitality, exhibiting all the class and courtesy of a drunken rugby team negotiating for a loose ball.

Some might have wondered why Raines had ordered the buffet set up here, as opposed to the church, where the news conference was going to be held, but the Reverend's reasoning was an open book to Gunner. Raines's beloved new church would be the perfect place for this mad horde of reporters to roll tape and snap pictures in the summit's aftermath: The cross in the background of every recorded image might serve to remind people who his "partner" in the endeavor had been. But he obviously wouldn't want anybody breaking bread in there.

God's house was no place for such vulgarity.

Gunner took in the debacle of the media's assault upon the buffet table and imagined himself in the center instead, a madman who had just brought Willie Raines's greatest hour to a premature end with a string of incredible allegations against the Reverend—allegations that, at this point, could neither be proven nor corroborated . . .

He made up his mind all over again: He would wait for the summit's end to make his move.

"I take it you're not hungry," somebody said.

The voice behind the investigator had been smart and sweet, and he turned around to find that the woman it belonged to fitted both descriptions as well. Early twenties, tall, with a medium-sized Afro and a smile that could melt ice faster than a microwave. The prim and proper mode of dress said she was an aide—but not a bad one to have around, to be sure.

"Actually," Gunner said, "I'm starving. But I'm not sure I'm up to fighting that mob for a plate."

"Would you like me to go in and get something for you?"

"No, no. Thanks, anyway."

"How about something to drink, then?"

Gunner shook his head. "I think maybe I'll just go back to the car, wait there for the news conference to start."

"Why wait in the car? You can wait in the church, if you like." She pointed to the pronounced steeple that was visible above and beyond the roofline of the school building just across the way. "Bobby's inside, he'll show you where to sit and everything."

She smiled again, making it an offer he couldn't refuse. "Okay. Thanks."

He started off, until she said, "But it's not going to happen, you know."

He looked back at her. The wonderful smile was still there, but different, somehow.

"What's that?"

"What you came here to see. Most of you, anyway. The summit's failure. Reverend Raines's humiliation. Some bloody fight between the gangbangers in his office that could ruin everything he's worked so hard for. Nothing like that's going to happen." She shook her head softly, placidly. "The Good Lord won't let it."

Gunner just nodded his head, admiring the openness with which the young woman shared her faith.

"I hope you're right," he said, showing her a smile of his own.

He reached the church proper a few minutes later and entered through an open side door, expecting to find "Bobby" waiting for him within, as promised. Bobby, however, was nowhere to be found. In fact, the church was empty; Gunner had the building to himself.

And what a building it was.

Like its exterior, the interior of Willie Raines's church was a definite departure from the classic Christian house of worship, in that it preferred asymmetry to balance, smoked glass to stained glass, and light pine pews to dark oaken ones. Still, it was no less eerie in the dark; its silence seemed just as deafening, and its massive chromium cross just as mournful. Gunner had to agree with Raines: This was no place to eat, drink, and be merry.

A series of tables had been set up end to end at the front of the church, before the altar, but that was the only sign of the impending news conference. Gunner sat down in a pew at the back and contemplated going home. It was now twenty-five minutes after twelve; Raines and his esteemed panel of gangbangers would be at it hot and heavy by now. Immediately upon his arrival, five minutes late or not, Gunner still might have been able to close Raines's circus before it had pitched its tent, but now that chance was gone. Now, there was nothing to do but try and catch Raines in between the summit and the news conference, to take him aside and remind him that Teddy Davidson was going to turn up eventually to blow the lid on things for good. Surely, Gunner thought, Raines would have to concede the point, and even be wise enough to use the news conference to make his fall from grace something less than a prime-time death-plunge straight to hell.

It wasn't much to hope for, Gunner knew, but it was worth a try. So he stayed put in the empty church, waiting for an even emptier event, and pondered the mystery of Bobby—the missing usher—as a way of passing the time.

Then somebody up in the balcony stifled a sneeze.

It had been a man's sneeze, squelched as well as two hands over his face could manage, but a sneeze just the same. With no other sound but Gunner's own breathing with which to compete, it had sounded like a cannon discharge. Gunner stood up and looked skyward.

"Bobby?"

Bobby, or whoever, didn't answer. Neither did he, or whoever, sneeze again.

Gunner stepped into the church's center aisle and took a few steps backward, moving toward the front to get a better view of the balcony, but could see little or nothing of what lay beyond its railing. The silence of the place had grown whole again, and it engulfed him. His stomach began to churn wildly; only dimly aware of it, he started down the aisle once more, this time heading toward the rear of the church, making a conscious effort to be quiet about it.

He found the staircase leading up to the balcony and began to ascend it. He gave no thought to reaching for the Ruger because he knew it wasn't there. Toon had gleefully confiscated it. The staircase was curved, a tight spiral that climbed up and to the left, so that by the time he had any useful view of the landing and beyond, he would be more than visible to anyone up there—as if they needed the extra edge.

He was gathering himself to make a kamikaze charge forward when the man on the balcony grew tired of waiting for him and came down after him, instead. He just hopped down into Gunner's view, staying to the other side of the staircase where he couldn't be touched, and said hello.

"Get up here and shut the fuck up," Teddy Davidson whispered angrily.

He had a short-nosed Colt AR-15 assault rifle in his hands and a look of great impatience on his face. His overall appearance was that of a skid-row bum as badly in need of a shave and a change of clothes as he was of a few hours sleep.

Gunner made him wait a whole tenth of a second before continuing up the stairs.

Up on the dark balcony above, a middle-aged black man with a gray-frosted Afro and a snow-white mustache lay prone upon a choir bench, one foot bare and a thick black dress sock stuffed into his mouth. His hands were tied with a leather belt behind his back. His eyes were open but lidded, dreamy; they seemed to be the only part of his body with any fight left in them.

Poor Bobby.

"You're supposed to be in New Mexico by now," Gunner told Davidson.

Davidson just stood there, out of Gunner's reach, showing no desire to play the investigator's game of Twenty Questions. "Ever hear of misdirection?" he asked acerbically, keeping his voice down to a dull, dry rasp.

Of course, Gunner had. Pro football was his life. The art of misdirection was a simple one: Fake one way, go the other. Induce the other guy to overcommit to one side, then head off in the opposite direction.

"Nobody west of Phoenix so much as gave me a second look," Davidson said, grinning.

"They should have known you'd come back. *I* should have known you'd come back."

Davidson merely shrugged. *C'est la vie.*

The last thing Davidson wanted to do was actually fire the gun. Gunner knew that. He had gone to a great deal of trouble to spring this one last, unforgettable surprise on Willie Raines and the world, and he would no doubt hesitate to throw it all away just to put a few gaping holes in a meddling private investigator if said investigator was to try something stupid . . . such as duck his head down and go for the gunman's knees. . . .

"*What the fuck is this?*" a strange voice boomed from the direction of the staircase.

Davidson whirled, to find a pair of teenage gangbangers standing at the top of the landing, one tall and one short, both in a foul mood. The tall one wore a full-length black leather jacket and the short one had a toothpick in his mouth, but that was all the extraneous detail Gunner had time to note before he seized the opening their appearance gave him and slammed a fist across the right side of Davidson's face, knocking him to his knees.

The AR-15 clattered to the floor, creating a hollow racket in the empty church. Dazed, Davidson clawed after it with both hands, but Gunner brought a right foot up to kick the wind from his midsection, and Davidson forgot the gun entirely. Gunner watched him double over, hugging his waist and gasping for breath, then snatched the heavy assault rifle from the floor and gave his two benefactors a good hard look at last.

The tall one in the long leather jacket had a dark, disconsolate face framed by a mane of shiny black jheri curls; the small one was short-haired and neckless, with a hard stocky body that made him look about two feet shorter than he actually was.

The small one said, "Who the hell are you, man?" in the same voice he had used before to ask what the fuck this was.

"I'm the law," Gunner said, trying to make that sound like something with which even a platoon of crazed gangbangers wouldn't mess. "Who the hell are you?"

"His name is Wheel," the tall one said, the words coming slowly, ponderously, from out of some dark, incalculably low vocal register. "An' my name is Dog. An' that motherfucker's name right there"—he aimed a finger at Davidson's general direction—"is Teddy goddamn Davidson."

His right arm came up out of his heavy coat, bringing the vague shape of a single-barreled pump-action shotgun with it.

Gunner could do nothing but get out of the way. Davidson had made it to his feet, still wobbly, when the three blasts came, one right after the other. The first one caved his chest in and sent him reeling; the second took his chin off; and the third blew his remains off the balcony, scattering a bloody mess over the pews below.

A fourth .22-caliber round put a jagged hole in the back of the choir bench behind which Gunner was hiding, but it was only fired in passing, so as not to make him feel neglected or totally unimportant.

"That was for my homeboy Casper," the big kid named Dog said matter-of-factly. He dropped the shotgun to his side, made the Cuz sign energetically with his left hand, and then was gone, racing the smaller Wheel down the stairs and out into the street.

Gunner slid the AR-15 across the floor to the other side of the balcony and tried hard to feel lucky to be alive.

chapter **sixteen**

．．

In a very odd way, Gunner felt sorry for
the Reverend Willie Raines. His post–peace summit news
conference was a disaster. The spectacular death of Teddy
Davidson not only forced the minister's little afterparty out of
the First Children of God Church itself—in deference to the
police investigation taking place there—but rendered it a veritable nonevent, as well. From the tiny confines of a hur-
riedly prepared Sunday school classroom, Raines had tried
hard to sell the just-concluded peace conference as a
qualified success, taking great pains to point out that tech-
nically, bad blood between rival gangs had played no part in
Davidson's death, but his audience was minimal and his witnesses—the six gangbangers with whom he had conferred—
were generally unavailable to either confirm or deny his
claims. The police were taking them aside a pair at a time for
questioning, and those who were with him at any one time
were too busy celebrating Davidson's assassination to talk
about anything else.

While their impromptu interrogation foiled Raines's
every attempt to turn the news media's attention from Davidson's murder to the story they had come here to cover in the
first place, it did manage to prove worthwhile. Rod Toon,

whose CRACK unit was directly responsible for the investigation at the scene, actually persuaded one of the gangbangers
on the Reverend's panel to admit that the homeboys who had
blown Teddy Davidson off the church balcony were his. It
was nice to get an unforced confession for once, Toon
thought, but hardly necessary. David "Cold-Bee" Bennett
was a nineteen-year-old runt and Little Tee with a passion for
red bandannas and dark sunglasses whose runaway paranoia
was legendary; there was no way he could have come here,
unarmed and naked to the world, to talk peace with several of
his worst and most-hated enemies without assigning a pair of
fellow Tees like Anthony "Dog" Lewis and Clarence
"Wheel" Mitchell to watch his back.

And yet, Bennett had confessed, anyway—glibly, matter-of-factly. Dog and Wheel, his boys, were heroes. They
had brought Teddy Davidson to justice, righted the great
wrong that had been done to Los Angeles gangbangers everywhere, and in so doing had brought immeasurable honor to
their set.

Willie Raines would never have admitted it, but the two
assassins had actually done a better job of bringing the gangs
together on this day than he had.

Gunner had no choice but to feel sorry for him.

Sorry enough, in any case, to wait until the klieg lights
of public scrutiny had gone down on the First Children of
God Church to approach its beleaguered founder with the
bad news Gunner had come here to deliver. Toon had read
Gunner the riot act in eight different languages and removed
his men from the scene, and the Reverend had lost the token
interest of one last, preoccupied member of the press when
Gunner finally requested a meeting.

Raines was tired and badly disheveled, but he led the
investigator to his private office on the grounds and issued an
official order that they not be disturbed. He made himself
comfortable behind yet another imposing desk and Gunner

did likewise on a burgundy leather couch backed up against one wall nearby.

"You don't look relieved," the investigator said.

Raines sighed heavily and smiled. "I couldn't be more relieved, I assure you. I'd been prepared to be exhausted at today's end, of course . . . but not for these reasons." Just like that, the smile was gone.

"I didn't mean that," Gunner said.

Raines looked at him quizzically.

"I was talking about Davidson. He's dead, and you don't look relieved. Why is that?"

Raines had to think about the question a while before answering it, still not certain how Gunner intended it to be taken. "I'm relieved in the sense that the poor devil's misery is over, Mr. Gunner, if that's what you mean. And I'm relieved to know that his senseless killing of children has come to an end, of course. But beyond that, I see no reason to feel relief. A man was murdered here today. Brutally. There is very little solace to be found in that."

"True," Gunner said, nodding. "Unless this particular dead man happened to take something more than his body with him to the grave. You're familiar with the expression 'dead men tell no tales,' aren't you, Reverend?"

Raines shrugged, reluctantly playing along. "I believe so."

"When Davidson died, he took the truth about a lot of things with him. Who it was that gave him Darrel Lovejoy's list of gangbangers to use as a guide for murder, for instance. Everyone seems to have assumed Lovejoy did it himself, simply because he wrote it, including the man who killed him. But Lovejoy could just as easily have written the list for someone else. Someone who asked him to write it under decidedly false pretenses, of course."

Raines stared at him blankly, waiting for him to make his point.

"I'm talking about you, Reverend. Teddy Davidson got that list from you, not Darrel Lovejoy."

Raines started shaking his head emphatically. "No. That's insane."

"Yes," Gunner said. "We do agree on that."

"You don't know Willie Raines! You couldn't possibly make such an accusation if you understood for one *moment* what Willie Raines stands for!"

"I know what you stand for. I think I even know what your intentions are. If I didn't think a decent man was buried somewhere underneath all the madness, I wouldn't be here now. I'd be telling this story to the police, not you. But I can't sit on it forever. Whether I can prove a word of it or not, I'll have to go to the authorities with it eventually. With or without you." He paused. "Unless, of course, you're as good at killing men yourself as you are at having them killed for you."

Raines looked at him for a long time, the light behind his eyes mirroring his vacillation between rage and guilt, grief and indignation. For Gunner, it was not unlike watching a ball kick around on a roulette wheel, waiting for fate to side with either red or black, the dark or the light within a man's heart.

Before the wheel could stop spinning, Raines got up and walked over to the lone window in the room, where he peered out into a world of leadership-starved people he had thought only hours ago was his own to command.

"You can't imagine how much I wish I *could* do my own killing, Mr. Gunner," he said. "But my conscience—and my faith—refuse me that luxury." He turned away from the window to face Gunner evenly. "So here I am. With no alternative, to hear you tell it, but to bare my soul and throw myself on the mercy of my fellowman."

"I'm afraid that's about the size of it," Gunner said.

"Considering everything I have to lose—and all the people I'll disillusion by doing so—do you honestly believe I'll feel any better about myself afterward?"

Gunner shrugged. "That depends on how heavy a load you've found it to carry. A man like yourself, in your line of work . . . I would think it's weighed a great deal on you."

Raines nodded his head slightly, acknowledging a great truth. Tears welled up in his eyes as he stood there, but refused to fall. "Yes. Lord, yes," he said. He looked out the window again and asked, "Do you remember Sam and Dave, Mr. Gunner?"

"Sure. The twins."

"The twins. Exactly. Well, there's only Sam, now. Dave has passed on." He took a deep breath and let it out arduously. "I had him put to sleep two days ago. I had no other choice. As I told you the day you met them, Dave was inherently antisocial, absolutely impossible to deal with. It was something all the training in the world could never have corrected, every trainer and veterinarian I ever took him to said so. It was in the blood. And yet despite his condition, I never would have given up on him had it not been for one thing: He was beginning to have an adverse effect upon *Sam*.

"That was inevitable, of course. The two dogs were inseparable; they did everything together. And Dave was the strong one, the more dominant personality; eventually, he would have ruined Sam completely, I'm sure of it. So I cut my losses. I destroyed one brother to save the other. Do you follow what I'm getting at, Mr. Gunner?"

Gunner said, "You played the good shepherd. You stripped the weed from the vine so that the vine might grow and prosper."

"Yes."

"And that's what you called yourself doing by killing the gangbangers on Lovejoy's list."

"Yes. I did." He looked Gunner's way again, smiling

sadly. "Perhaps you'd have to be an ordained minister your-self to understand."

Gunner shook his head. "I doubt that would help."

"On the contrary. I think it would. I think if you had some insight into the realities of a clergyman's calling, if you could imagine for just one moment what it's like to feel com-pelled to save the world when your power to heal is woefully insufficient to the task, you would understand perfectly. No servant of Christ can save everyone, Mr. Gunner. No matter how hard we may try, no matter what methods we may adopt, it is a simple fact that our every victory is doomed to be tempered by some defeat, somewhere down the line.

"Therefore, it is imperative that we learn to keep our losses to a minimum. That we make the commitment to rec-ognize the forces of evil at work against us in all their forms and deal with them accordingly. Disbelief, for example. Hardened skepticism. We cannot allow these poisons to run wild among the good people of a congregation and still ex-pect that congregation to be saved. Doubting Thomases breed, Mr. Gunner. Dire hopelessness is transmittable."

He crossed the room to a silver bar cart parked behind his desk and began to make himself a drink, never thinking to ask Gunner to join him. "I had to work with the children in this community a long time before I could admit that, but now it seems as clear to me as the heavens above. I can only reach my hand into the quagmire of this insanity called gang-banging and pull so many kids out. I have to draw the ones up who wish to be drawn up, and let the others go. And I cannot stand idly by and let those who prefer the darkness to the light to impose their will—*Satan's* will—upon young people who might otherwise choose to come with me.

"Those boys on that list were *demons*, Mr. Gunner! *Demons!* I know that to be true because that's exactly what I asked Darrel to give me: the names of Lucifer's most power-ful emissaries on the street. I was in the early stages of organizing this morning's peace summit, and I had made up my mind long before that I was going to do everything in my power to see that it succeeded. The summit was going to prove to the world that the poor black youth of this nation are not yet an expendable commodity, that there is still great worth and pride and potential behind our children's pain and hatred, fear and resentment, and I was not going to permit the agents of Satan to render it stillborn by infecting the entire gangbanging populace with their impenetrable pessimism and contempt. I'd had it happen to me too many times in the past."

"So you hired Teddy Davidson to do some killing for you," Gunner said.

"No. That's not true." Raines shook his head again, his mood descending as his thoughts turned to Davidson and his violent death earlier in the day. "Teddy never took a dollar from me to do anything. What he did for me, he thought of as doing for God. He was a very . . . *disturbed* young man. He'd lost his fiancée and the child she was carrying several years ago in a gang-related shooting, and of course, there was always Rookie to contend with. . . ."

"How did you come to find him?" Gunner asked, already familiar with Davidson's unenviable history.

Absently, Raines said, "Oddly enough, through Darrel. Darrel brought him to my attention. It was Darrel with whom he had had words at the Christian Youth Fellowship meeting I told you about before, the one that had preceded Teddy's decision to leave the church. Darrel had told me afterward that Teddy had said some things about the Patrol and its value to the community, generally expressing the opinion that anything done for the benefit of a gangbanger was a waste of time and money, and had literally turned violent. Darrel threatened him with expulsion from the church, and he decided to leave voluntarily, instead. We thought that was the end of it, but a few weeks later—"

"He started making crank calls to Darrel's home."

"Yes. Scared Darrel's poor wife Claudia to death, Darrel said. How did you know?"

Gunner started to cite the appropriate verses from the book of Deuteronomy, but instead just said, "Lucky guess," and let it go at that.

"Darrel asked me to talk to him, to see if I could reason with him before the police had to be asked to try," Raines went on. "So I did. I asked Teddy to meet me here one afternoon, and we talked about his problems in depth." He took a long swig of his drink and said, "I'm no clinical psychologist, Mr. Gunner, but it was immediately clear to me that this was a man who could become homicidal at any moment. I knew if he didn't get help, he would almost certainly kill some gangbanger somewhere, sooner or later."

"So you gave him Lovejoy's list and turned him loose."

Raines nodded, eyes cast downward. "That's a very harsh way of putting it, but I suppose that's exactly what I did. Yes." He shook his head at the insanity of it, trying to dislodge its hold on reality through the force of denial alone. "I looked upon it as utilizing his madness *constructively*. I told myself that Teddy was a sick man who would kill senselessly, indiscriminately otherwise. So I gave him direction, a purpose. I convinced myself that the work we were doing together was a necessary evil, a mere sacrifice of the few for the overall good of the many."

Raines laughed, taking no pleasure in it. "But I was nearly as great a failure at living with the guilt of commissioning murder as I would have been with the guilt of actually committing it," he said. "I read about the first killing in the paper and saw it on the news and suddenly I understood—I *understood!*—what it was I had done and was about to be a part of. In your very words, Mr. Gunner, I had turned a madman loose upon children. *Children!* Sick children, demented children, children possessed by the devil himself, yes, but *children* just the same! All my good intentions aside, what I had done in just one week's time had made a lie out of every oath I have ever made to God the Almighty. It reduced me to the worst and most despicable thing a man of the cloth can ever become: a charlatan and a hypocrite; a *fraud*.

"So I tried to call it off. After the very *first one!* But it was too late by then, of course. Teddy wouldn't listen. He had a mission now. A *holy* mission, assigned to him by a messenger from God. And there was nothing that messenger—*this* messenger—could say or do to rescind what Teddy liked to look upon as his 'divine orders.'"

This time the laugh turned into something else, and his tears did fall. The proud man Gunner had always thought Raines to be would have ignored them, but this one didn't. This man, humbled by a fall from the greatest height known to mortal man—self-anointed sainthood—used the palms of both hands to wipe them away, oblivious to Gunner's presence and indifferent to his judgment.

Gunner found himself looking away.

"And so the killing went on," Raines said, struggling to compose himself. "And all I could do was watch, and pray. For his soul, and for mine."

"And go through with your plans for the peace summit."

"Yes. I had to do that above all else! After what I'd set into motion to ensure its success, I *had* to make it work. The summit had to be everything I promised it would be, and more. And the sad thing is—the *criminal* thing—is that it was. It *was!* Those boys in that meeting hall with me today . . . they were truly beautiful. Truly beautiful. When you consider all the garbage—the pain and the misery, the filth and the poverty, the anger and the rage—they had to put aside to come, to leave their homeboys and colors and sets behind for one day just to join hands and discuss the prospects for peace in their neighborhoods—you have to love them. You have to *love* them!

"The story here today should have been those boys, and the message their presence here was meant to send to every man, woman, and child in this country: Gangbangers want a *chance*. They want hope. They want a reason to believe in *something*, *any*thing, besides the basic rules of survival. There is no greed in that, Mr. Gunner. No greed, at all."

Gunner just nodded his head. The irony of the cruel turn Raines's fortunes had taken was not lost on him. The minister had gone to great lengths to see to it that his beloved peace summit became nothing less than a front-page, film-at-eleven media event that could demonstrate, far better than anything he had ever tried previously, the true plight of the inner-city Los Angeles gangbanger—and it had all been for nothing. The very man to whom he had given the task of removing the summit's most likely obstacles—a heartsick psychopath with a king-sized grudge to bear against all things gang-related, named Teddy Davidson—had with his death almost certainly guaranteed the summit a negligible role in tomorrow's headlines, despite its relative "success."

"Were you aware that Teddy Davidson was being black-mailed?" Gunner asked.

"Yes." Raines nodded his head again. "But not right away. Teddy didn't tell me he'd been paying a witness to one of the murders—Whitey Most—until after he'd tried to kill Most and failed. He called me up one day and it all came out at once. I think he called it making a confession."

Gunner remembered the shattered driver's side window on Most's car and what the dealer had asked him upon their first meeting that night in San Fernando: *"You the mother-fucker tried to kill me the other day?"*

"Most never tried to put the squeeze on you?"

"No. He never knew about me. Teddy would never have told him about me. That was the one thing I never had to worry about, Teddy telling anyone that it had been me who'd put him up to killing those boys, not Darrel."

"Until Sunday."

"Yes." Raines nodded. "Until Sunday. I had his complete faith, his complete loyalty right up until then. But when he came to me after shooting those police officers, and I tried to convince him to turn himself in . . . he ran. He saw it as a betrayal. I promised him both the church and I would help him with his defense in any way possible, and I thought I had him resigned to surrender, but when I actually made the call to the police, he turned on me and fled. I knew from that moment on I had lost him. If the police were to find him, he would tell them everything. *Everything.*"

"But he never got the chance."

"No. He never did."

The two men fell silent for a moment. They knew there was only one place for this discussion to go from here.

"What do you intend to do now?" Gunner asked, finally.

Raines gazed at him strangely, somewhat confused. "I should be asking you that question, shouldn't I?"

Gunner shrugged. "Not really. We both know the same story, but only one of us has a snowball's chance in hell of getting anyone to believe it, and it's not me."

"But you assured me you'd tell it, anyway."

"That's true. And I will. My professional ethics would give me a hard time, otherwise. The question is, am I going to have to make my statement alone, or are you going to make one of your own first?"

Raines didn't say anything.

"It'd be better for everyone all around if you took the initiative here, Reverend," Gunner went on. "Because when you get right down to it, I'm not the one with any real stake in where we go, or what we do from here. You are. Whether I go to the police with what I know today, or sit on it for a week, the consequences for me are likely to be about the same. The number of times a night, for the next few nights, I'll have to roll over in bed before nodding off—that's about the only difference it may ever make to me. But I don't think the same can be said for you. Can it?"

Raines watched him stand up with the haunted eyes of an abandoned child. "No. No, it can't."

"It should help that you've had a few months' practice in deceit, but then again, it may not. Your conscience has had quite a workout; it'll be interesting to see how much it has left."

They went to the door together and shook hands.

"I'll be praying for you, Reverend," Gunner said.

Then he left the good pastor of the First Children of God Church to the business of praying for himself.

chapter **seventeen**
....

It was a 1967 Chevrolet Nova with a horrid guacamole green paint job over a lime green base. The right-rear fender was crushed like the vanes of an accordion and its left-hand headlight was just an empty socket spewing wires from its core. Rod Toon circled the car three times, but he knew even before his first pass was over that this was the vehicle for which his department had been looking for well over a week now.

"What do you think, Toon? Am I still a total fuckup, or have I finally done something right?"

Gunner was standing off to the side, giving the LAPD detective all the room he could possibly want to conduct his study of the car. They were working by flashlight inside the fetid and decaying garage of the Imperial Blues's old weapons cache, the condemned home Gunner had visited five nights ago on 117th Street south of Imperial, in the as-yet-uncast shadow of the new 105 Freeway.

"Bigger accidents have been known to happen," Toon said, pouring the flashlight's beam into the Nova's interior. "How the hell'd you find out it was here, anyway?"

"I took a guided tour of this place last Friday night. This is the former Blues safehouse Rookie Davidson ripped off to get hold of the gun Whitey Most used in the Darrel Lovejoy killing. Toby Mills's gun. I never got inside, but I could see the garage was in pretty good shape. I called CALTRANS this afternoon, and they told me they'd had to replace a padlock on the main gate sometime in the middle of last week, it just kind of fit."

"It fit. Right."

"You still haven't answered my question, Toon. Does this get me off your shit list or not?"

"I don't see a weapon. You want off the list, I've gotta have a weapon."

Gunner started to argue but decided against it. "You try the trunk yet?"

"The trunk. Yeah. Good idea."

There was nothing to keep it closed but a coil of heavy-gauge insulated wire. Toon yanked it off and lifted the lid with the fervor of an archaeologist on a history-making dig, the flashlight's narrow column of light spraying across the pitch-black garage every which way as he moved.

But the Uzi wasn't there.

"I'm not sure I like the looks of that," Gunner said, peering over Toon's shoulder into the car's empty trunk.

"Forget it," Toon said. "It'll turn up."

And so it did.

A burst of gunfire exploded through the garage door and both men went down under the barrage, Toon because he had to and Gunner because he instinctively thought it wise. Something had taken a piece out of the policeman's left leg just below the kneecap and he was lying there trying to pretend that the pain wasn't killing him and the blood wasn't scaring him half out of his mind.

"Jesus Christ Almighty!"

Gunner kept his belly pressed low to the ground, and crawled over to him. "I don't suppose I have to tell you who that is out there," he said.

"I know who the fuck it is," Toon said angrily. "Why the hell didn't you tell me from the start what this little field trip of yours was all about? I'd've known we might run into Cube and his pals, I'd've brought along some goddamn backup!"

"That didn't sound like Cube and his pals to me. I only heard one gun."

"It doesn't make any goddamn difference! You don't go up alone against a psycho like Cube Clarke unless you've got no other choice!"

He had pulled off his tie and was struggling to make a tourniquet with it. Gunner took it out of his hands and did the dirty work for him, his mind on the Ruger P-85 he was still without and badly missing.

"I was hoping to surprise you," the investigator said. "And I thought a couple of grown men like ourselves could take one teenager without much trouble."

Before Toon had a chance to answer that, the Uzi outside abruptly barked again, sending them rushing for cover. Gunner helped Toon claw his way to the rear of the Nova and they huddled there together, staying low, waiting for a seemingly endless, whining wave of bullets and shrapnel to come to an end.

When it did, and silence had descended upon the garage once more, Toon said, "He's not gonna do that all night. He's not that stupid. You know what I'm saying?"

Gunner nodded his head somberly. He had felt something sharp cut his cheek a moment earlier, just below his left eye, and now he could taste his own blood in his mouth.

"He'll be coming in," he said.

"Yeah. Any minute now. He's been around long enough to know, he messes around out there much longer, after the racket he's just made, he's gonna have a squad car on his ass before he can finish us off."

"Okay, so he's coming in. Any ideas on what we can do about it?"

"Yeah. Just one." He let his eyes play over the Nova. "You ever hot-wire a car, Gunner?"

Gunner didn't bother answering the question, just said, "You're out of your mind, Toon. He makes his entrance before we can get the damn thing started, we'll be easier to hit than two fish in a barrel."

"So what? We're gonna be that anyway, if we just wait around here. I don't catch him with a lucky shot coming in, he's gonna cut us to fucking pieces, and you know it." Using the Nova's rear bumper for leverage, Toon was already struggling to his feet. "So quit arguin' and help me into the backseat, will you?"

Gunner wasn't mollified, but he did as he was told.

When both men were in the car—Toon in the back, Gunner behind the wheel—Gunner asked, "What am I supposed to do once we're out of here?"

Stretched out on the Nova's sickly vinyl upholstery, Toon tried to grin through his pain and said, "If you're lucky, you won't have to do anything. You'll put about ten thousand miles' worth of tire tread on that little fucker's ass and save somebody the expense of burying him."

"And if I'm not lucky?"

"If you're not lucky, you use this," Toon said, holding his service revolver out for Gunner to take. "You do him before he does us. You put the pedal to the metal and give him all six in passing, as fast as you can count that high. You read me?"

Gunner took the gun. Toon saw the expression on his face and recognized it immediately. "I know what you're thinking, Gunner," he said, "and you can forget it. I don't give a fuck what his birth certificate says; that's no fifteen-year-old kid I've just told you to blow away—that's a *man*. A man who gave up being a baby three goddamn homicides ago. And if you don't do what I tell you and treat him like one, he's gonna put both of our sorry asses in the ground. Make no mistake about it."

His eyes bore into Gunner until the investigator had no recourse but to nod his head in agreement, unable to refute Toon's logic.

"I hear you," Gunner said.

Without any further discussion, he ducked his head under the Nova's steering wheel and went to work on the car's ignition, using Toon's flashlight to guide him. He had to break the wires he needed with his hands and strip the insulation back with his fingernails; he had one wire done and the other broken when the garage door started to rise, groaning like an old man haunting a graveyard.

"Gunner!" Toon warned him.

Gunner lifted his head to peer out of the car's windshield while he fought to prepare the second wire, no longer able to see what he was doing. The door before him was rising fast now; it would be Cube Clarke's intention to surprise them, to shove the door out of the way and be on top of them before they could adequately defend themselves.

Though it was a wreck and an eyesore, a mistreated and neglected piece of machinery more than twenty years old, Gunner understood that the Nova would have to start on the first try. There would be no time for a second.

He touched together the two naked wire ends beneath the dash and held his breath as the garage door swung all the way open.

"*Gunner!*" Toon roared again.

The Nova sputtered awake and bucked forward violently, given full throttle by Gunner's right foot mashing the gas pedal to the floorboard. He caught a glimpse of Cube Clarke standing directly in the car's path in the pitch-black darkness outside the garage before the Blue opened up with the Uzi and the investigator was forced to duck his head again, below windshield level, driving blind.

Almost immediately, Gunner felt the Nova collide with something. The sound of the impact was dull and sickening, a sound Gunner hoped soon to forget, but the car sped on unfazed, bouncing and careening off an unseen curb. The Uzi fell silent and Gunner looked up just in time to see Clarke's body roll off of the car's perforated windshield and disappear, tumbling over its right front fender to the ground below.

Gunner sat up behind the wheel and eased up on the gas, bringing the car to a stop in the middle of the pulverized remains of 117th Street. As the investigator looked back over his shoulder at Clarke, who was trying to command his broken body to its feet less than ten yards away, Toon fought to lift himself from his prone position in the backseat and said, "What the hell are you doing? Don't stop, you dumb shit! Get us the hell out of here!"

"He's hurt," Gunner said flatly, getting out of the car.

"Are you out of your fucking mind? Get back in the car, Gunner! Use your fucking head!"

Toon opened his mouth to go on, but Gunner was already moving away, toward the fallen Blue.

As Toon watched through the Nova's murky rear window, the investigator reached Clarke just as the latter was completing a painful crawl along the street's craggy landscape to the Uzi, intent on regaining possession of the weapon from which he had been temporarily separated.

"Let it go, Cube. You need help," Gunner said, standing over him. He had Toon's service revolver in his right hand, pointed at a spot just between Clarke's shoulder blades.

Toon's voice was barely audible in the distance, shouting Gunner's name all over again.

Both Gunner and Clarke ignored it as the Imperial Blue once more took hold of the automatic rifle and tried to stand, forcing a shattered left leg to carry some part of his weight.

Finally teetering on his one good leg like a drunken sailor, he swung the Uzi up in Gunner's general direction and, through a mouthful of blood, said, *"Fuck you."*

To Toon's amazement, Gunner followed his advice and emptied the police detective's gun. He fired six rounds in rapid succession and made them all count, leaving nothing to chance. Clarke went down under the fusillade as if hit by a train, firing the Uzi into the night sky as he descended.

He was dead before the gun's last muzzle flash had melded with the darkness all around him.

Gunner gave the Blue's pitiable form a short, silent examination, then pitched Toon's revolver and turned away, walking toward the sound of sirens and a pair of red dome lights that were closing fast upon him.

chapter **eighteen**

....

You've gotta put it out of your mind, Gunner. You wanna go crazy?"

"Thanks for the sterling advice, Toon. Dear Abby couldn't have said it better."

"You're seein' quite a bit of the Lovejoy woman, I understand."

"She's a chiropractor. I've got a bad back. It's a romance made in heaven."

Toon just grinned. "Look, this is getting off the subject a little, but I got a call from Willie Raines this morning. He says he wants to see me this afternoon. Very important. You wouldn't have any idea what that might be all about, would you?"

"Me? Why would I know?"

"Just an idea I had."

"You shouldn't get so many ideas, Toon. Your line is law enforcement, not advertising."

They were standing out in the parking lot of the Seventy-seventh Street Station, on an overcast Friday two weeks after the death of Cube Clarke. The LAPD had just completed its investigation of the Darrel Lovejoy homicide and decided Gunner had done nothing while under the employ of Kelly DeCharme to warrant either prosecution or suspension of his license.

So he was getting his Ruger back.

"You asked me a few weeks ago if you were off my shit list," Toon said. His next words weren't even out of his mouth yet, and already he hated the sound of them.

"That's right. I did." ·

"For the record, yeah. I guess you are. Until the next time, anyway."

Gunner started for his car. His *real* car. He'd given Del the Hyundai back and taken the red Cobra out of mothballs. "There isn't going to be a next time, Toon," he said, tossing the comment over his shoulder.

"Shit. Guys like you, there's *always* a next time," Toon said.

Gunner turned the Cobra's engine over as Toon stood over him. "Remember what I said, Gunner. Serious business. You've gotta put it out of your mind. Cube Clarke was no kid. You hear what I'm sayin'? Repeat after me: Cube Clarke was no kid."

"Cube Clarke was no kid," Gunner said, humoring him.

"That's right. Keep sayin' it. Over and over. 'Cube Clarke was no kid.'"

Gunner nodded his head condescendingly and started the car rolling. "Goodbye, Toon," he said.

On the way home, with the Cobra's top down and the wind freezing his face, he made a concerted effort to concentrate on the fifty thousand dollars he had "inherited" from Whitey Most, having kept one last little secret from Rod Toon, but his mind would not stay put on anything so auspicious. Instead, it gravitated toward the world of gangbanging, as he had known it would. He had been able to think of nothing else for days.

Up to this point, he had fought the compulsion tooth

and nail, but today, as an experiment, he tried a different tack: He went with it, hoping the flood of black images would somehow revive the blissfully blind hatred he had held for gangbanging and all its participants only five short weeks ago. Deliberately, he thought about drive-bys and baby-faced wannabes, killers without conscience making hand signals for TV cameras, and walls and fences obliterated by overlapping layers of prideful, grotesque graffiti. He thought about crack and PCP, shotguns and Uzis and AK-47s, scars across beautiful throats and heavy black bellies—in short, every bleak, soul-crushing, and heartbreaking aspect of the L.A. street-gang culture he could possibly imagine.

And still, the pure, uncomplicated abhorrence he had once known for gangbanging would not come.

So he reverted to Toon's exercise in his search for peace, the same one he himself had come up with the very night Cube Clarke—too young at fifteen to see an R-rated kung-fu movie without a parent or guardian in tow—had died.

Cube Clarke was no kid.

Cube Clarke was no kid.

Cube Clarke was no kid . . .

Someday, he knew, the self-hypnosis would take hold— and he would actually begin to believe it.